Legacy

A DiMarchese Case File

Bill Mesce, Jr.

IMPRESS
BOOKS

First published 2017
by Impress Books Ltd
Innovation Centre, Rennes Drive, University of Exeter Campus,
Exeter EX4 4RN

© Bill Mesce, Jr.

British Library Cataloguing in Publica

A catalogue record for this book is av   itish Library

ISBN 13: 978–1–911293–019 (pbk)
ISBN 13: 978–1–911293–026 (ebk)

Typeset in Garamond MT
by Swales and Willis Ltd, Exeter, Devon

Printed and bound in the UK
by ImprintDigital.com

To the gang at FDU — this one's for you.

Prologue

"C'mon, Fat Ass! Hit or whiff so we can all go home!"

Libby flushed. "Geez, Mo, that's your *husband*!"

"I *know* it's my husband, Lib," Maureen said as if her friend had been providing an unpleasant reminder. "You think I'd talk like that to a stranger? Have him come up here with that bat and club me like a baby seal?" Her attention went back to the flushed, wheezing, 48-inch-waisted man at home plate. He'd stepped out of the batter's box, at a loss as to how to deal with the meteors that the slightly leaner younger fellow on the pitcher's mound had been shooting across the plate. "Oh, come *on!*" Maureen said impatiently. "Don't spaz out on me, hon! Get those big buns back in the box and finish up!"

Libby shook her head. "Geez, Mo, show a little mercy! I mean … *Geez!*"

Libby – who'd been so spooked by the nuns in her Catholic school days that she'd say an Act of Contrition if she'd so much as scratched an itch "down there" – always marveled at her friend's fearless shamelessness. Just on the ride out, Maureen had Libby pull her SUV up alongside some pimpled kid in daddy's BMW who'd cut them off. Once they'd caught up with the kid, Maureen had put her Daisy Duked bottom up in the window, slapped it and yelled at the kid to "Kiss it 'til your lips chap!"

"Hey," Maureen said, "I'm supportive as hell. I'm sitting out here watching these beer-gutted spazzos while I'm frying like bacon under this goddamn sun! After that, I'm entitled to an opinion, and my opinion is my big-bottomed bastard couldn't connect with that ball if it was nailed to his bat."

"Mo, *geez!*"

Not that Libby didn't agree with Maureen, at least as far as the frying like bacon part went. A ruthless summer had beat the life out of Flushing Meadows, turning the grass the color of straw, wilting the leaves on trees too sparsely spaced to offer much shade. Beyond the park, with the jets in and out of LaGuardia lending pained screams to the picture, Queens looked like it was dissolving in the heat.

The few – *very* few – wives and girlfriends and kids who had braved the scorching temperatures to cheer on their softball-playing husbands, boyfriends, and dads were as beaten lifeless by the relentless sun as the bleached grass and dying trees. The ladies fanned themselves listlessly with whatever they had – sunhats, paper plates, copies of *Cosmopolitan* or *Us Weekly* – while the kids whined about headaches and sunburn. By the bottom of the seventh inning with two outs and the at-bat team down two runs, few cared who won, the predominant sentiment having become one of simply wanting the game to be *over*.

Libby and Maureen had crammed their folding beach chairs together in a lollipop-shaped bit of shade the size of a kiddie wading pool about ten yards off first base, a small circle of microscopically cooler air cast by a sapling with leaves curled and dried like parchment.

On the next pitch, Maureen's husband managed to clip the ball enough to send it bouncing erratically across the infield. The ball took a wild bounce in front of the shortstop, caroming left just as the shortstop dove right which was enough for Maureen's husband to make it to first base, driving the man who'd been on first to second.

"Shit," Maureen hissed. "Now we're stuck here for another batter."

Maureen's husband looked over to where she and Libby were sitting and clasped his hands over his head like a champ.

Maureen flashed a smile of laser-whitened teeth, waved back to her husband, and muttered to Libby like a frozen-lipped ventriloquist, keeping up her smile, "I gonna kill 'at hat huck i' this game isn't o'er in a next ten 'inutes."

"Ah, my Gabe is up," Libby said, then gave up a moaning, "Ohhhhh ..." She began frantically rooting around in her shoulder bag and pulled out a digital camera.

"That the new camera?" Maureen asked. "Nice," which Libby knew meant that by this time next week, Maureen would have one, too.

"Well, it's *Gabe's* new camera. I can't figure out what half these buttons do. He asked me to record him whenever he's up. I almost forgot all about it."

"Somebody's gonna get a spanking!" Maureen said with a leer. "Which isn't necessarily a bad thing."

"*Mo!*" Hot as she already was, Libby could feel her face grow hotter. She fumbled with the buttons. The camera made a few different kinds of beeps but didn't seem to be doing anything.

"Let me see that," Maureen said and grabbed the camera out of Libby's hands. "I programmed Fat Ass's new laptop for him. This should be snap. See? This little red thing, that's to record. It even says on the screen it's recording. Here's your zoom. Ooooh, *niiiice* ..."

"What?"

Maureen angled the camera's view screen around so Libby could see. Libby cupped a hand around the screen to block the sun's glare.

"Check out the guy on second," Maureen said.

"Freddy Bushka?"

"Why would I tell you to check out Freddy Bushka? Freddy Bushka's got an ass like an empty knapsack! The *runner!*"

Maureen meant the man her husband had driven to second. They had noticed him when they'd first gotten to the ball field, looking so different from the rest of the players that the two women had joked he'd must've come to the wrong game. The other players were factory workers, construction workers, mechanics, deliverymen, all in their 30s and 40s, all wearing sagging Bermuda shorts and T-shirts with logos stretched tight across bellies swollen from summer diets of beer and char-broiled meat.

But the runner taking a long lead off second was younger, late 20s maybe, lean and hard ... except in his round, almost babyish face.

Maureen zoomed the camera in on the runner's face. "Cute, hm?"

Libby leaned over for a better look. "Oooh, yeah." She immediately recoiled at her own appetite.

"Jesus Christ, Lib, are you blushing? You're allowed to think he's cute," Maureen said. "It's not like you're gonna run down there and jump his bones. *I* might."

Libby looked across the field to second and noticed a pattern crawling down the runner's left leg. "Let me see that a sec," she said, taking her camera back.

"Ahhhh!" Maureen nodded approvingly. "Want a better look, hm?"

"Ooooh, he's *bleeding!*"

"Really?" Maureen took the camera back.

"See?" Libby said. "His leg."

"Oh, *yeah!*" Maureen said in a husky voice.

"Mo! *Geez!*"

"For Chrissakes, Lib, the most manly thing my guy does is crack a nail opening his beer! It's not like I'm gonna run off with this kid. I love my big-assed bear. I don't know *why,* but I do. But I got my fantasies, ya know. I'm married; not dead. Don't you ever –. Oh, Lib, don't tell me you *never –*"

"Oh!"

4

Libby's husband connected with the pitch with a rifle shot of a *crack* and the ball bulleted just over the second baseman's outstretched glove.

"*Run, Gabe! Run, baby!*"

"*Move, ya fat fuck 'fore Gabe runs up your ass!*"

The center fielder charged in to nab the decelerating ball, spied a sprawl of negligently left dog crap in his path, tried to sidestep, twisted his ankle and went down.

A moan went up from the fielding team's supporters as the other two fielders charged after the ball now bouncing off into far center.

Libby kept the camera on her Gabe who was rapidly catching up with Maureen's huffing-puffing husband.

"*Bring it home, Sweetcheeks!*" Maureen screeched. She was on her feet now, stamping her sandaled feet and squealing.

Prompted by Maureen's screeches and squeals, Libby swung the camera to home base in time to see the cute runner lower his head and barrel in toward the stocky catcher now blocking the plate and screaming for the fielders to, "*Throw me the fucking ball!*"

A group "*Oooof!*" went up from the onlookers as the runner slammed into the bigger catcher, impacting so hard the catcher's mask went flying one way, his mitt another. The runner stumbled over the catcher's sprawled body and limped across home base. The ball clanged into the chain link backstop a half-second later.

"That's my cutie!" Maureen beamed. "Rock hard!"

"Hey," Libby said.

As soon as he'd crossed home base, the runner had turned to the prone catcher. Libby had thought there'd be some good-sportsman kind of gesture, the runner helping the catcher up. But instead the runner went for the bat Libby's husband had dropped nearby after his hit. The runner was screaming at the catcher who was trying to get to his feet. Instead of reaching out a helping hand, the runner bayoneted the catcher in the midriff with the bat, then put a sneakered foot on the catcher's stomach to push him back down onto the dusty base line.

The runner was screaming loud enough that Libby could hear him clearly across the field: "I said stay the fuck down you son of a bitch! *Stay the fuck down or I'll end you!*"

Players from both teams were running toward home base.

"I hate a fight," Libby said, looking for the off switch.

"Are you kidding?" Maureen grabbed the camera and kept recording. "That's my cutie in there! I didn't think he'd take any – *Oh shit!*"

Libby didn't need the camera to see it. Over the heads of the men charging toward home, she saw the bat raised up over the runner's head, and as it started to come down on the catcher she turned away.

That night, when she couldn't sleep, she would tell her husband she could still hear the noise of the bat coming down on the man in the dirt trying to crawl away. She would later tell people, "It sounded like somebody dropped a watermelon off the roof."

1

Dante DiMarchese resettled himself in the guest seat. He tucked the tail of his suit jacket under his rear so it wouldn't pucker at his shoulders, neatly arranged the open jacket down his sides, displaying his vested stomach, which, even at 43, he'd managed to keep nicely flat, crossed by a gold watch chain anchored at one end by a conspicuously dangling Phi Beta Kappa key. He had ever so lightly dusted the chain and key with face powder; just enough to keep it from flaring on camera, not enough to completely dull its gleam.

"We're back from commercial in two minutes," the floor manager called from where she was kneeling by the center camera, in the shadowy pit in front of the banked seats of the TV studio audience.

The makeup girl flew out of the wings to give the host sitting across from Dante a quick retouching; a few dabs of this, a smear of that. The makeup girl turned to Dante. He smiled a no-thanks and politely waved her off.

Dante did his own makeup. The studio people tended to be *too* flattering, they took the character out of a face. Dante had learned, as he had with his watch chain, how to treat his face with *just* enough to keep the bright studio lights from turning him into a bleach-faced zombie without erasing the lines around his mouth and across his forehead which he felt gave him an air of authority, of maturity – of *gravitas*. He kept the gray in his temples, even touched it up to make sure it showed on camera. Even his toupees were tailored not to cover too much; a certain amount of forehead looked dignified.

The host was flipping through the notes on her clipboard, cramming during the commercial break so she could give the impression she knew what she was talking about when the studio lights came back up. She looked up just for a second to give Dante a practiced smile and touched his knee; another practiced move intended to comfort a nervous guest. "You've done this before, Doctor, so you'll be fine. Just relax, have fun with it."

Dante gave her a thank you nod, pretending he appreciated her concern, all the while thinking *My dear, I could probably do this better than you.*

"One minute," the floor manager called, and the host turned back to her notes.

Dante crossed his right leg over his left, tugged on his trouser leg to make the crease run straight and smooth, took a quick glance to make sure there was no embarrassing gap between his trouser cuff and the top of his sock. He shot his cuffs, set his elbows on the arms of his chair and linked his fingers sagely across his chest, making sure the onyx cufflinks that complemented his dark eyes were on full display.

"Thirty seconds ..."

Dante cleared his throat a few times, closed his eyes and took one deep breath, consciously relaxing his vocal chords, an exercise he'd found could cheat his tone into a lower, warmer, more authoritative register.

"Ten seconds ..."

His eyes opened, he turned his own studied smile toward the host.

He ran down the checklist in his head: jacket, make-up, posture (erect but not too rigid), trouser crease, his best TV toupee … It was all fine …

Except for them putting him in the wrong fucking stage-left seat.

"We're back in five, four, three …" The floor manager silently held up two fingers, the studio lights came up and Dante, with disciplined effort, managed not to squint under the sudden rising glare, the floor manager held up one finger, then pointed to the host as the red light over the center camera came on.

"Hi, and we're back," the host chirped brightly into the camera. "You might remember our next guest. He was with us last year to talk about his book *Shadow Hunter,* which was about his role in solving the Bailey Beach murders. He's back with us again to talk about his new book, something a bit different from *Shadow Hunter …*"

She picked up the book propped up on the end table near her chair. The cover showed a man's head from the eyes up, his eyes looking worriedly at the cartoon figures in orbit around his cranium: a dollar sign, an occupied hospital bed, two children in a sandbox, a house, a woman expressing spousal concern.

"… *Minding Your Mind: Safeguarding You and Yours for the Day You Can't,*" the hostess said, reading the title. While the camera focused on the book cover, she quickly glanced at the clipboard in her lap. "In this book are strategies you can use to protect yourself, your family, and your financial assets as you get older and may not be able to make decisions for yourself. Would you please welcome back the man famous for his work with criminal minds: Dr. Dante DiMarchese."

There was a round of sign-instigated applause, and Dante nodded in acknowledgment, smiling at the audience.

"Nice to see you, again, Doctor."

"It's a pleasure to be back, Lisa."

"Before we discuss your new book –"

Shit, Dante thought. *It's a three-minute segment, my dear; let's not dawdle! It's enough you have me sitting stage left so you can look prettier!*

9

"– let's clear up something for our viewers. I think the popular view of a forensic psychiatrist is what you showed in *Shadow Hunter;* someone who profiles serial killers and other criminals for the police. But that's not the whole picture, am I right?"

"Quite right, Lisa." He could hear his impatience tighten his voice a bit. *Bring it down,* he warned himself, *down …* "Yes, some forensic psychiatrists – and actually I'm a forensic *psychologist,* not a psychiatrist – are involved in that area, but for most of us in the field, the bulk of what we do is not nearly so glamorous. In a given year, most of my work will involve civil cases, a number of which I use as case studies in my new book." *Nicely done, Dante,* he told himself, *Nice way to bring it back around to the book.*

"But you have worked with law enforcement?"

Dante smiled, a way to catch a mental breath so his exasperation didn't show through. "I do, occasionally, consult on criminal matters, yes."

"Which was the case on the Bailey Beach murders a few years ago."

Dante's smile became a bit more forced. "Yes, Lisa, but, as I say, that kind of work is atypical for most working forensic psychologists. More often you'll find us dealing with the kinds of cases I discuss in *Minding Your Mind." Remember that, Lisa? That's the book I'm here to sell to all those housewives who sit through this drivel, so can we please get back to –*

"Before we get to your new book –"

Christ, woman –

"– I hear rumors *Shadow Hunter* is being developed as a movie?"

A topic which, if Dante wasn't going to be allowed to shill for his new book, he was certainly happy to publicly lobby for. "Well, it's just a rumor at this point," he said with precisely feigned modesty. "Fingers crossed!" which he did, looking out at the audience in equally feigned good humor. A gratifying chuckle rippled through the seats.

"Any talk about who would play you?" Lisa the wayward host asked.

"As I said, it's just a rumor."

"But if it happened, you must have a wish list."

"I don't know. I hadn't thought about it. Naturally, the first requirement would be, in the interest of accuracy, that the actor would have to be *extraordinarily* good looking." He turned to the audience, expertly bringing them with him on the joke. "Don't you think?"

The audience laughed, they applauded without help from the sign.

Which almost made Dante forget the stage manager signaling to Lisa that there was only one minute left in the segment and they had yet to discuss his goddamned new $27.95 book.

* * *

"Ya know, my wife bought that serial killer one a yours, Doc," the driver said. "Couldn't put it down."

"I commend her on her taste."

The jabberer behind the wheel wasn't helping with Dante's mood, constantly interrupting a perfectly good sulk. He'd had to cram his three-minute pitch into the last minute of his interview, in the process sounding like a shrill tobacco auctioneer while sitting in that goddamned stage-left seat.

"I guess we'll be seein' you next year when you got another book?"

"No doubt," Dante said, though hoping it would be a different driver. And that there would be another book.

His cell phone let out a few tinny bars of Vivaldi's "Spring" from *The Four Seasons Suite* signaling a text message.

"Hey, I heard that in a movie once!"

Not nearly as impressed with the driver's keen ear as the driver himself seemed to be, Dante ignored him as he pulled on his reading glasses to check the text. As he machine-gunned out a response he told the driver, "I've changed my mind, if that's alright. I won't be going home."

"Fine with me, Doc. Station said to take you wherever you wanted to go."

"You know the little park across the street from the United Nations? There."

"The UN?" The driver nodded, impressed. "Those guys could use a shrink."

The town car pulled up at the curb in front of the Ralph J. Bunche Park on the west side of First Avenue. Dante waited for the driver to open the door for him, then stepped quickly past knowing what was coming.

"Hey, Doc, when I heard I was gonna be drivin' you, I brung my wife's copy with me. Would you mind autographin' –"

"Sorry," Dante said, hurrying on, "Don't have a pen," although he had a quite stunning $375 gold-trimmed, diamond-studded Mt. Blanc Meisterstuck in his inside jacket pocket.

"*I* got a pen!"

Dante pretended not to hear, waved goodbye without turning, and headed for the stairs curving up out of the park along the polished granite of the Isaiah Wall to the medieval-flavored towers of Tudor City. The man who had texted him stood on the overlook at the head of the stairs, leaning on the iron railing. He was short but thin, almost gaunt, a gray-templed 40s. Consequent to the afternoon heat, his suit coat lay over the railing, his collar button undone and tie loosened, his sleeves rolled up past slim but sinewy forearms.

George Stavros was looking across First Avenue, his heavy-browed eyes fixed on the massive slab of the UN's Secretariat building, the look on his face … Dante could only characterize it as one of woeful disappointment. The man was so lost in it he didn't notice Dante sidling up to him on the railing.

"The eagle flies at midnight," Dante said furtively.

Stavros turned, surprised to see Dante there. "What the hell was *that?*"

"A joke. Secret meetings, code phrases."

Stavros nodded. "Oh, yeah, that's funny." He smiled graciously. He held out a hand. "Thanks for coming, Doctor."

Dante took the hand. "Good to see you again, Sergeant."

Stavros held up a finger. "Lieutenant."

"Congratulations. When did that happen?"

"Couple months ago. You don't write, you don't call. No wonder you don't know."

"A promotion well-deserved, Sergeant. I'm sorry – *Lieutenant*. It's going to take some getting used to."

"Hey, you're a smart guy. What *is* that thing?" He pointed to the park below, at the 50-foot-high stainless steel obelisk jutting up out of the narrow patch of sun-bleached grass, burning bright with the afternoon sun.

"Daniel LaRue Johnson."

"That's what it's called?"

"That was the sculptor. It's called *Peace Form One*."

"*Peace Form One*." Stavros mulled the words, and that air of disappointment closed over him, again. He looked back across the avenue toward the sprawl of the UN grounds: the Secretariat, the flag-bordered plaza, the once-considered-futuristic curves and dome of the General Assembly. Stavros' face wrinkled in a meditative frown. "I read somewhere – I don't remember where – there used to be slaughterhouses over there along the river, right where they built all that. Slaughter houses. Something about that seems appropriate to me." He nodded down at the Isaiah Wall. "They must've had high hopes when they put that up there."

He meant the quote from the Book of Isaiah where, carved into the granite blocks over the stairs, read the words:

THEY SHALL BEAT THEIR SWORDS INTO
PLOWSHARES, AND THEIR SPEARS INTO
PRUNING HOOKS. NATIONS SHALL NOT LIFT
UP SWORD AGAINST NATION. NEITHER
SHALL THEY LEARN WAR ANY MORE.

"I could see where they'd thought people had learned a lesson," Dante said.

"You would think. How many people died in the Second World War?"

"They say fifty million, fifty-five, no one really knows. I've seen some estimates as high as eighty million"

"Jeez, eighty million, you'd think they'd've learned a lesson. You know, I read somewhere – I don't remember where ..." "Anyway, it was that in all of recorded history, all those thousands of years, they could only find a couple hundred years where nobody was fighting a war somewhere."

"Sounds tragically right."

Stavros nodded at the Isaiah Wall. "That makes *that* pretty naïve, don't you think? That just because it was a bigger war than most, people'd give up the habit?"

"Maybe not naïve. As you said: hopeful. It is, after all, something of a prayer."

"Mind if we walk? I can't stand still when it's this hot."

Dante nodded. Stavros threw his suit jacket over his shoulder and Dante let him lead them across the narrow street behind them into the slightly cooler shade cast by the tall, slim trees of Tudor City Green. Dante followed Stavros through the garden gate and along the gravel paths to a wrought iron fence overlooking a small playground.

There were white moms and black and Spanish nannies watching their kids play in the dirt, climb on the monkey bars, hang on the swings, finding a dozen different ways every second to draw a warning shout from whomever was watching over them: "What did I tell you about playing with sticks? ... What is in your mouth? Spit that out! ... Are you *trying* to give me a heart attack?"

Stavros leaned against the fence, watching the children at play. He smiled, but at the same time his chest heaved in a silent sigh. "You have kids, Doctor?"

14

"I'm divorced. There's a boy. I don't see him much."

"That's too bad. How old?"

Dante wasn't quite sure. "High school."

Stavros looked at the ground, his thick brows drew close together. There was something going on in that gray-templed head, but Dante didn't press him.

Stavros led them back through the garden, and then along Tudor City Place. "Were you ever in the service, Doctor?"

"The military? No."

"I'm in the National Guard. You didn't know that, did you? Almost 15 years. We got called up for Iraq in oh-seven, they extended our deployment, we came home, three years later we were re-deployed in Afghanistan, tour ended, we came back, 13 months later they sent us back to Iraq *again*."

"I suspect that must be quite … grueling."

"I guess that would be the polite word. *Grueling*. You watch the news much, Doctor?"

"You mean on TV? No. I find TV news is like the famous New York egg cream."

"How's that?"

"An egg cream doesn't have an egg or cream in it. They call TV news the news, but I've never detected much news in it."

Stavros chuckled. "I wouldn't disagree with you there, Doctor. Well, if you *had* been watching yesterday …" Stavros winced at the recollection. "It was all over TV. FOX was calling it 'Sports Rage' … with two exclamation points."

They crossed the street again, to another overlook on the 42nd Street overpass. From there they had a clear view over First Avenue and the FDR Drive to the East River. Past the small pile of rock that was Belmont Island, a river tug slowly shoved a barge upstream. On the Brooklyn side were the Long Island ferry slips, and just beyond them, newly sprouting overpriced waterfront high rises, half-finished and rippling in the summer haze. Dante remembered – had it been that long ago? – when the Brooklyn riverfront had been a less tony arrangement of grim-faced factories.

"A beer league softball game over at the old World's Fair grounds," Stavros went on. "One of the players clubbed another guy with a bat. Cracked his skull. Some jackass recorded it. By the evening news it was on every station; by this morning, all over cable and the Internet." A pained look as Stavros unpleasantly marveled at how fast bad news could spread in the Digital Age. "The vic's on life support, the family's going to pull the plug. That makes it a homicide."

Dante shrugged. "Hot day, too much beer, tempers flare –"

"This wasn't like that."

"Flushing is a bit off your beat, isn't it?"

"The Queens DA would have my ass for butting in, especially for butting in on behalf of the perp."

"I don't follow."

"The kid's name is Abel Gant. I'd like you to look into this. As a favor."

"I'm still not sure what you're asking me to do, Lieutenant."

"I'm asking if you can help this kid out, Doctor."

"By which you mean conjure up some mental defect so he can walk away from a murder charge."

A flash of anger crossed Stavros' face, but it quickly turned to a rueful smile. "Doctor, you've done it for guys a lot worse than this kid."

It was the faintly pleading tone which finally put it all together for Dante. He wagged a gently chiding finger at Stavros. "This is *personal*. You *know* this young man. He served with you."

Stavros was taken aback for a moment, then he shook his head and chuckled. "Not bad. You mind telling me how you came up with that? Was it with all that talk about the war?"

"That was part of it. And meeting like this. And the way you've had to work your way up to why we're here. But mostly, it was the way you were looking at those kids in the park."

"What way was that?"

"Someone with a fondness for children would've been amused watching them at play."

"I wasn't?"

"There was something else there. The word that comes to mind is … melancholy."

Stavros looked away, across the river. "I see why you get the big bucks."

"Something about this young man reminds you of one of your kids?"

"Something about *all* of them reminded me of my kids. I had 40 men in my platoon. I was old enough to be a dad to most of them. You're not supposed to think like that, that's not good military thinking. But no matter how hard I tried, that kept coming back to me: that each one of them was somebody's kid."

"Like *your* kid."

"You want to do for them what you hope somebody would do for yours."

"Even here at home."

"Even here at home." Stavros's chest heaved the way it had when they were looking at the children in the park. He turned to Dante with a softness in his face that Dante had never seen there before. "So, I'm *asking*, Doctor."

He's not asking; he's begging.

It was Dante's turn to look away across the river. "Who's handling his case?"

"Vance, Vance, Wallach & Troy." Stavros rifled through his jacket pockets. "I have their card here somewhere –"

"Don't worry, I have the number." There were few New York law firms of any substance for which Dante *didn't* have the number. "Lieutenant, if you're asking me to have a conversation with the boy, I'd be happy to do that for you as a favor. But anything more …" And Dante shrugged.

"Worried about your fee, Doctor?"

17

Dante shrugged, feeling guiltless that he was, indeed, worried about his fee. After all, this Gant boy may have meant something to Stavros, but he was nobody to him.

"Don't," Stavros said. "Vance is picking up the whole tab."

"Well, then, there's no reason not to say yes, is there? I'll call their offices to make arrangements as soon as I get home."

"Thanks, Doctor."

"You don't have to thank a man who bills for his time."

They shook hands, then Stavros headed for the stairs that led down to 42nd Street as Dante headed back toward the Isaiah Wall. Dante had a thought, turned and called back to Stavros: "I don't remember Vance being noted for their pro bono work. How'd you get them to do this? Did you ask them for a favor, too?"

Stavros smiled sadly as he called back, "I didn't have to. Vance Junior served in my outfit, too. He left a leg back in Iraq." And then another thought: "You should spend more time with that kid of yours."

But Dante had already turned his back on Stavros, walking on and pretending he hadn't heard.

2

Dante lived in a townhouse on the Upper East Side. It was narrow, as most old brownstones tend to be, but on the Upper East Side one paid exorbitant prices not for square footage, but for the privilege of living on the Upper East Side. There were three floors above ground, and a separate entrance beneath the front stairs leading to what had been, at one time, a cellar. A small space around the front was set off by a high wrought iron fence with an electrically locked gate. Poking at the keypad by the gate, Dante noted the withered flowers in the planters beneath each window and atop the balustrade of the front stoop. Dante had a contract with a so-called "horticultural service" which sent around – or, rather, was *supposed* to send around – an over-aged hippie woman in a peasant skirt, wooden clogs, and macramé bracelets twice a week to keep the flowers from looking like the desiccated disasters he was now seeing. The poor condition of the floral décor caused him no small irritation, but then Dante was, at that moment, quite predisposed to being irritated.

"Mrs. Froe-*lich!*" he bellowed as he came through the lower entrance.

The downstairs front room served, in part, as a waiting room and had the usual waiting room accoutrements: sofa, a couple of cushy chairs, a tension-easing bit of Hudson River school art on the wall.

The room also had Esther Froelich sitting just inside the door entrenched behind a paper-littered three-sided desk. Behind a breastwork of PC, office phone, printer/copier/fax machine, and in/out boxes, she referred to her emplacement as Checkpoint Charlie.

Esther Froelich barely topped out at five feet and had the willowy shapelessness of a corn stalk, although, paradoxically, to those who knew her, she seemed about as willowy as an iron bar. Her sharply angled face, completely and persistently devoid of any touch of makeup, was mature yet ageless; a few light lines and lightly gray-streaked hair pulled into a sloppy but convenient bun suggested an age range, depending on the light and her attitude at any given moment, from late 30s to early 50s. Her heavy-lidded eyes behind wire-rimmed glasses were so small Dante, even after all these years, was unsure of their color, knowing only that they rarely displayed anything more than barely expressed disinterest and/or an equally minimal display of disdain. She wore the kind of blandly patterned, carelessly chosen clothes one acquired, Dante suspected, at some plebian cache, i.e., Walmart or Target, and which looked all the more bland and careless hanging, as they did, on her lean frame as straight and formless as a window curtain.

She had not bothered to look up from whatever it was she was working at on her PC, pausing only long enough to point at two piles of correspondence on the desk at her elbow: "That's for you to read, those are for you to sign."

Always fearful of neglecting anything Mrs. Froelich told him needed doing, Dante began rifling through the piles even as he continued his railing: "Did I or did I not explicitly direct you to explicitly direct that so-called producer to seat me camera *right?* The *right* side, Mrs.

20

Froelich! *Right!*" Dante demonstrated with his two handfuls of paper. "Very simple. Leeeeeft, riiiight."

The sarcasm did little to interrupt Mrs. Froelich's typing. "So you did, and so *I* did. Unfortunately, Little Miss Lip Gloss also thinks *her* left side is her good side. And it happens to be Little Miss Lip Gloss's show."

Dante was too irritated to concentrate on the correspondence in his hands, realizing he'd read the same line twice without taking it in. "Which am I signing?"

She turned from her work with an impatient sigh, tucked the to-read material safely out of the way to prevent further confusion. He began signing without reading, and Mrs. Froelich turned back to her keyboard.

"Might just as well have put me up in front of a fun house mirror," Dante grumbled.

"I'm sure you are, as usual, overreacting," Mrs. Froelich said.

Dante turned to one of a pair of small gold-framed Trafalgar mirrors on a near wall and made a sour face. "Brutally realistic self-appraisal. A four rating of the New York metropolitan TV-viewing audience will collapse in their homes gagging over this … this … appalling … *ach!*" Dante threw up his hands in disgust at the image in the glass. "My, God, I look like some kind of *mutant!*"

"You look adorable from either side. Did you see the letter from the Criminalist Association of the Dakotas?"

Dante snuck a look back in the mirror, but wasn't any happier at what he saw. "The what?"

"The Criminalist Association of the Dakotas. They want you to speak at their annual whatever in Bismarck."

Without turning from her keyboard, she found the letter in the sheaf of papers she'd taken away from Dante and handed it to him.

"How many criminalists could they possibly have in the Dakotas?" he said, taking the letter.

"Not many which is why I guess they come from both Dakotas."

"What do they want me to lecture on? Cattle rustling?" He quickly scanned the letter. "*Omaha?*" He let the letter slip out of his fingers to Mrs. Froelich's desk. "I think not."

"There's an honorarium," Mrs. Froelich pointed out.

"Oh?" Dante retrieved the letter. "How much?"

"Four figures."

"Oh," he said, and let the letter fall back to the desk.

"*Low* four figures."

"Tell them I have a scheduling conflict. I'm off ... *somewhere* on that date."

"They actually offered a spread of dates."

"Them I'm off somewhere *else* on those other dates! And what happened to the flower people?"

"The – ?"

"The flowers outside! They look ... *irradiated!*"

"I'll call them."

"Also, put in a call to Vance, Vance and whatever. I have the number somewhere –"

"*I* have the number somewhere."

"Yes, talk to Vance Junior, tell him I spoke with our mutual friend and I'd like to come in and discuss it further."

"He'll know what all that means?"

"Presumably." Dante turned for the door leading to the rest of the house.

"Oh," Mrs. Froelich added, saying it in such a way as to freeze Dante with his hand on the doorknob and set the space between his shoulder blades traditionally reserved for dagger pokes twitching.

"Yes?"

"Your brother-in-law is in your study."

Dante's hand dropped from the doorknob. "My brother-in-law."

"In your study."

"Correction, Mrs. Froelich: my *ex*-brother-in-law."

"Fine. Your *ex*-brother-in-law is in your study. Better?"

22

"Hardly. And why, pray tell, did you let him into my study?"

"I didn't *let* him anywhere. But since you won't let me bring my bazooka to work, I was at a loss as to how to stop him."

Dante opened the door. "Mrs. Froelich, from now on, please feel free to bring your bazooka to work."

* * *

If Mrs. Froelich's Checkpoint Charlie was the brains of Dante DiMarchese, Inc., which it was, then Dante's study was its heart. It was the room in the house in which he spent the most time; understandably so, since it was the room he'd spent the most time pulling together. Dante had spent a fortune on designers and decorators throughout the rest of the house, but this room was his *sanctum sanctorum,* and this room he'd assembled himself.

It was an idealized synthesis of images he'd collected over the years; a blend of bits and pieces of dark, regal-looking studies he'd seen in movies, read about in dense period novels. A floor to ceiling window looked out over a narrow balcony to the street, flanked by heavy, dark drapes. The side walls were floor-to-ceiling book shelves, the yards of leatherbound volumes broken up by a variety of curios and little *objets d'art* Dante had picked up here and there – a small Grecian vase, a Revere pewter cup, and so on. The open rear wall was paneled with oak – not Home Depot sheets of paneling, but real slats of oak – and on either side of the double sliding doors were mounted more Hudson River idylls. A hand-woven Persian rug covered the polished parquet floor. On one side of the room, angled into the corner, was a Steinway baby grand, and in the other corner, by a pedestal-mounted bust of Bach, a violin parked on its stand near an easel carrying sheet music. On the other side of the room, a pedestaled globe, a brass-and-glass liquor stand, and in the rear corner against the oak paneling, an antique roll-top desk.

The furniture had been selected with care, positioned just so, and each shelved book and antiquity arranged as part of a pattern pleasing

23

to his eye. Dante had once driven Mrs. Froelich nearly mad one day as she'd watched him fidget endlessly with the violin stand, moving it a few inches this way, a few inches that. "Does it make a difference?" she asked. Then he began rearranging the books for the umpteenth time. "Have you even *read* any of these things?" she said before she shook her head and left the room.

But for Dante, these little flaws mattered. This was his room; this was *him*.

So after such efforts at perfection, it was something akin to sacrilege when, as he stepped through the open double doors, he found Dominick Castellano slouched in his already rumpled off-the-rack suit deep in the studded leather chair behind the roll-top desk, his scuffed shoes parked on the immaculate baize blotter.

"Hello, Dominick."

Dominick's face was buried behind an open copy of *Minding Your Mind,* only the tangle of his thick, black, uncombed and uncombable hair visible over the cover. "I liked the last one better, Danny."

Dante winced at "Danny." "I'll try to do better next time."

Dominick clapped the book shut and tossed it on the desk. "Too many big words. No pictures."

"I'll see about having cartoons in the next one. That should please you."

"That'd be nice." He was a short, broad-chested man in his late thirties. Dante had always thought Dominick's thick, heavy features unpleasant, was always unsettled by those constantly moving caterpillar eyebrows of his, felt the permanent shadow along his heavy jaw was offensive somehow. "Oh, hey, sorry, I didn't mean to take your seat." Dominick stood, made a show of dusting off the chair, stepped back and, with a sweeping gesture of his arm, offered it to Dante.

Dante ignored the offer and went to the liquor stand, mixed himself a whisky and soda in a crystal tumbler. He did not offer Dominick a drink.

"I heard you were on TV this morning," Dominick said.

"It was just the taping. It'll air later today."

"Gee, I gotta be sure I'm home to catch that. I hope it doesn't go up against SpongeBob. The taping went well, I trust?"

Dante took a sip from his glass. He liked the weighty, full feel of the crystal in his hand. "Very well, actually."

"Really?" Dominick's ever-mobile eyebrows wigwagged an expression of mocking skepticism. "'Cause you didn't sound too happy downstairs when you came in."

Dante smiled tolerantly. "The problem with having exacting standards is one is rarely satisfied. I envy you, Dominick. I envy you that you always seem so easily satisfied."

Dominick grinned too broadly. "Hey, that was a shot, wasn't it? Good one, Danny!"

"What do you want, Dominick?"

"I don't know what you're worried about with the TV thing. You'll look bee-*u*-tee-ful! You always do! All those stay-at-home ladies watching their afternoon gabfests, they'll get a load of you decked out like an uptown peacock, then they'll look over, see ol' Ralph lugging out the garbage with his butt crack hanging out ... That'll get 'em wondering why they never hooked up with *this* kind of Prince Charming!" Dominick scooped *Minding Your Mind* off the desk, turned to the glamour headshot of Dante filling the back cover and pretended to pinch the photo-Dante's cheek. "Mm-*mmph,* what a catch that woulda been! That kind of soccer mom hot-and-horniness has gotta be good for moving a few copies, eh, Danny?"

Dante finished his drink and set his tumbler firmly down on the liquor stand with the harsh noise of glass on glass. "What do you want?" he asked, again, icily.

And just as icily, Dominick said, "Business." He reached for his stuffed, uncloseable briefcase at the foot of the desk, a sagging affair of cracked leather Dante recalled Dominick had been given as a gift from his parents when he'd graduated law school ... and continued to use all these years later even though it looked like it might fall apart in his hands. Dominick dug into the mass of papers in the briefcase, pulled out a smudged manila folder and dropped it on Dante's desk.

Dante made no move toward the desk. "You know my retainer."

"This is contingent."

"Lawyers work on contingency, Dominick; one of the many reasons for which I am grateful I am not a lawyer."

"There's a guaranteed payment once there's a resolution –"

"Which is the definition of contingency. Which is what I don't do. Fee for service."

"Yeah, I know, your pro bono days are long dead and gone. Just look at it and then tell me no."

"I took on a case just today. Even if your client could afford me, I wouldn't have the time –"

"Because it would kill you to take ten minutes to look at it."

Dante looked to the folder on his desk. It was thin. He nodded a possible concession.

"Thank you," Dominick said, and turned for the door.

"How is …?"

Dominick stopped in the doorway. "I'm sorry, did you say something, Danny?"

Of course he heard it, the taunting little shit. Dante found himself clearing his throat, hated that that made him seem faltering. "How is your sister?"

"She's doing fine. Thanks for asking."

"It would've been impolite not to."

"And God knows, you'd never do anything impolite. She's seeing somebody."

"Really? How very nice for her." Dante turned to the liquor stand, mixed himself another drink.

"It *is* nice for her. He's a good guy. She likes watching *him* take out the garbage. Butt crack and all."

"As long as she's happy."

"Yeah." Dominick nodded at the file on Dante's desk. "So you'll look at it?"

Dante shrugged noncommittally. "If I do, I'll call."

Dominick nodded, realizing that was as much of a pledge as he was going to get. He started for the door but stopped, again. "I know these days it's all about royalties and residuals for you. But you know something, Mr. Pignatello?"

Dante closed his eyes at the name, could swear he felt an actual physical pang behind his eyes at hearing it.

"Maybe," Dominick continued, "every once in a great while, it should be about something else, don't cha think? That's just *my* thinking." He pointed at the folder on Dante's desk. "Those are real people in there, Danny. And some of them are hurting." He started out the door. "Hell, maybe you'll get another book out of it." And as he headed down the stairs to Checkpoint Charlie: "Oh, by the way, your son is fine, too. I know he'll appreciate you asked."

Dante stood at the great, front window of the study, drink in hand, looking down at the dying flowers on his balcony. He heard the brownstone's lower door open, the wrought iron gate squeak, saw Dominick step out onto the street. Dominick turned – it rankled Dante that Dominick would know he'd be there – made a little pistol of his fingers, aimed it at Dante and fired.

* * *

The room beyond Checkpoint Charlie had, at one time, been Dante's office, back in the days when he had still treated patients in his home. Now, it was what the realtors called an "informal living room," and what Dante referred to as "the lounge." There was a bar, casual furniture, and the only television in the house.

Dante was comfortably ensconced in one of the sofas, a drink on the coffee table in front of him. The TV was on but, for the moment,

Dante's attention was on the *New York Times* crossword puzzle in his hand.

He heard the outside door open, some mumbled greetings between Mrs. Froelich and someone else, then heard her say, "Be with you in a minute, Eddie. Just let me freshen up and we're gone," and off she went upstairs.

It then occurred to Dante, with a chill, that he'd left the door to the lounge open.

"How you doin', Doc?"

Mr. Froelich was a broad-faced fellow, maybe just a few years older than Mrs. Froelich, always showed up for her wearing workman's twills and boots, and even though he'd been doing so for years, Dante didn't have a clue or an interest in what the man did for a living. What he did know about Mr. Froelich, and which irritated him no end, was how Mr. Froelich always insisted on being conversational.

"Ahh, crosswords," Mr. Froelich commented from the doorway. "Never had a head for that."

This surprised Dante not a whit.

"I used to try the one in *TV Guide* but I couldn't lick it."

"Well," Dante said, "*TV Guide*."

Mr. Froelich took a step into the room, pointed to the flat screen TV on the wall. "Ya know, a lotta times I like the TV on just to keep me company, too."

Dante sighed noticeably, signifying that this was not an exchange he wanted to maintain. "Actually, I'm going to be on in a few minutes. Otherwise …" and he made a dismissive *humph*.

"Yeah, there's not much on's good these days."

Dante sighed, again, and when Mr. Froelich still seemed unable to correctly interpret the signal, Dante stood, put a hand lightly on Mr. Froelich's arm and guided him back through the door. "Mr. Froelich, you've always seemed a nice enough fellow, but you shouldn't feel obligated to maintain a conversation I doubt either of us really wants to have. Please tell your wife good evening for me and I'll see her in the morning." And at that, Dante – gently, mind you – closed the door in Mr. Froelich's face.

Back on the sofa, adjusting his reading glasses as he re-focused on *The Times,* he heard Mrs. Froelich.

"Sorry I was so long," she said.

"Man, I hate when you keep me waiting like that," Mr. Froelich said.

"So don't talk to him. And keep your voice down. That's not that thick a door."

"I was just tryin' to be nice."

"He doesn't want you to be nice, trust me."

She might've called out a good night, he wasn't sure, wasn't even aware of the outside door opening and closing, because by then, his interview was on the TV. At his first close-up, Dante threw his newspaper down, disgustedly hit the "off" button on the remote, and sulked deep down into the sofa.

"Hideous," he said.

* * *

He made himself dinner – a light chicken osso buco over brown rice with a small garden salad – and brought it into his study, eating at his desk. He'd brought up a bottle from the small wine room – so he called it; it was really just a big closet off the lounge – a '97 Jacopo Biondi Santi Sassoalloro to compliment the wine in the chicken. As he sat at his antique desk in his precisely appointed study eating his fine dinner with its fine accompanying wine he felt that sense of wholeness and self-fulfillment few people ever feel … ever. That they are where they should be, as they should be.

But then, not quite.

That folder left behind by Dominick … He'd pushed it aside when he'd sat down to eat, had generally ignored its finger-smudged cover. Yet it just *being* there nagged at him.

Dante poured himself a second glass of the '97, pushed back from his desk and took a seat at the Steinway. He opened the cover over the keys, wanted to play something … *anything* … thinking it would put the thought of the file folder on his desk out of his mind.

He struck a single note, a bold middle C which echoed through the empty house, hanging in the centrally air-conditioned coolness for the longest time. He took a sip of his wine, sighed, went back to his desk. He pushed the dining tray out of the way, set the folder in the middle of his blotter. He reached for the folder tab, stopped. *Once it's open, it's open.*

Dante flicked the folder open.

There were no documents, no paperwork, reports, depositions … none of the usual legal case file-stuffers. There were only photographs, the small kind taken by family cameras from pre-digital days. No captions, no notations; just the pictures.

As Dante flipped through them he quickly realized Dominick had put together a portrait gallery tracing the life of a family.

Husband/father, wife/mother. Nineteen sixties, maybe seventies, in front of a small, drab home jammed up against others. Queens, maybe; Brooklyn, possibly. Dad is tall, a little gawky-looking, slightly stoop-shouldered. Mom is short, stocky, a rough but not too displeasing peasant face.

There are two children: a bobble-headed, dark-haired two-year-old boy standing in front of his father, Dad's hand on his shoulder; and a blonde baby girl squirming out of focus in Mom's lap.

Dante flipped through the pictures and the boy grew up: a pimpled, vacant-faced teen, then a good-looking if still vacant-faced young man. The daughter: blonde, growing slightly thick in the middle, probably not unattractive if she put a little work into it … but she didn't.

As the family grew up, Dad grew prosperous. Him in front of a corner grocery, then a picture of him proudly standing by as workmen knock through into the building next door, expanding the store, then the whole family in front of a supermarket, a "Grand Opening" banner hanging over the front door. Then, another "Grand Opening," Dad holding up a boasting three fingers: third store. The cramped little house was replaced by an airy suburban split-level.

They grew prosperous … but sad. Dad grew older, but Mom grew sickly, aging faster than her husband. Then, Mom in a wheelchair. A last birthday: "Happy 60th Mom" banner hanging over the dining room table, the woman now frail as blown glass, still in her wheelchair only now with an oxygen line running to her nose. It was the last photo of Mom.

A wedding, the son's, to a gorgeous young thing with hair too blonde to be natural.

The daughter, no wedding, but pictures of her with a young man, only the one young man. A bespectacled, pleasant-looking fellow. A serious relationship as the pictures covered a span including a Thanksgiving, a Christmas … then nothing. No more young man.

Dad grew elderly, he proudly held his grandson at his baptism … but then no more photos of Dad with his son or his son's wife or his grandchild. Just Dad and his daughter.

Dad's birthdays thereafter were sparsely populated: no son or daughter-in-law, no grandson. Dad seemed to age quicker now, looking frail, his daughter – doting daughter – always nearby.

Dante squared the photos into a neat pile in the folder, closed the cover, sat back and took a mulling sip of his wine. He reached for the phone on his desk, stabbed at the keypad.

"Hello?" Woman's voice.

"Hello, Sylvia? It's –"

"Danny, is that you?"

She didn't mean it as the poke Dominick had, but still, "Danny" stung.

"Yes, is your –"

"Wait a sec, Danny, hold on. Dominick Junior! For Chrissakes, would you leave that poor dog alone? She was laying there all nice and quiet; why'd you have to get her all cranked up …? What …? I don't care who started it! Go wash your hands and go to bed right now! … Because I said so, that's why! I swear to Christ, if I have to put this phone down … Jesus, I'm sorry, Danny. You must want Dom, right?"

"Yes, I –"

"Hold on. Dominick! Phone! Is that them jumping on the beds? I swear to Christ, if I come up there, I'm coming with the wooden spoon!"

Then a rattle as Dominick picked up the extension and Sylvia hung up. "Hello?"

"It's me," Dante said.

"I didn't think I'd be hearing from you so –"

"It's me."

"Ok. And?"

"And I thought we might have lunch tomorrow."

3

Vance, Vance, Wallach & Troy did well enough as a law firm to afford an entire floor of the Grace Building in midtown, high enough to have an unrestricted view in any direction; south to the narrows, east to Brooklyn, west to Jersey, north clear across Central Park to the low jumble of Harlem.

Dante had dealt with the firm before, respected both their depth of talent and integrity. It was to their credit, in his mind, that they'd gotten rich by being good. As corporate as it appeared, however, Dante also knew that, at heart, it was an old-fashioned, autocratic family firm. Grandpa Vance had launched the firm 50 years ago. Then, in the '80s, Vance Junior had seen an opportunity in the City's rehabilitation of the once-notorious 42nd Street/Times Square neighborhood. He'd become expert at handling the flood of complex real estate dealings and zoning issues which went with booting out the porn shops and grindhouses and bringing in family-friendly theaters and multiplexes, eateries, souvenir shops, and the New York branch of Madame Tassaud's, building the firm into a powerhouse in the process. Grandpa Vance had since gone to his higher reward, but Vance Junior, despite the other names on the letterhead, had taken his place as the supreme ruler of the firm.

Which made Vance, Vance, Wallach & Troy's taking on of Abel Gant's case all the more mystifying; for all the great standing the firm had in the legal community (and it was considerable), criminal law was not, by general consensus, their forte.

Dante found Vance waiting for him in the reception lobby, silhouetted against the bank of windows filled with a panoramic view of a southern Manhattan already aglow with a brutal summer morning sun. Dante found this curious in that, unfailing gentleman though Vance was, he did enjoy his kingly role at the firm and it was more the custom to be brought before the king for an audience than to have the king come before the guest.

As soon as Dante stepped off the elevator, Vance came toward him, hand extended. He was shortish, a bit thick but a good Brooks Brothers tailor had made him look more solid than chubby. He had the kind of heavy face which could as easily fold into an intimidating fleshy frown as into Santa Clause jollity.

"Dr. DiMarchese. Good to see you, again."

"Mr. Vance."

Vance held the handshake a second too long, and Dante caught a nervous flick of his eyes, a very uncharacteristic, un-kingly demonstration of a rare moment of indecision. Then, without having yet let go of Dante's hand, Vance guided him toward a pair of leather chairs in a far corner of the reception room.

"Doctor, if you don't mind, I thought maybe we could talk for a moment before I brought you in."

"Certainly."

Vance looked past Dante, out the window. "This Abel Gant case …" He shook his head, settled deep in his chair with a sigh. "This is my son's thing, Doctor. I advised him against getting involved."

Dante smiled. Vance commanded, ordered, directed ... but he didn't advise. "Why was that, Mr. Vance?"

Vance's face folded into a configuration Dante hadn't seen before: pained. "According to my daughter-in-law, Tom has just gotten to the point where he can go two, three nights without waking up in a cold sweat and screaming about what happened ... over there. I don't see how involving himself in this case is going to accomplish anything more than poke at a wound that still hasn't healed. Particularly a case where the evidence is so damning."

"And where you're picking up the tab?"

Vance smiled wryly, sadly. "Mark your calendar so you can remember the day, Doctor, because this is one of those rare occasions when the money doesn't matter to me. I'd give it all away tomorrow – everything I own – if it'd make my son whole, again." And, in case Dante doubted, a reaffirmation: "I would."

"I don't doubt it," Dante said. He pointed to the glass wall by the entry doors where the firm's name was etched in 18-inch Times New Roman letters. "Yours is the first name on the wall, Mr. Vance. From what you're saying, it seems there are practical reasons for your firm to refuse the case."

"He's my son, Doctor, and he wants to do this. He's already threatened to go off on his own and take on the case if I don't let it through our doors. It was an enormous concession on his part just to let me bring in a criminal litigator; you know this kind of thing really isn't our line. I don't know what's going through Tom's head. When it comes to criminal cases, he's never handled so much as a parking ticket. That's a hell of a situation, eh, Doctor? I don't want him to take the case because I'm his father, and I can't say no to the case –"

"Because you're his father."

"Do they have a word for that in your professional lexicon?"

"Parenthood."

Vance Junior nodded in unhappy amusement.

"I understand your dilemma," Dante went on, "but I'm not sure I understand what you're asking me to *do*. I'm not even sure you *are* asking me to do something."

Vance Junior took a breath, rearranged himself in his chair. He was, now, again, the king. "To bring this to as quick and clean a close as possible," he said sharply. "The longer this case drags on, the more I'm worried about what it'll do to my son. I almost lost him once, Doctor, and some part of him is still back there in Iraq. I don't want to lose another piece of him."

"Mr. Vance —"

"Just keep it in mind is all I'm asking. Can you do that much without compromising your professional integrity?"

"I can do that."

Vance Junior then led him through the offices. It was what one might expect from an established, respected firm: a lot of dark wood, dark paneling, dark carpet, dark suits. But once through the door marked "T. Vance III," the visual tone made an abrupt change.

Open, airy, blond wood. On the walls, Rothko prints favoring bright blues and reds popping against the light paneling. Instead of the usual heavy desk, a comfortable seating area, some light blue cloth-covered chairs and sofas around a coffee table where sat a silver coffee service and trays of Danishes and mini-bagels accompanied by assorted spreads.

There was a tall, gray-topped black gentleman named Brundage, another Brooks Brothers type Dante remembered as the firm's office manager; he'd handle the paperwork and payments. There was a woman also in the Brooks Brothers professional uniform, Rachel Blume, she was the gun-for-hire criminal attorney Vance had brought in.

"This is my son Tom," Vance said, pointing to the lean, handsome man sitting across the low table.

"Make it Tommy," he said, holding out a hand without standing. Dante noted how Tommy Vance's left pant leg didn't fill out the way the right one did; that would be the prosthetic. A scattering of small, almost unnoticeable scars on the left side of his face. "Pardon me for not getting up. Have a seat, Doctor. Coffee? Hungry?"

Dante settled in a chair, unbuttoned his jacket, carefully crossed his legs, and shook his head to decline.

Tommy Vance didn't wear Brooks Brothers. Tommy Vance wore Armani. He didn't wear his hair in an immaculately shellacked TV news anchor helmet like the rest of the Vance personnel, but in a stylishly shaped mop. The office, the Armani, the rest of it ... Dante now understood why Tommy Vance's father had been unable to "advise" his son to do anything.

"Funny we never met," Tommy Vance said. "I mean, as much as you've worked with us."

"If I remember, I think the first time you were still away at school."

Tommy nodded, smiled, clearly appreciating that Dante remembered ... or had studied up (it was, in fact, the latter).

"And the last time you may have been overseas," Dante said.

"You come highly recommended."

"By your father?"

"Among others."

"You mean our mutual NYPD acquaintance."

"When even the opposition respects you, I give that a lot of weight."

Dante acknowledged the compliment with a nod.

"Rachel, why don't you show the doc what you've put together on Gant?"

Gant. He calls him "Gant." Not "Abel."

Rachel Blume passed Dante a portfolio. "There's a contents sheet in there, but the quick rundown: arrest report, transcript of Mr. Gant's initial statement to the police –"

"He agreed to be questioned?"

"Apparently without hesitation," she said unhappily, and then, even more unhappily, "The icing on the cake: he waived his right to counsel during questioning."

"Ah," said Dante, understanding Ms. Blume's unhappiness.

"I couldn't put it better myself. So, you have his statement, preliminary ME's report on the victim, witness statements, and a DVD copy of the video of the attack."

"Not that you need it," Tommy Vance said. "You could find it on a thousand Internet sites."

"How do you get an impartial jury in an age where *everybody* shares *everything* online?" Brundage said.

"Change of venue is pointless," the elder Vance said. "Everybody in the world has seen the goddamned thing."

He said "Gant." "Well, I'm glad that's your concern, not mine," Dante said. "I'd like some time to look over this material," indicating the portfolio, "but if I could get in to see Gant tomorrow? Tomorrow morning if possible?"

"Rachel'll set it up," Tommy Vance said while the woman was already making a note for herself.

"I presume he's being held at The Tombs?" Dante asked Blume. "Let my office know what time and I'll meet you there. Then afterward, maybe we can compare notes over a coffee."

She smiled in a way that said she was more interested in the "over a coffee" than the "compare notes" which pleased Dante.

"Gant." "Mr. Vance –"

"Tommy."

"Of course, sorry, Tommy, you don't know Mr. Gant personally, do you?"

"He was in my unit in the Guard. I thought George Stavros told you that."

"Oh, he did. But quite a few men were in your unit, yes? What was your position?"

"Battalion XO. Executive officer."

38

"And headcount for a battalion is?"

"An infantry battalion, we deployed with 847 men."

"I'm impressed that you remember that so precisely."

Tommy Vance smiled. "It is said that a battalion XO's job is food, bullets, and people. And I like to think I was pretty good at my job."

"Still, almost 850 men, you couldn't possibly know them all, could you?"

"Believe it or not, I could put a name to a face on quite a few of them. They were my people, Doctor."

"I understand, but how many were you *friends* with? That's what I'm asking; were you a friend of Mr. Gant?"

"Does it matter?"

Dante could tell from the looks of the others that Tommy Vance wasn't the only one wondering.

"No. If you were close, I was hoping you might be able to tell me something about him; changes in behavior, that kind of thing."

"I didn't know him well, but I knew him. His name came through battalion headquarters. He'd been decorated. He'd been wounded."

"Seriously?"

"He was returned to duty in a few weeks as I remember."

"We have a request in to the VA for Gant's medical files," interjected Rachel. "Although the VA being the VA, God knows when we'll get them. We also have a request in with the National Military Records Center in St. Louis. We're hoping – and I repeat, *hoping* – we should have them by today or tomorrow. I'll have copies made and sent over to your office ASAP."

Dante nodded a thanks, turned back to Tommy Vance. "How did you find out about Mr. Gant's trouble? Did you see it on the news?"

"I feel like I'm being interrogated," Tommy Vance said.

Dante smiled. "Just curious."

"No, George Stavros ran me down. He told me."

"And you immediately stepped into the case."

"Yes."

"For a man you don't really know that well."

"Yes."

"Even though the evidence – as I understand it – seems fairly –"

"What's your point, Doc?" Politely smiling, but wary.

"As I said. Just curious."

"About?"

Dante quickly looked over at Tommy's father who seemed as interested in the answer as his son. "About *why*."

Tommy Vance seemed to relax at that, his smile turned understanding, sympathetic. "I told you," he said in a way which said he was sure Dante couldn't really understand. "He was one of my people." And as far as Tommy Vance seemed to be concerned, that said it all.

* * *

Dante accompanied Vance and Brundage to Brundage's office to deal with the clerical formalities.

"Oh we few, we happy few, we band of brothers," Dante murmured.

"Hm?" Then Vance, nodded, understanding. "Tom and this Gant fellow. I guess it's true. I never served. How about you, Milt?"

"I've been fortunate enough to miss that particular life experience," Brundage said, stepping aside and letting them into his office. He asked his assistant to gather up the paperwork while the three of them took seats around his cluttered desk. "You hear about it," he said musingly, "this bond between guys in the service. You see it in all the movies and on TV. I guess if you haven't been through it, it's hard to understand."

"It's probably why he doesn't like the idea of sitting on the sidelines while Ms. Blume carries the firm's colors into battle," Dante said.

Then the assistant was back, and they quickly dispensed with the matter of fees, signed necessary papers. Dante stood, shook their hands – with a special nod to Vance to let him know Dante hadn't forgotten their earlier discussion – and he turned for the door. "Oh, I almost forgot." He dug into his inside jacket pocket for a small slip of paper and set it on the desk in front of Brundage.

"What's this?"

"Receipt. For the cab ride over here. In case you've forgotten, Mr. Brundage, it's a thirty-day turnaround on expenses. And with that, gentlemen, I bid you *adieu*."

* * *

"I saw you on TV yesterday," Dolly Moffitt said. Her large, dark eyes brightened behind her designer frames as she smiled with the kind of down-to-the-bone sincerity which comes from endless practice.

"Hideous," Dante said slumped in his chair across from her desk.

"I think you came off quite well," she insisted.

Dante huffed just as insistently.

Dante's publisher was housed in a stone, steel and glass monolith just off Times Square along with its corporate cousins in recorded music, magazines, and TV production. It was an impressive edifice on the outside, and the cavernous lobby was equally intimidating with banks of large LED screens and the sound of commercials and ADD-rhythmed videos booming off the polished granite walls.

Inside, on the print side at least, the offices were about as intimidating and impressive as a company of tax preparers. The publishing floors were a crowded rabbit warren of cluttered cubicles, college interns on the verge of tears as they banged on rebellious copy machines, and bleary-eyed editors Dante was sure saw proofreading marks dancing in their sleep from plowing through the never dwindling piles of manuscripts and galleys on their desks.

It was no doubt a sign of the ebbing fortunes of publishing that Dolly Moffitt, despite being a senior editor, had an office about half the size of Dante's waiting room. The book shelves lining one wall were jammed and groaning with copies of the various editions of the dozens of books she'd done, along with the complementary copies that arrived every day from pitching agents, pitching authors, and gloating colleagues, all shoved unread and jumbled on the shelves wherever she could find room. She never got to read them because she was too busy with the half-dozen or so books she was working on at any given time.

She was pixy-cute 40ish, her trim figure never in anything other than a simple if well-fit black suit. She had been all smiles and warm hugs before she had taken him by the arm to her office because that's how she was with her writers – but God forbid you weren't one of her writers. Dante had known Dolly Moffitt for nearly four years, and damned if there didn't seem to be a new assistant outside her office each time he visited, although the truth was she didn't always fire them. Many of them quit. A few before the end of their first day. Some before lunch.

"It was fine," Moffitt said to Dante.

"Considering I spent most of the time being asked about the *wrong fucking book,* it was *fucking perfect!*" Dante held up a hand. "Pardon the language."

Moffitt smiled that it was ok as she smoothly rose and closed her office door. "So, then, they buy the old book, too," she said. "Win-win."

"Then at least they'll be buying *something.* I've been looking at the sales numbers on *Minding Your Mind* –"

She took her place back behind her desk. "I asked you not to do that, Dante In fact, I *told* you not to do that." She moved her head slightly side to side, a polite signal for him to shut up. "Dante, dear, at the beginning, I warned you this one would be a slow starter."

"Slow? This isn't *slow,* Dolly! This is an *ooze!*"

Moffit's smile never faltered, the easing tones never broke. "Dante, we believe in the book. If we didn't, I wouldn't have recommended we take it on. Right now, no matter what you think of the numbers, it's tracking more or less the way we thought –"

"More or less?" Dante said suspiciously. "More or *less?* How much *less?*"

"Now shush. I told you what to expect. Did we think it was going to be another *Shadow Hunter?* Of course not. Telling people how to protect their assets in case their brains turn to oatmeal hardly has the dramatic electricity of chasing down a serial killer."

"Doomed," Dante muttered.

She broadened her smile a bit to let Dante know they were done with this particular, non-productive topic. "It'll be fine," she said with finality.

Dante gave her an if-you-say-so sigh, though he was hardly convinced, and started to pull himself out of his chair. "I'm sorry to just pop in like this," he said, tugging at his jacket to remove the slump-induced wrinkles. "I had a few meetings in the neighborhood, it occurred to me to stick my head in, but I shouldn't have."

She nodded that no apology was necessary. "I only wished you'd called because we could've done lunch or at least run out for coffee. As it is, I've got someone coming in in a few minutes, so I'm going to have to shoo you out."

He reached for the door.

"The thing is," she went on, "I *wanted* to have lunch because I thought it might be time for a chat."

Dante took his hand from the doorknob and lowered himself back in his chair, wary now. "About?"

"It's time for you to be thinking about your next book. Well, *past* time, actually. Given any thought to it?"

"Not really, since, as you've pointed out, I've been busy obsessing about *this* one."

Moffitt chuckled. "Dante, we want to keep some heat on your name. I would think you'd want that, too. Publishing isn't what it used to be; the market has a short memory, it doesn't pay to have your brand off the shelves too long. If we could have something out next year, that'd be ideal. I'm not saying we *have* to, but that'd be, well, as I said, *ideal.*"

"Next year. Ideal."

"If we had a manuscript in hand by, say, November, we could make Christmas next year."

"November." It came out something like a groan.

"Listen, my dear, I'll look at anything you bring me, but if you want to see the same numbers you saw on *Shadow Hunter,* bring us another *Shadow Hunter.* It's that simple."

"Another *Shadow Hunter.* Simple."

"I know serial killers don't grow on trees – at least I hope not – but …" She frowned, and that bothered him. "As I said, I was going to call you, so it's actually kind of funny you stopped by."

"Yes, funny."

"Do you know Eldon Stewart?"

"I don't believe so."

For just the briefest moment, Dante saw Dolly Moffitt's practiced, polished poise and smile and cheery eyes falter. And at that, Dante was no longer morose about his lousy sales numbers or being taped from the left on TV or anything else. He felt a tingle on his neck, strong enough that his fingers went to the electric sensation at the top of his spine. "Who is Eldon Stewart?"

She looked out her sooty windows at the sooty windows of another monolithic block of glass and concrete across 43rd Street. "He's Joss Lee's lawyer."

Odd, Dante thought. His face felt like it was burning, yet his stomach seemed to be holding a ball of ice. "What happened to what's-his-name? Castin?"

Moffitt shrugged. "Maybe he chopped him up, has the body parts in mason jars in his basement. Ok, not funny. Anyway, it's Eldon Stewart, now. He brought us a proposal from Mr. Lee. Just day before yesterday. I've been trying to think how to bring it up to you –"

"A book proposal?"

"Well, that *is* what we do, Dante. Maybe you noticed it on the sign downstairs: we publish books. Yes, a book proposal. For a collaboration."

"With me?"

Something about it struck her as funny and she laughed a small, incredulous laugh. "I know!"

"Joss Lee wants to do a book with *me*?"

"My mother told me if I lived long enough I'd see everything."

"Your mother got one thing right."

"Come on, Dante, you've got to admit that's a hell of a twist. The Shadow Hunter does a book with the shadow he hunted."

"Is that even legal?" Which wasn't really Dante's concern. Finding a way to say no without saying no was.

"There might be some way around the Son of Sam law. Our lawyers are looking into it. Maybe if he doesn't get paid, or his share goes to some worthy cause, or … I don't know. I get the impression he's not particularly concerned about money, which, I guess, proves he's *totally* crazy! Legally, it might *not* be possible. And even if it is, I'm not saying we should do it … or that *you* should do it. I could see where it could be very uncomfortable for you."

"Oh, yes, 'uncomfortable,' that's the word that comes to mind."

"But Eldon Stewart brought it to us, it is an interesting concept, and I feel obligated to put it out there for you to at least think about. Maybe at least talk to this Stewart guy and see what Lee has in mind. Like you said, serial killers don't grow on trees –"

"*You* said that."

"– and here's one you already have hooked and in the basket."

Dante cleared his throat, pretended to look at his watch, and stood. "I've got a meeting."

Moffitt nodded, crossed her office to hold the door for Dante. She gave him a formal editor/author hug, set a hand on his arm and gave it a squeeze. "To make a next-year date, we need a proposal in hand in, say, a couple of weeks. Make it two weeks … although one week would be –"

"Ideal."

She squeezed his arm, again, harder this time, as she said, "No pressure, of course."

"Of course."

45

4

Dante was still brooding about his conversation with Dolly Moffitt, so much so he almost walked past Virgil's. It was one of those brew and beef saloons for young white collars working in the Times Square area. Dante pegged the median age of the clientele at 30 and the bartenders and table staff as even younger. Wood paneling, heavy wooden chairs and tables in a vague attempt at rustic casualness; big screen TVs at both ends of the bar, each blaring out a different sports event, the din of screaming commentators and noisy fans ebbing and flowing against the jukebox and its four-wall sound system.

Just looking through the window made Dante's head hurt. He spied Dominick at a table against one wall under what was supposed to pass for country inn décor – a rusted ox bow. Dominick was studying *The New York Times*, but when Dante stepped through the door up to the barely post-adolescent hostess he saw Dominick had switched to *The New York Post*, no doubt solely for his benefit. Dominick was holding it up and open so Dante would be greeted by the front page. Wars in Africa, riots in the Middle East, the world economy dallying with collapse, and the front page of *The Post* concerned itself with an uproar the previous night at Yankee Stadium when the benches had emptied over a too-close brush-back pitch.

"Dominick?"

"Hey, Danny! I didn't see you come in."

Like hell.

Dominick set aside his paper and checked his watch. "I should've known. Right on the button. Still, I figured a guy as fashionable as you would be fashionably late."

Dante slid into the chair across from Dominick, a tight fit against the loud, crowded table behind him. "Good manners are never unfashionable, Dominick."

"What?"

"I said good manners are never unfashionable," Dante repeated, raising his voice above the baseline racket. "An alien concept to you, no doubt."

"Oh, hey, that was another shot, wasn't it?" Dominick smiled, a broad imitation of good-naturedness. "Man, you like giving me those shots. That's ok. I've got a sense of humor."

"I would think you'd have to. I presume there's some sort of table staff—"

"Don't worry, I already ordered for you."

Oh God …

"So," and Dominick leaned forward, grinning expectantly, "you going to take the case or what?"

Dante held up a slow-down hand. "Husband, wife, son, daughter. Son's maybe two years older than the daughter. Should be in his early to mid-30s about now."

"Mr. and Mrs. Harlan Bick," Dominick detailed. "Son: Harlan Junior. Daughter: Emeline."

"Harlan Senior. Worked hard."

"Very."

"But never forgot his family."

Dominick's grin and his tone turned more pointed. "Amazing he could balance them out like that, isn't it? I mean, work and family."

Dante ignored the poke. "Mother Bick falls ill."

"Lung cancer. Passed in 2000."

"Harlan Junior meets someone."

"Dorothea Meader."

"Marries, moves out, starts a family."

"Little Harlan III, though I'm thinking they must secretly hate that kid to hang that tag on him. That boy's looking at 18 years of getting his ass beat."

Dante sighed not quite patiently over the digression. "Be that as it may, Emeline also moves out, meets someone. But something happens. Father Bick also falls ill."

"Small stroke."

"And ever the dedicated daughter, Emeline returns home to tend to Daddy. Nevertheless, he deteriorates."

"Series of mini-strokes."

"Whatever plans she had for herself go by the wayside, and her life becomes centered around taking care of Father Bick." Dante held up a questioning finger. "But where's Harlan Junior?"

Dominick responded with a melodramatic flourish: "Ahhhh, where *is* Harlan Junior?"

"The wife, Dorothea Bick nee Meader."

"Ah-*ha!*"

"She has ambitions for young Harlan, and that becomes a source of friction, and then schism —"

"Ah, yes, *schism!*"

"— and consequent estrangement between father and son."

"*Cherchez la femme!* Didn't know I knew French, did you?"

"You don't. Now, unless I miss my guess, there has recently come to light a re-drafted will —"

"Doesn't there always?"

"– in which a once fair division of the estate between the siblings has been re-apportioned in provocative fashion."

"Which I guess is your nice way of saying Mr. and Mrs. Harlan Junior had a shit-fit when they saw the new terms. Junior's practically iced out. He gets a token twenty grand, and that's in trust for his kid, and he only gets that at the suggestion of Daddy's lawyer."

Dante looked the question at Dominick.

"Nope, not me," Dominick said. "Someone who handled all of Daddy's affairs back to the year one. Now Emeline figures she's in a bar fight and Daddy's mouthpiece isn't the guy for it."

"Enter your firm."

"She likes me. She thinks I'm 'scrappy.'"

"That's one word for it. Who's on the other side?"

"Shanahan & Shanahan."

Dante nodded, impressed.

A waitress who looked barely old enough to be allowed to walk Manhattan without a parent was standing over the table skillfully manipulating a loaded tray. "Your friend timed it out just right, didn't he?" she said familiarly to Dominick.

"The guy's like a fine Swiss watch," Dominick said.

"Breitling, to be specific," Dante said.

The waitress smiled uncertainly, not knowing what that meant. She set down two frosted mugs of beer and two oval platters of what appeared to Dante to be orders of ribs struggling for breath in a pool of lava-thick barbecue sauce.

"If you need anything, give a wave!" the waitress said cheerily and disappeared.

Dante frowned at the oozy mess on his plate, then frowned at Dominick who was tying on a plastic splatter shield on which was stenciled in barbecue sauce-colored letters designed to look like they'd been splashed there: "Rib Bib." Dominick grinned hungrily at his plate and made a show of rubbing his hands together appetizingly. "Dig in, Danny!" then he picked up one of his ribs, pushed his lips through the gooey coating of sauce and began gnawing.

Dante looked on either side of his plate for utensils. There were none.

Dominick gave a dripping grin and held up his sauced fingers. "They're ribs, Danny. Nobody eats ribs with a knife and fork."

"Actually," Dante said, pushing the plate away, "I ate before I left the house."

"No you didn't."

"No, I didn't, but out of habit, I was trying to be polite. How much of an estate is in question? For Harlan Junior and Emeline?"

"Dad liked to live simply."

"Ah, a man after your own heart."

"You bet your ass. *He* would've eaten the ribs. Didn't spend much on himself. I guess he was socking it away for the kids. Depending on which way the market's blowing, we're talking maybe three, four million or so in stocks, bonds, cash. To hear it from Emeline, neither of the kids knew he had that much. Then there's the house."

"Where she's been living. Where she takes care of her father."

"And which is still in the old man's name." Dominick sucked the last bit of sauce clear of his rib, let the denuded bone splash back onto his plate, started trying to work something loose from between two of his front teeth with his tongue. "I supposed *you'd* call it modest, but as sucky as the real estate market is, it's still good for another couple hundred grand.

"The big enchilada is the business. One of the supermarket chains has expressed an interest in picking up Ol' Man Bick's three stores. That would mean a throw-in to the kitty of maybe another five, six million and some change, maybe more. All together, it's not Anna Nicole Smith money, but a tidy little nest egg nonetheless." He lapped up some loose sauce from a finger and fished another rib out of his plate. He narrowed his eyes as if targeting the meat. "Wouldn't buy the movie rights for a half-decent true-to-life serial killer story, though, would it?"

Dante briefly thought back to Dolly Moffitt and her too-enthused broaching of the subject of Joss Lee, then pushed it out of his mind. "Close, but not quite, no. And speaking of money –"

"You're gonna put me off my food."

"Please, if you can eat that, you can stomach anything. I want a guarantee, in writing, on your firm's letterhead, that win, lose, or draw, I will be paid my fee immediately upon settlement of the case. With interest appropriate to the delay."

Dominick set down his rib, wiped his hands on his napkin, and reached into the briefcase at his feet. He came up with a pair of envelopes and held them out to Dante.

Dante eyed them, but did not take them. "The fee does not cover my expenses, and those are not deferred. I don't care if you have to go into your own pocket, Dominick. Reimbursement within thirty days of submission. And I want it –"

"Guaranteed in writing. Done and done." He pushed the envelopes closer.

Mindful of Dominick's sticky fingerprints on the envelopes, Dante took them and quickly read over the letters inside. "You were awfully sure of yourself."

"I had a feeling," Dominick said, turning back to his ribs.

"Paperwork?"

"Messengered to your office. Should be there when you get back late this afternoon."

"Late this …? Dominick, I do not intend to sit here that long watching you grind your way through that poor mutilated cow."

"I'm meeting with Emeline at my office after lunch," Dominick said, pausing for a silently heaved burp. "I figured you'd probably want to be there, get yourself introduced. Hey," and he nodded at Dante's plate, "if you're not gonna eat those …"

"Oh, please!" Dante quickly pushed his plate toward Dominick. "Be my guest."

5

They stood on the sidewalk outside the restaurant, Dominick, with what Dante never doubted was intentional obnoxiousness, sucking loudly at bits of rib meat still stuck between his teeth. Dante turned right for Dominick's office, but Dominick stopped him with an, "Unh-uh," and nodded the other way, toward Grand Central Station.

"You said your office."

Dominick grinned with a finalizing *thup*-ing of his tongue behind his front teeth. "*Home* office. Shorter schlep for the lady."

"But longer for me."

"She's the client, Danny. So charge me for mileage."

There was a dare in Dominick's eyes. Dante considered, smiled and nodded, then followed Dominick toward the train station.

"By the way," Dominick said, "You got gum on your shoe."

Dante teetered awkwardly on one foot while he picked his other up to check out the sole of his Italian loafer. There was nothing there.

Dominick grinned. "Made you look."

At the New Rochelle train station, they picked up Dominick's

SUV, its interior littered with kids' coloring books, broken crayons, DVDs of cartoons, fast food debris, toll receipts. Fifteen minutes later, they were pulling up in front of Dominick's house, a colonial bought more for its spaciousness than its looks, with a front yard looking like a steroidal extension of the SUV's interior: toys, dolls, balls, an upended Big Wheel.

Two kids – a cherubesque four-year-old girl topped with a loose tangle of brown hair, and a slightly younger boy whose looks were obscured by something akin to clown make-up – exploded out the front door and charged directly toward Dominick.

Dominick dropped his briefcase, held up his hands protectively – "Nonono! Don't jump on Daddy! *Don't jump on –*" and then they jumped on Daddy who struggled to get his arms around the two as they squirmed and wormed their way up his torso. "You're gonna give Daddy a hernia!"

"What's a hernia?" the boy asked.

"Something you don't want." Dominick set his kids back down on the ground and blinked at his son's face. Actually, not much like a clown at all, Dante reappraised. Sort of a cross between Alice Cooper and something from *The Rocky Horror Picture Show*. "What the hell happened to you?" Dominick asked.

"Dommie let me do make-up on his face," the little girl beamed.

"She made me pretty," Dommie said with his own beam.

"Make-up?" Dominick dabbed at the streaks of color on his son's face. "This doesn't look like make-up. This looks like *marker!*"

"Mommy doesn't let me use her make-up," the little girl explained matter-of-factly. Then she frowned at Dante. "Who's he?"

"Don't you remember your uncle?"

"He's not my uncle."

"Smart girl," Dante said.

The house was furnished for comfort, not to impress, but even so, Sylvia Castellano maintained a losing battle to quarantine the contagion of kid litter: building blocks, decapitated action figures, at least a

53

ream of paper scattered about crayoned with just-learned letters, stick figures, and abstract squiggles. Sylvia was, at that moment, trying to scrub some pastel stain out of the living room sofa with a heavy dose of Resolve.

"Syl," Dominick called from the hallway where he held on to little Dommie trying to squirm his way free, "what's with Picasso here?"

Sylvia ignored him, looked up just long enough to flash a smile at Dante, carefully push back a wayward strand of blonde hair from her wide, blue eyes before she went back to applying another dose of Resolve to the sofa. "Hi, Danny! Long time."

"You're looking well," Dante said.

"You sweet-talk your patients like that?"

"Only the nice ones."

Dominick ahemmed his way into the conversation. "Dominick Junior here —"

Sylvia plopped on the sofa in surrender. The stain wasn't leaving, and, from what Dante could see, it wouldn't be alone. "You're the one who gave 'em that big speech yesterday about not fighting and learning to play together. So, they played together. Relax. It'll fade in a couple of weeks."

"A couple of —"

"Why are you home so early?"

"I've got a client coming by. She should be here —" Dominick glanced at his watch "— well, any minute, really." Dominick nodded at Dante to follow.

"Wait!" Sylvia called. "Whaddaya think?" She disappeared through an archway into the dining room which, from what Dante could see, was used as a Play-Doh sculpting workshop. She reappeared with a huge shopping bag. She reached in, pulled out a flowered quilt, started wrestling it out of its plastic zipper bag. "How 'bout it, Danny? You always had good taste."

"Well —"

"It's *June!*" Dominick said. "What're you doing buying quilts in June? What's wrong with the old one?"

"*That's* what was wrong with it: it was *old*. I was tired of it."

"You gonna do the same thing when you get tired of me?"

"In a heartbeat. There's a bag boy at the Shop Rite been looking really good."

"He's welcome to the mortgage, too. C'mon, Danny."

They turned for the hall leading deeper into the house, but Dante's way was blocked by what could've been a dog but looked more like a three-foot high dust mop. The dust mop had teeth, which it bared with a low growl.

"Ignore him," Sylvia called. "He's harmless."

The dust mop growled again.

"Are you sure?"

"Gee," Dominick said, "he's usually pretty good with strangers." He smiled mockingly. "You must be special."

Dante followed Dominick down the hall, sliding along the wall past the dust mop which kept its teeth-baring snout aimed at him.

"Don't you want to see the pillow shams?" Sylvia called after them. "They're really pretty."

"Until I married you, I got along just fine without pillow shams," Dominick called back as he headed down the narrow stairs leading off the kitchen to the basement, Dante following. "I didn't even know what a pillow sham was. Little did I realize I had this voice deep inside me, this gnawing ache in my heart! What was I missing? *Shams!* I needed *shams!* Thank you, God, for bringing this angel of mercy into my life with her pillow shams!"

"You're making your own dinner tonight," Sylvia's muffled voice came through the floor. "You know that, right?"

Most of the basement had been converted into what had been intended as an adult rec room. Paneling, a wet bar, a pool table. But the intended adult atmosphere had been overrun by the same riot-at-the-daycare debris field Dante had crossed upstairs, with the addition of expressive crayoning on the cheap paneling.

"See what you're missing, Danny?" Dominick said as he stepped around this, stepped over that. "You should get married, again. You know what they say; fourth time's the charm."

"Who says that?"

"The woman behind Door Number Four?"

A louvered door led to a cramped, windowless, paneled office: a scuffed self-assembled particle board desk, a cheap desk chair, and two mismatched padded chairs whose threadbare condition suggested this was where Dominick's old living room chairs came to die. A rather large doll, one rolling eye frozen in a permanent blink, sat at the desk, its puffy-cheeked face apparently another example of Dominick's little girl's make-up-by-marker skills. Sitting across from her in one of the padded chairs was a Buzz Lightyear.

"I tell 'em not to play in here," Dominick mumbled, tossing the dolls out among the rec room junk. "Oh, hey, don't sit down yet." He pulled a lint roller out of a desk drawer and ran it over both chairs, quickly picking up a thick coat of dog hair. "They're not supposed to let the dog in here, either. There you go, that's fine. Can I get you something while we're waiting? Beer? Nothing like that tinny taste you get drinking straight from the can."

"Hey, Mr. Smartass Shams!" Sylvia called down the stairs. "I think your client is here!"

Dominick held up a cautionary finger as if he was worried Dante might bolt, and went upstairs. Dante fidgeted in his seat, felt something sharp in his posterior, reached around and extracted a red Lego from the cushions. He turned to toss it out the open louver door and found himself facing the oversized, growling dust mop again. Dante carefully set the Lego down on Dominick's desk.

"Right down here, Ms. Bick," he heard Dominick say. "Be careful on the stairs."

The dust mop turned away, then Dante heard a woman's voice: "Oh, what a friendly thing he is!"

"Yeah, he's usually nice to nice people."

Then Dominick ushered Emeline Bick into the office. Dante stood, took her hand.

She had the same unnecessarily plain look he'd seen in the family photos Dominick had given him, though the pictures hadn't quite caught her slump-shouldered, resigned air and why-bother dowdiness.

"A pleasure, Ms. Bick," Dante said and showed her to the other chair. "Sorry about the circumstances."

"I've actually seen your books," she said as she settled into her seat, letting herself hunch forward a bit. "I mean, I haven't read them, they look a little … . I'm afraid I'm not that, you know …" She made some sort of vague gesture in the direction of her head. "But I see them in the stores. I can't thank you enough for, well, somebody like *you* …"

"Please," Dante said with perfected false modesty.

She frowned at something on his sleeve. "Oh, you have a loose thread."

Dante plucked the long, wavy strand of hair free and made a face at Dominick. "Not a thread. Dog hair."

Dominick shrugged an insincere apology.

"Seems like such a nice jacket, too," said Emeline Bick.

"It was."

"Can I get you coffee or something, Ms. Bick?" Dominick asked.

"I don't want to be any trouble."

"No trouble."

"Coffee would be fine."

Dominick stuck his head out the door. "Hey, Syl! Think we could get some coffee?"

"You're not crippled, Dom! I've got dinner going here!"

Dominick smiled an apology at Emeline Bick. "Back in a sec," and off he went before Emeline could, as she'd apparently intended to do, object.

"Yeah, right, dinner!" they heard Dominick yell as he started up the stairs. "This is just because I don't care about your damn shams! And how many times have I told you about letting the damn dog in my office! That's *my* damn office! Not the damn *dog's*!"

"I don't go near your damn office. Talk to the kids."

And at that point, the upstairs door mercifully closed. As insurance, Dante closed the office door, returned to his seat and turned to Emeline Bick.

"So, Ms. Bick, Mr. Castellano has only given me the roughest idea of your situation."

Emeline Bick would've had not a pretty face, but at least a moderately pleasant one were it not sagged into a permanently depressed look. "It's so sad. I didn't think this kind of thing happened until *after* somebody ... somebody, you know, *passed*. You hear about people fighting over wills and that kind of thing, but my father is still *alive*!"

"And well?"

"You mean in his head, don't you?" She managed to firm those pulled-down cheeks into a look of conviction. "My father knows what he's doing, Doctor."

Dante nodded.

Then, her face softened and sagged again, and so did her voice. "What's sad is we were so close."

"You mean you and your brother?"

"All of us. We were a happy family. I know you see these talk shows and it doesn't seem like there is such a thing anymore, but we were. You look at where we were and ... and you wonder how it winds up like this."

Dante nodded, again. "Yes, well, normally, Ms. Bick, you and I probably wouldn't meet until later in the process."

"Process?"

"Usually, I'd interview your father first, and there's a good deal of paperwork to evaluate – medical records and so forth – and then, at some point, you and I would have a conversation."

"I thought since I was your client –"

"Excuse me, but you're Mr. Castellano's client. I'm being engaged by his firm. You should be clear on my role, Ms. Bick. It's not my job to support your side of the case, or anybody's side. I perform what you might call a psychological reconnaissance on your father for Mr. Castellano; nothing more, nothing less. What Mr. Castellano does with that information and how he chooses to present it, that's not my concern."

"Oh." Dante was beginning to feel the only emotions she was capable of expressing were various degrees of sadness and/or disappointment. Even puzzlement came across as disappointingly sad (or sadly disappointed). "I didn't … understand."

Dante smiled comfortingly. "Ms. Bick, there are people in this profession who feel it's their mandate to provide only what supports the case of the people paying them."

It took her a second, but then she smiled, sadly of course, with comprehension. "They lie."

"Well, I wouldn't call them liars. Let's just say they're highly interpretive."

"They play with the facts."

"There are no facts, Ms. Bick. You go to a doctor, you say you have a headache, he does an x-ray, an MRI, he sees a mass, he does a biopsy, it's cancer. That's working with facts. We're talking about mental states; someone's *mind*. Ms. Bick, I could tell you exactly what part of your father's brain he uses when he's making decisions, or when he's figuring out a dinner check. I could show you his brain at work with an MRI, show you what part of his brain fires when he's thinking about something he loves, and what part fires when he's thinking about something he hates. But I cannot show you *why* he loves what he loves or hates what he hates. I'll speak with him, I'll make observations, make some conclusions, render an assessment, which is a very glorified way of saying I'll make an educated guess."

She frowned. "Then there's no way of knowing the truth."

59

"Everybody finds their own truth, Ms. Bick."

"It's all kind of … confusing. I didn't know how it worked." She shook her head, tsk-tsking herself.

Too much poor-little-stupid-me. Poor-little-stupid-me doesn't pick Dominick Castellano for a courtroom street fight.

"There's no reason you should've known. People's conceptions about this are based on what they see on TV and in the movies. As Mr. Castellano will explain, our first order of business will be to set up an interview between myself and your father. Does he still live at home with you?"

"No, he's in an assisted care facility." Immediately defensively apologetic: "He insisted! His mind, in his head, he's fine, but his health …"

"I see."

"I didn't mind taking care of him. Really! But he didn't want me to go through that."

"How did your brother react when your father moved into the facility?"

"You'll have to ask him. We don't talk."

"Not at all? Is that since this business with the will?"

"From even before. You know what's funny, Doctor? How you can stop loving somebody you loved your whole life. My brother and I …" A nostalgic wistfulness passed over her face, then a sigh and she looked down into her lap. "But now …"

"How does your father feel about your brother?"

"That's why my brother's fighting this! He can't accept that Dad feels this way."

"Meaning your father more or less cutting him off. Well, I would think that's understandable. We sometimes feel guilty about expecting something when the time comes, but it's also natural to feel you're due –"

"Oh, I don't mean the will! I mean, yes, the will, but that a father can stop loving his son. You know, you meet somebody, you think you're in love, you make plans, then something happens, you break up …" That wistful looking back, again. "I don't know; somehow you can accept that. It happens.

"But a sister is always supposed to love her brother, and a father is always supposed to love his son. But I *can* stop loving my brother, and H-J – that's what I always called him – he doesn't get that. Doctor?"

That was when he realized he'd been drifting. "I'm sorry. I was listening, Ms. Bick. Just thinking."

"It does happen that way, doesn't it, Doctor?"

Dante smiled with his own bit of nostalgic wistfulness. "Tolstoy thought so."

Emeline Bick's face went blank.

"Each family has its own miseries."

Then Dominick was in the doorway with a tray with cups, a coffee pot, and the usual trappings. "Here we go. You two getting to know each other?"

* * *

For Dante's purposes, the rest of the meeting was superfluous: Dominick discussing the legal end with Emeline, outlining possible strategies and the like, finalizing her getting in touch with her father's doctors to set up a face to face between him and Dante. Then Emeline was gone, Dominick called a cab for Dante and walked him outside to wait on the front lawn.

"You'll probably be meeting with the old man tomorrow or the next day," Dominick said.

Dante nodded. "If it's tomorrow, make it late in the day. I have something on for the morning. Something *non*-contingency, so you can see why that gets priority."

Dominick made a dismissive face, then continued on: "I'm also going to be deposing Bick Junior and his wife later this week. I'd like for you to be – . Well, son of a gun! Now isn't this a co-inky-dink!"

A yellow VW Beetle was pulling up at the curb. Dante recognized the silhouette behind the wheel even before the driver climbed out of the car. "Coincidence my –"

"Hi, Dom!" Then her eyes settled on Dante, first soft, then hard, then resigned, then – as she always ultimately was – unfailingly polite: "Hello, Dan."

"Edie."

Edie DiMarchese nee Castellano was a quiet kind of pretty, the kind you didn't notice until you'd been talking to her for a while, then couldn't get out of your head. At least, that was how it had worked for Dante back at the beginning. She was short, had a pleasantly full body not quite hidden by the oversized Giants football shirt and loose knee-length skirt, a wide face and large, dark eyes designed for smiling, which made it all the more painful when she had no reason to. She ran her fingers through her loose, short brown hair – a familiar nervous tic while she took a second to mentally fix her place.

She stayed there at the foot of the walk, by her car, smiling automatically at Dante.

"Hey, Sweets!" Dominick called. "Would you believe I forgot all about you coming over for dinner tonight? I must be going senile."

Dante and Edie shared a doubting smile, neither believing Dominick had forgotten a goddamned thing.

And then they shared a second, doubting smile when Dominick said, "Hey, is that Syl calling? Probably gotta help her in the kitchen or beat the kids for her or something." He turned for the house. "I hear you, Syl! I'm coming! Dammit, I said I'm coming!" and he disappeared inside the house.

"He should be disbarred," Dante said heading down the walk.

"He was always smooth," Edie said walking toward him.

"Smooth as an old dirt road. Don't worry; I'm not staying. Dominick has me consulting on a case. My cab should be along any minute."

"I wasn't worried."

They stood a few feet apart on the walk. The sun was behind Dante; she had to squint up at him. There were new lines around her eyes, he noted, but they took nothing away from her.

"I think this is just your brother's idea of a joke."

"Not too funny, is it?"

"Not too, no."

She looked away for a moment, at nothing, smiled at some thought flitting through her head, then looked back up at him. He used to tease her that she was the perfect height for him; that when they hugged, he could rest his head atop hers.

"I saw you on TV yesterday," she said.

He groaned which made her smile and shake her head; the reaction hadn't surprised her.

"You looked fine," she said. "Came off quite well. Very … polished. As usual."

"You're generous. I must say, you're looking quite well yourself."

"Thank you."

"Dominick tells me you're seeing someone."

"Yes. A fireman. Why would that interest you?"

"I only wanted to say I hope it goes well for you."

"Thank you. And you?"

He could almost feel how it'd be, her head against his chest, his cheek resting in her hair. "Never seems to be time." Then he saw his taxi pull up behind her VW. Inwardly, he sighed. He beckoned the cabbie to wait a second. "Well …" he said.

She'd turned at the sound of the cab pulling up. "Yeah."

He began to step past her, stopped. "I meant to ask … How's the boy?"

She had never had an angry stare, even when she was livid. Her face simply lost its warmth.

"You mean your son?" she said flatly. "He's starting to look at colleges. He's a good kid, smart, doesn't quite know what to do with himself, though. He's … He's at a point where he's asking a lot of questions."

"About us? That's natural."

'Well, that may be. He wants to know what happened with us. I can only tell him my side. I would think you'd want him to hear your side."

He pretended to look at his watch, make some motion about the cab. "I, uh —"

"I'm sure you do."

And before he could say goodbye, she'd walked by him and into the house.

* * *

The brownstone's backyard was small, deeper than wide but nothing that couldn't be covered in a dozen steps or so — which almost made the amount of work that had gone into it overkill, but it was as Dante had wanted it. There was a short, flagstone patio, then, alongside much of the length of the yard on either side set off with white cobbles, beds rainbowed with a half-dozen varieties of chrysanthemums backstopped by trim shrubberies along the whitewashed fence. Down the center of the yard, laid out in an aesthetically pleasing easy S, were flagstone stepping stones set on a path of crushed white gravel. The path led to swath of grass across the rear of the yard, as immaculately manicured as a putting green, in the middle of which sat the small white-painted gazebo, where Dante sat in a padded wicker chair at a small, glass-topped wicker table. Across its surface, he'd spread the contents of Rachel Blume's portfolio on Abel Gant, leaving just enough room in a corner of the table for a flowered teacup of featherweight porcelain.

It's that simple, Dolly Moffitt had said. *Find another serial killer. That simple.* He paged through the file, ostensibly to brief himself, but with some just-below-consciousness part of him — almost an autonomic reflex — wondering if maybe something in these typed sheets and filled-out forms might be luridly commercial enough to satisfy her.

64

He turned the pages and read the words but nothing registered. His mind kept going back to the conversation he'd had with Emeline Bick.

"Mrs. Froe-*lich*!" He did not look up as he held his teacup aloft, assuming that would be signal enough.

A moment later, Mrs. Froelich came down the flagstone and gravel path carrying a steaming teapot. She stepped up into the gazebo and poured Dante a fresh cup of green tea.

"I don't know how you can drink this stuff," she said. "It looks like somebody peed in your cup."

Still without looking up, Dante beckoned her to another padded wicker chair across from him. Dante took a sip of his tea, set his reading glasses on the table, sat back in the chair, the cup nestled in both his hands. He closed his eyes and enjoyed a quick, late afternoon hush of a breeze that had somehow found its way past the bulwark of brownstones and into his yard. When he opened his eyes, Mrs. Froelich was sitting in somewhat bored patience, the teapot in her lap.

"Mrs. Froelich, I would like to ask you a question. About your family."

"My family?"

"You have children, yes?"

"It's nice that after eight years you would ask."

A patient smile: "You have children?"

"Three."

Dante shuddered. "Three!"

"Three."

"Ages?"

"Christopher is thirteen; Russ is twelve; and Tee-tee —"

"Tee-tee?"

"Tricia, but when the kids were small, the boys couldn't say Tricia, so —"

"So Tee-tee."

"Tee-tee's, well, she'll start driving next year."

Dante took another sip of his tea and set the cup back down on the table. "Hypothetical question, Mrs. Froelich."

She squirmed in her seat as if preparing herself. "All right."

"What would it take for you to stop loving one of your children?"

"Excuse me?"

"Let's say one of them stole. Or maybe killed someone."

"Are you serious?"

"Always."

"I don't know. I can't even picture something like that. Hm. I might hate something they've done, but ... They'd still be my kids. Is that all, Doctor?" She started to rise but Dante waved her back down. "You know this teapot is hot."

Dante crossed to her, took the pot, wincing as he noted it was, indeed, hot, and set it on the gazebo floor. "Are both your parents still living?" he asked as he took his seat, again.

"Yes."

"Are you close?"

"Well, it's hard. They retired to some place in Arizona a few years ago, we hardly see them."

"So, you don't feel ... affectionate."

"It's not that, it's just ... Well, they're not *here*."

Dante tapped his finger restlessly on the arm of his chair. "Another hypothetical situation. Let's say your father passed away –"

"Maybe one of my kids killed him."

"Let's say he passed away –"

"He's actually in pretty good shape. I think my mother would probably go first."

"Let's say," Dante continued a bit more insistently, "*hypothetically*, your father passed away. There is an estate of some worth."

"That's a hell of a hypothetical. I don't think they have much –"

"And you find he leaves you nothing," Dante pressed on.

"Nothing?"

"Nothing."

"Well …" Mrs. Froelich shrugged prosaically. "It's his money."

"You wouldn't feel hurt?"

"Maybe. I don't know. It depends."

"On?"

Mrs. Froelich considered for a moment. "Who he left it to. I mean, let's say he was stepping out on my mom, you know, with some frisky 62-year-old down the block, and he left *her* the money. I'd be pretty pissed. I'd dig the old bastard up just to beat the hell out of him if he pulled some crap like that."

"What if he left it all to your brother?"

"I don't have a brother."

Dante frowned.

"Oh," Mrs. Froelich said, nodding.

"Yes, another hypothetical."

Mrs. Froelich thought it over for a few seconds, then another of her philosophical shrugs. "It depends."

That "it depends" of Mrs. Froelich's was beginning to irritate the hell out of Dante. "On?"

"Why."

"And if you didn't think it was a good enough 'why'?"

"Like I said; it's his money."

Dante sighed, stood, handed her the teapot. "Thank you."

"Was I any help?"

"A blinding beacon in the dark."

"I hope your damn tea is cold," and she headed for the house.

6

The interview room at the Manhattan Detention Complex – more commonly and grimly known as The Tombs – was a small, bare-walled room, a door in one wall, a one-way mirror for observers in another wall, painted in what was supposed to be (but wasn't) a soothing blue. The bare walls had no acoustic give at all, and even the slightest noise – a pencil dropped on the metal table bolted to the middle of the scuffed linoleum floor, say – sounded empty and harsh.

An uncomfortable folding metal chair sat at each long side of the table. On one side, Dante's side, sat the open file on Abel Gant he had received from Rachel Blume. Next to the file, an open leather-bound portfolio, Dante's Meisterstuck laying on a blank pad of yellow foolscap.

In front of the chair opposite sat a large take-out cup of Dunkin' Donuts coffee, two packs of Marlboro cigarettes, and a book of matches.

Dante stood with Rachel Blume on his side of the table facing the metal door. Her loose-fitting pantsuit and flats, blocky tortoise-shell glasses, no-nonsense bun and absence of make-up displayed the quiet assertiveness of a woman who had worked jailhouses before.

And so had Dante. He didn't want Abel Gant looking at him as another authority figure, so he wore a sand-colored two-piece suit and had picked out a toupee with a full but relaxed head of hair.

The metal door swung open, and, for a moment, the daytime din of the cellblocks – the irritatingly incessant, reverberating murmur of men marking time – bled into the interview room before a corrections officer brought in Abel Gant dressed in a Department of Corrections orange jumpsuit. The CO looked to Dante and Rachel Blume for a cue, Blume nodded him out, and the metal door shut with a metallic clang that, in the small, hard room, made Dante and Blume flinch.

Abel Gant was an unexceptional looking young man, average height, a bit lost in the baggy DOC jumpsuit. He still wore his blond hair in a military cut, just a shadow on top and cut down nearly to the skin on the sides. He was 27 according to his file, but there was a puffy-cheeked boyishness to his face that, at first glance, made him look considerably younger.

Until he stepped closer under the flat, white light from the caged bulb over the table. The tours overseas had toughened and lined his skin, and it made for an odd mismatch: that boyish face and the lines of someone much, much older around his eyes and the small, baby-lipped mouth.

Blume pointed Gant toward the coffee and cigarettes. "I remembered."

A small crooked smile as he slid into the chair across from them. "So you did. Thanks." He peeled open one of the packs of cigarettes and lit one. He took a deep, basking drag. "I ran out yesterday. I been climbing the walls."

"Well, aside from that, how are you getting along?"

He shrugged as he pried the lid off the coffee. "Ah, it's no worse than basic training. Maybe noisier. And if you drop the soap in the

69

showers, you're advised to leave it there." He gave an if-you-know-what-I-mean wink.

Blume pointed to Dante. "This is –"

"The shrink," he said without looking up, then taking a sip of his coffee.

Dante held out his hand. "I'm Dr. DiMarchese, Mr. Gant."

Gant ignored Dante's hand, looked up for the first time. He had small, hard, blue eyes, studying eyes. The crooked smile, again, but there was nothing to it; no feeling, no mirth, no more emotion to it than if it were a tic. "You the guy supposed to get me my NGRI?"

Dante shook his head, puzzled. "NG –"

"Not Guilty by Reason of Insanity." Gant looked to Rachel Blume. "I thought he was supposed to be some kind of pro."

"I'm just surprised at how quickly you've acquired the vernacular," Dante said.

"Remember: I'm in here with a thousand legal experts all offering me advice."

"I'd take their counsel with a grain of salt, Abel," Blume said. "Remember: they're still *inside*."

The empty smile, again. "According to them, it's all because they had lousy lawyers."

Blume gave no sign she'd even heard him. "Everything you say to the doctor is confidential. Even I'm not privy to it without your permission. We both thought you might be more comfortable talking freely if I left the two of you alone, but if you need me, I'll be in the observer's room. Just wave me in." Then she was gone with another flinch-inducing clang of the door.

"You think I insulted her with that crack about lousy lawyers?" Abel Gant asked.

Dante slid into the other chair. "She's a criminal lawyer. I'm not sure it's possible to insult her." He reached inside his suit jacket and pulled on his reading glasses, reached for his pen, checked his watch and wrote the date and time at the head of the first page.

Gant slouched in his chair, feet wide apart, a too-studied picture of unconcern. "Nice suit."

"Thank you."

"Watch. Pen. I'll bet even those specs go a good dollar. You do pretty well for yourself."

"Observant."

Gant nodded at the pad of foolscap. "You gonna note that?"

"Should I?"

Gant sighed tiredly. "Jesus, we gonna play *that* game? 'What do *you* think, Abel? How do *you* feel about it, Abel?'"

"I just didn't think it was that important."

"Why do shrinks do that? You pay somebody a hundred bucks an hour and he just sits there and nods and you do all the work; what the fuck *is* that?"

Dante smiled tolerantly, patiently. When Gant saw he would get nothing back, he nodded at Dante to go on.

"I want to ask some basic questions first, Mr. Gant —"

"Make it Abel."

Not friendly, Dante thought. *Acting friendly.*

"Seems stupid to be formal if you're gonna be in my head," Gant went on. "You got a first name?"

"Dante."

Gant wrinkled his nose. "I'll go with Doc. Hey, Dante; wasn't that the guy wrote something about heaven and hell?"

"It was a little ditty called *The Divine Comedy*. Sort of a guided tour of hell, purgatory, and heaven."

"Never read it. It's supposed to be a big deal. Is it? I mean, why's it such a big deal?"

Dante set his pen down, and gave his tolerant, patient smile again. "Mr. Gant —"

"Abel."

"Mr. Gant, I'd love nothing better than to enlighten you as to the joys of medieval literature, but I don't think that's why Tom Vance

71

and George Stavros have gone to the trouble and expense – considerable expense, I might add – of bringing me in."

Gant made a conceding motion of his hand. He took a sip of his coffee, a drag on his cigarette, and let out a long, noisy stream of smoke. "Why *did* they bring you in, Doc? I mean, nothing's bringing that guy back, right?"

From evasive to aggressive.

Dante picked up his pen. "By 'that guy' I take it you mean –"

"Brian Kinney." The crooked smile, again, but feeling something for the first time; rueful. "He was my co-star in that video everybody's talking about. Has anybody set it to music yet?"

"Not yet."

Gant frowned into his coffee. "He had a wife, he had three kids. Two girls and a boy. You want to know their ages?"

"You seem to know a fair amount about him."

"They get newspapers in here, Doc. Taxpayer's expense, too."

"You're reading a lot about him?"

"You know how when you die, everybody's always saying nice things about you – good father, good husband, good neighbor – even if you were a miserable shit-heel. But it seems like he really was a nice guy. I'm just glad his kids weren't at the game. Course, that goddamn video is all over the place, so they've probably seen it anyway."

"You didn't know him before the game?"

"I didn't even know his fuckin' *name* until … well, after."

"His death troubles you?"

Gant fixed Dante with those small, hard eyes. Not angry, not quite; but cold. "No, actually, Doc, I get off on it. I lay awake nights beatin' my meat to it. What the fuck kinda question is that?"

"Actually, I didn't ask a question. I was just remarking that as much violence as you must have seen overseas –"

"You think maybe I'm so used to bashin' in brains, this time didn't bother me?"

"Did you do much brain-bashing overseas?"

"Nothing like this."

"But you saw combat."

Something about the question amused Gant enough to bring an almost-chuckle out of him. "Well, probably not like what you think. *You* say combat, you're thinking a fire fight, rat-a-tat-tat ka-chow ka-chow, but it's almost never like that. You're escorting a supply convoy – that's what we did, we were convoy security – there's what looks like an old garbage can by the side of the road, you pass it and it's an IED. It takes out a truck, you pull a guy out, he looks like overcooked bacon. Maybe, sometimes, a couple ragheads toss off a few rounds for dessert before they fly, but it's not much of a fight. Now you, you say combat, that's not what you think. But that's what it was … day in, day out."

Makes it sound like a general comment, but it's a specific memory. It's in his eyes. But no emotion.

"No downtime," Dante said.

"Downtime is when you got nothing to worry about. But you don't trust the fuckin' Afghan soldiers, you don't trust the fuckin' Afghan cops, you don't trust the fuckin' Afghan ol' mama does the laundry. So where's your downtime?"

"And then they sent you back. More than once."

"Then they sent me back."

"And it's worse because then you know what it's going to be like."

"Yeah."

Dante turned to Rachel Blume's file. "You were decorated on your last tour. And wounded. Silver Star and the Purple Heart."

A short, bark of a dismissive laugh. "The Purple Heart I got for not keeping my ass down! Literally!" Gant rose up on one haunch and patted his right buttock. "Want to see the scar?"

"No, thank you. And the Silver Star? That man you pulled out of the burning truck. You did that under fire."

"Didn't help him any." Again, flat, affectless.

"Did you lose many friends over there?"

73

"A few."

"Any seriously wounded?"

"A few." A pause, another sip of coffee. Then, "I never got the chance to go through all those stages," he said too lightly. "You know, that stages of death thing? What are they? Denial, getting pissed off –"

"Denial, anger, bargaining, depression, acceptance. I wouldn't think, under the conditions you experienced overseas, you would have had the time."

"Especially acceptance. Never got to acceptance. I've got friends who are dead, Doc. They died bad. How do you 'accept' that?"

He's mocking the idea, but he's hoping I can give him something.

Dante set down his pen and sat back. "When Kubler-Ross came up with the concept of the five stages, she wasn't talking about dealing with the death of others, but with one's own death. Grievers seem to have 'adopted' them I suppose you could say. Initially, she hadn't even broken the process down into those five steps. The story goes it was an idea that came to her while she was working on the book that would make them famous.

"The concept has an understandable appeal: it's simple and most of us like simple. And, it's so … orderly. Like a good recipe. It suggests that if one goes through all of these stages, if you add a teaspoon of this and a soupçon of that, somehow you come out the other end at some kind of peace. However, it bears saying, with all respect to Dr. Kubler-Ross, forty-odd years of subsequent research suggests people rarely behave simply; according to the rules. Emotionally, psychologically, they bounce here and there, sometimes hitting several of the five stages at once, sometimes not experiencing some of them at all."

Dante gave Gant a few moments to process it all, then leaned forward, picking up his pen. "That kind of constant stress you were describing; did you have any problems readjusting to being home?"

"Oh, I dunno. One day you're picking up body parts, two weeks later you're here. You think there might be an adjustment problem there?"

"You ever talk to anybody about that? Army psychiatrist? They talk to you before you're discharged, don't they?"

"Doc, you just want to get out."

Again, evasive.

"Talk to anyone since then?"

Gant smiled drolly. "You."

"Do you have any family?"

"My father died when I was a kid. My mom …" No change in his flat tone, but a long pause. "The first time I deployed."

"Nobody else? Aunts, uncles, cousins …"

"Nobody I keep in touch with."

"Girlfriend?"

"There was nobody special."

"Not even since you've been back?"

Gant overdid a leer: "You want to know if I'm available, Doc?"

"Nightmares, night sweats, drinking problems –"

Gant suddenly took to his feet, paced restlessly in the little spare space afforded in the room. "Look, I'll save you some time. You g'ahead and write down PTSD, I'll get labeled a bug-eyed loony vet, I'll do a few months at Bellevue … and then it's over. Well …" He stared into one of the corners of the room. "… not for Mrs. Kinney and the kids."

"You feel responsible."

"I've seen the video. That did look like me with the baseball bat."

That's the third time he's brought up the video..

"What do you remember about that day?" Dante asked.

"I don't have to remember! Go home, sign on to YouTube, you can watch it all fucking day! You can watch it in super slo-mo!"

"What do you remember?"

Pacing, again. "I killed the guy. That's what I remember."

"You don't remember it, do you?"

Gant stopped his pacing. He was facing the one-way mirror, looking at his reflection, turning those hard little eyes on himself.

"I mean," Dante continued, "the actual event. I'll wager you don't remember anything until you were in detention." He turned to Rachel Blume's file, again. "When the police questioned you, you didn't ask for a lawyer for which Ms. Blume will never forgive you." He found the line with his finger: "'Then I just got mad and I hit him,'" he read. "That's what you told the police. I've seen the video. That's not quite what happened. There was more to it than that. You were running for home, the catcher blocked the base, you ran into him, *then* you picked up the bat –"

"I know what happened after that," Gant snapped. "I've seen the video, too."

The video, again.

"How's your leg?"

"Hm?"

"Your leg."

"Ok."

"How'd you hurt it?"

Gant took his seat. "Must've happened when I ran into the guy." Something in Dante's face made him ask, "What?"

"Nothing," Dante said, making a note.

Gant studied his fingertips dancing along the rim of his Styrofoam cup. "What you were saying," with a forced casualness, "about that Kubler guy and the five stages thing?"

"Gal, actually. Elizabeth Kubler-Ross. What about it?"

"If you don't go through those stages, how do you get through it?"

It's not curiosity. He's looking for an answer.

"There's no rule that says you need to go through those five stages. It's like anything else; different people find different paths. Some people get through it on their own. Some need help."

Gant's empty, crooked smile. "A shrink."

"Sometimes," Dante nodded. "Sometimes just a friendly bartender. But in your situation, sometimes it's not so much grief you're dealing with as stress, trauma. The violence of the loss, the suddenness, the randomness. To stay effective, at the time maybe you compartmentalized it; tucked it away somewhere. But eventually, maybe consciously, maybe subconsciously, it comes back. The realization that it could've been you as much as anyone else; maybe the feeling of guilt that it wasn't you.

"Back in World War II, soldiers could lose their combat effectiveness if they were on the front line too long. They found that a little time off the line, back in a secure area, and they could, more or less, recharge their psychological batteries. But what we found in Vietnam was there are wars without a secure area; the front line is everywhere. There is no place to recharge. And that was the case, I suspect, where you were."

"So, again, I'm asking: how do you get past that?"

"I don't know that you do. I had a patient once who'd been in Korea. He was in the fighting at the Chosin Reservoir. Look it up if you want some new bad dreams. Here it was, decades later, and he was still having nightmares. Sometimes he would see something – a commemoration ceremony on Veteran's Day, something on the History Channel – and it would all come back to him. I don't know that you ever really do get over it. Best case is, hopefully, you find a way to live with it."

"With a friendly bartender?"

"For something like this, maybe somebody more professional."

"Like you?"

Dante buried his eyes in his scribbled notes. "I don't practice therapy anymore. I'm a forensic psychologist, Mr. Gant. A consultant. If, afterward, you're interested in therapy, I can make some recommendations –"

"Ahhh, you're like a general," Gant said with a certain epiphanic satisfaction.

"How so?"

Gant grinned a so-I'm-not-the-only-one-with-a-problem grin. "You want somebody else to do the killing for you. You'll tell me I might be nuts, but after that, you'll just tell me where to go. That's it, right? You're telling me where to go?"

"I have a feeling, Mr. Gant," and Dante set down his pen, "that right now, you're telling *me* where to go."

Gant took a last sip of his coffee, then dropped the butt of his cigarette into the cup where it died with a quick hiss. He scooped up the two packs of Marlboros. "You're a perceptive guy, Doc," and he headed for the door.

7

Dante knew a coffeehouse not far from the White Street detention complex which catered to the young legal crowd hovering about the neighborhood. The place worked a little too hard on a sleek modern look, and Dante would have preferred something more Parisian bistro than Ikea showroom, but he recalled they offered a respectable espresso and, on occasion, the scones were not too reprehensible.

He and Rachel Blume sat at an isolated corner table, sipping lattes. Dante fiddled with a scone – this was, thankfully, one of those less reprehensible occasions – while Rachel picked the berries out of a blueberry muffin.

"He's hurting," Dante said.

"Wouldn't you be more worried if he wasn't? I would." She didn't pop the berries in her mouth. The pink tip of her tongue flicked out to scoop them off the tip of her finger.

"Do you really need those?" Dante asked. "The glasses? Or are they just a way of throwing cold water on the jailhouse natives?"

"I'm afraid I do. Normally I wear contacts."

"That coif doesn't look very comfortable."

"My face feels pulled tighter than a drum. It's like a bad nip-and-tuck."

"Something of which I doubt you'll ever have need."

"Aren't you sweet." If she took the compliment as a ploy, she didn't seem to mind.

"Please, feel free ..."

She smiled, reached back behind her, and in a second she was shaking her hair loose, roughly shaping it with her hands. "Ah, that's better."

"Indeed," Dante said. "I was going to suggest lunch, but I have something on this afternoon. How would you feel about dinner?"

"Hungry." Then she frowned. "But not tonight."

"Oh."

"Now, *tomorrow* night ..." She smiled.

"Be ready by seven."

"Seven-thirty. I have work."

He nodded the concession.

"How shall I dress? Something like this?" and she plucked at her jacket lapel.

"You might consider it. I'm just as liable as the prisoners to riot."

"Really? A riot?"

"Well, at the very least, a serious disturbance."

She squinted at his hair, puzzled. "I don't want to embarrass you ..."

"Yes?"

"It's been bothering me all day."

"Please."

"Didn't your hair look different up at the Vance offices?"

"And it will probably look different yet again tomorrow night."

"That'll be nice," she laughed. "It'll also be nice that we'll have more time to discuss Abel Gant."

Dante sighed rather melodramatically at her bringing things back around to business. "Yes. Abel Gant. He's hurting ... but he won't allow himself to feel it. He *acts* emotions, but doesn't really feel them. I think he's afraid to. He wants release, but he won't emotionally engage with events that are painful, and as long as he refuses to engage, there's no catharsis."

"We're not talking about what happened in Queens, are we?"

"We are, but any number of things he experienced overseas as well. He's guarded; he puts up a lot of walls. He evades, sidesteps, distracts, maybe as much for himself as for me. He hasn't made any substantive emotional connections since he's been back. There's some survivor's guilt there, and also the very understandable view that no one who hasn't been through what he's experienced can truly understand what he has boiling inside."

"Are we talking PTSD?"

"Possibly, probably, at least to a degree. He doesn't remember what happened, you know."

"He never told me that."

"He didn't tell me, either. But he doesn't."

"Why wouldn't he tell me?"

"He wants to be accountable. He's not looking for an out."

She mulled this over, then there was a slight shake of her head as if she'd made some decision. "If he tells me he doesn't remember the attack, as his lawyer I'll accept it. But is it true? Do you think maybe he was playing you?"

"To work up an insanity defense? I don't think so. I asked him about his leg."

"His leg?"

"He hurt it that day. I asked him about it, and he thinks he might've hurt it when he ran into the unfortunate Mr. Kinney."

"So he does remember!"

"Watch the video closely. Before he runs into Kinney, when he's still standing on second base, you'll see he's already hurt. Even if he's faking not remembering, there's no reason to lie about this; there's no advantage."

"A blackout."

"He didn't just go berserk. His reactions aren't generalized. You know, like a World War II vet who won't drive a Volkswagen; a general animosity toward all things German. That's not the case here. Watch the video. A very specific sequence of responses was triggered which suggests that whatever he tapped into that day was also very specific."

"All of which sounds like grounds for an insanity defense."

Dante picked meditatively at his scone, tearing off small pieces and moving them around his plate with a fingertip. "Except ..."

"Yes?"

"I'll bet you the cost of dinner tomorrow night he won't allow it. I wouldn't be terribly surprised if he eventually says he wants to plea guilty."

The logic of which completely eluded her ... maybe because logic had nothing to do with it. "Why?"

Dante smiled sadly. "He *wants* to be punished. For Kinney. For other things. Maybe things he did overseas. Maybe for making it home in one piece."

She pried another blueberry from her muffin, held it to her mouth, a quick flash of pink as her tongue did its work. Dante's mind was already on tomorrow night.

"Is it treatable?" she asked, bringing Dante unhappily back to the present. "Tommy Vance will ask."

"Part of my evaluation will include a recommendation for intense therapy. If Gant works at it, if he stops flagellating himself, yes, it's treatable."

"Would you take him on? I'm sure Vance would be willing to pick up –"

Dante shook his head, focused his eyes on the swirls of foam in his cup. "I don't treat patients anymore. Sorry."

"This is more lucrative?"

"That, too."

* * *

Dante brought his bow down, stretching out the last note of the violin concerto, letting it linger in the air of his study. Then silence as he held his violin and bow across his chest, and looked to the little round man with the white, untamed tufted hair sitting in Dante's desk chair set in the middle of his Persian rug. A small end table had been set alongside on which sat a crystal carafe of sherry and two small crystal wine glasses.

The little round man was a rumpled 60-ish sort, wearing an ill-fitting green corduroy jacket much too heavy for the time of year mismatched with the blue vest underneath and baggy maroon slacks. His scuffed, cracked brogans wouldn't match anything ... ever. He had a broad, congenial face, but that was rumpled, too, fleshy with deep folds and wrinkles, and two thick eyebrows of exploding white hair.

But Levi Kaminski didn't care – obviously – what people thought of how he looked. As Dante had come to know, the fate of the state of Israel, his wife of 43 years Tessie, and music were just about all Kaminski cared about to any serious degree, and when it came to music, he particularly cared about the violin.

Dante stood for a full minute, holding his violin and bow as if he was afraid Levi Kaminski would snatch them away.

But Kaminski didn't snatch them away. His rumpled face grew even more rumpled as he fell into deep thought, then he poured himself a glass of sherry – he'd already polished one off during Dante's performance – took a savoring sip, then sighed.

After another long silence, Dante prodded with a "So?"

"So."

Another pause.

"Who told you to do the Vivaldi?" Kaminski asked.

"I wanted to try something on my own. I wanted to stretch."

"Ah, stretch. That's nice you got that ambition."

"Is it better? My playing?"

"Better than what?

"Better than last week? Better than the week before?"

Kaminski took another sip of his sherry, splashed some into the other glass and brought it over to Dante. "You got other hobbies?"

"I think of this as more than just a hobby."

Kaminski returned to his seat. "It's nice you think of it like that."

Dante felt an unpleasant pang in his chest. He put his glass down on the book shelves behind him and carefully returned his violin and bow to their stand in their corner of the room.

"Look," Kaminski said, "I don't want it should be God in heaven turns to my mother and says, 'Oy, Ruthie, a thief you raised!'"

"God says 'oy'?"

"*Our* God. *Your* god says maybe 'Goodness gracious.' But a thief my mother did not raise. Hey, I like you pay me every week with a check – a nice check, thank you – that clears to come to your nice house, drink your nice wine, and how you play is not too hard on the ears. God knows I hear worse." Kaminski tossed the rest of his sherry down in a single gulp, sighed and shrugged with a sense of philosophical resignation.

"But you should take that money, my good doctor friend, and maybe do something else for you that's fun. Take a nice girl out to a nice dinner. My sister's daughter is down from Buffalo, thick ankles but not a bad-looking girl, very successful ENT specialist up there, has her own money. You want, I'll fix it up. But this –" and his wildly tangled eyebrows wagged toward Dante's violin, "– how good it is is how good it's ever gonna be. It's *been* like that. Maybe something I should've said before, but my mother also always told me to be nice."

Dante stood there, cool and stoic, nodding understandingly at everything Levi Kaminski said. He took his sherry from the book shelves, struck what he thought was a casual pose leaning against the shelves, the bell-like crystal glass cupped in both palms.

"Maybe," Dante offered, "I pushed too far ahead with the Vivaldi. I might have overreached –"

"My friend," Kaminski said, holding up a hand to tell him to save the effort, "I could take you back to 'Hot Cross Buns,' but better it ain't gonna get. You got the heart, but it ain't in the fingers. What can I tell you? You can't be great at everything. Maybe this is the one thing you do only so-so." He rose on his short bandy legs … waiting.

Dante finished his sherry, then smiled at the little man. "I'll see you next week."

"It's your money," Levi Kaminski said, gave a small respectful nod of his head and left.

Dante stood alone in his study, waiting until he heard the downstairs door close behind Kaminski. He picked up Kaminski's glass from the end table and started for the study door, then stopped, looking at the violin on its stand, the afternoon sun coming through the great study window and giving the dark, shellacked spruce a warm glow, then toward the bust of Bach.

"Fuck you," Dante said and left.

8

When Dante had been a kid, the Caldwells had been a cluster of white-bread-and-mayonnaise communities along what was then the outermost ring of Newark's suburbs. Sometimes on summer week-ends, his dad would load them into his rust-splotched Chevy and they'd drive out and away from Newark, away from the little dying factory towns that clustered close to the city, then further out to where single families had homes all to themselves with green back-yards and lawns with flowerbeds set off by painted white stones. They'd drive through neighborhoods with kids riding new bikes on the wide, elm-lined streets, then past where the houses stopped at a borderland of thick woods, and then on to where the trees gave way to the airy expanse of Essex County Airport. It was a single strip field where people who could afford to – and until his dad took him there, Dante didn't know there were any such people – flew for fun.

The tree-framed airport seemed like the end of civilization. Roads headed further out into the west and Dante knew there were towns out there somewhere, and even further was Pennsylvania which seemed as distant to him as the moon, but for him, this was where the known world ended.

By one corner of the airfield, just outside the perimeter fence, there was always parked a hotdog truck. There would be a few cars scattered around the small square of ground, other families watching the brightly-colored single-engine Cessnas and Pipers fly in and out of the field. Dante's father would buy them hotdogs and sodas, and they would sit on the hood of the old Chevy, reclining against the front windshield. His father would keep up a running commentary on the coming and going planes.

For the flyer practicing touch-and-go take-offs and landings, his father would provide a Disney-Goofy pilot's voice as the plane touched down, taxied a bit, then revved its engine and took off again: "Woops, what the *hey!* This isn't Pomona! Gotta try again!"

It seemed funny at the time, but then maybe not so much funny as fun. He was lying on the sun-warmed Chevy's hood between his mom and dad, chomping on a dirty water dog on a summer afternoon, and if this was all his family could afford in the way of a good time on a weekend, it certainly seemed plenty enough.

The airport was still there, but the Caldwells were hardly the remote end of anything anymore. The once sleepy downtowns now had their tony coffee bars and sushi houses, and the border forests had been mowed down for new residential and commercial developments. Strip malls, clusters of town houses, roadside fast food franchises – it now all rolled on in unbroken ranks along the westbound strips of blacktop as far as Dante could see.

The airport had been out of his way, but he'd swung by in his rental Lexus. The patch of ground where his father had parked their car all those years ago was still there; Dante pulled up onto it, nosing up to the perimeter fence. But there was no hotdog truck, probably hadn't been one in years. The thick, summer-seared grass showed no sign of ever having been parted by a tire or footfall.

He reached for the door handle; an impulse to walk the old ground.

Dante backed the car away from the fence, pressed the gas pedal and lurched back out onto the busy county road and put the airfield behind him.

* * *

Dr. Quamdr Singh, the gray-templed, dark-complexioned director of the West Essex Assisted Living Village, was a short, thin-limbed man, whose little well-defined ball of a belly didn't quite mesh with the rest of his almost petite body. Dante liked that Dr. Singh didn't play any power games, had immediately come from around his large mahogany desk to shake hands and then sat with Dante on his office sofa, peer to peer, Harlan Bick's file open between them.

"He's losing mobility?" Dante asked, quickly scanning notes in the file. "Any other physical deterioration? Mental deterioration?"

Singh's face split in a smile of brilliant white teeth. "That's not exactly what it says." He spoke with the slightest holdover of a Hindi sing-song. "He didn't *lose* anything."

"It says —"

"It says he's become less mobile. Have you handled many geriatric cases?"

"Some."

"There's a difference between *losing* your faculties, and giving them up."

"So he *can* walk?"

"With the help of a cane, but he can toddle around rather well."

"He just chooses not to."

The bright, white grin, again, and a waving, confirming finger: "Ah."

Dante read further: "You suspect depression." He turned to Singh. "'Suspect'?"

"Mr. Bick does not like to discuss his situation. Mr. Bick does not like to discuss much at all. It's hard to get a read on his mental state when he clams up. Depression is an informed guess."

"Informed by?"

The other doctor sighed. "We try to make this place as comfortable as we can. We try to make it nice, give the residents fun things to do, keep them active, interested, engaged. We don't look at them as patients, but guests. But some of them still feel … useless. It doesn't do much for their feelings of self-worth when they feel like their families are warehousing them here, which, sad to say, is the case with some of them. Take somebody like Mr. Bick. He went, in a rather short stretch of time, from being a successful business guy to several small strokes to this."

"No offense to your facility, but *I'd* be depressed."

"Hell, it depresses me just talking about it."

"But my understanding is Mr. Bick *wanted* to be moved to a facility."

"I know," Singh said with a skeptical frown. "That's what he said, that's what his daughter said. But since the day he arrived, Mr. Bick has not once acted like someone who ever wanted to be here. I've seen the attitude before: he feels like he's doing time until he goes into the ground. For whatever reason – and he's dedicated to keeping it to himself – this guy's just given up."

Dante asked to see Bick's room and Singh escorted him through the complex. Dante was pleased to see the place was kept immaculate, the halls were filled with floral scents rather than acrid, grim hospital smells, photos and postcards from family and crayoned drawings from grandkids and great-grandkids were taped to the doors of residents' rooms.

"We've got a five-to-one ratio of Certified Nursing Assistants to patients, which is better than the recommended seven-to-one," Singh said with a well-modulated but justifiable pride. "Some places, it's as bad as fifteen-to-one. And you won't see us using antipsychotics just to keep our people quiet."

Dante nodded, suitably impressed.

Then they were at a door that was bare. The name plate beside the door read, "H. Bick."

"Is he in?"

Singh shook his head and opened the door for Dante.

"Visitors?"

"His daughter was coming regularly at first," Singh said, "several times a week. Now, she shows up maybe once a month."

"And his son?"

"That was *always* occasional."

The room was comfortable enough, maybe the size of a decent motel room with a bed, dresser, cable TV on a stand, a little snack fridge, a closet. But the walls were bare, no photos on the dresser top as he'd seen through the open doors of other rooms. There was, in fact, no sign anyone actually lived there.

"When the son came, did he bring his wife?" Dante asked.

"I don't recall ever seeing her here."

"The son had a child. Do you allow children?"

"Not only do we allow children, but we arrange family occasions. You know: things for the holidays, maybe put something together for someone's birthday. We try to foster a connection between grand-parents and grandchildren. It seems healthier for our residents and, I think, for the kids."

"Very progressive of you."

Singh nodded at the compliment. Dante saw a moment of sad rumination pass over the other man's dark face. "I brought my father over from India as soon as I could afford it," Singh said. "He was already quite old by then. When his health started to fail, well, I didn't have the money to – . Well, to do *this*," and he gestured at the complex around them. "That's the bar I've set for what we do here: if I'd had the money back then, what would I have wanted my father to have? I would have wanted him to enjoy himself, and to have his family spend time with him. Isn't that what you'd want?"

Dante turned away, pretending to continue to study a room so empty he'd long passed the point where there was anything left to see.

"Anyway," Singh continued, "to your point, I never saw the grandson here."

"No pictures, no mementos. Is this how he always kept the room?"

"No. I can't allow you to go through his drawers, but if you did, I think you'd find family photos stuffed away there. When he arrived, the daughter –"

"Emeline."

"Yes, she brought him, fixed up the room very nicely, very homey. As soon as she left ... this."

"*He* did this."

Singh nodded.

"Where is Mr. Bick?"

Singh led him to a solarium that looked out on the complex grounds. The area had originally been forest, and when the complex had been built a thin curtain of trees had been kept for privacy. Between the complex and the trees was a band of well-manicured grass marked with paths and small, hedged enclaves.

Harlan Bick, dressed in faded pajamas and an equally faded bathrobe, sat in a wheelchair parked by the tall solarium windows, but he seemed uninterested in the scene outside or much else. He was slumped in the chair, his head, topped with a thin, uncombed tangle of stringy gray hair, sunk between his shoulders. He seemed focused on ... nothing.

Singh asked by a pointed finger if Dante wanted to be alone with the older man. Dante nodded and Singh quietly withdrew.

Dante stepped up to the man in the wheelchair, cleared his throat. When that didn't attract the man's attention, Dante ahemmed again, and quietly said, "Mr. Bick?" then more firmly, "Mr. Bick."

The man's shoulders heaved silently, and his head slowly turned, face frowning, to Dante. His long, hollow-cheeked face was unshaven

91

and pale. At first, his gray eyes, hidden under heavy, wild brows, seemed vacant, as unfocused as the mind behind them.

"I'm Dr. DiMarchese," and Dante held out his hand. "I believe your daughter told you I'd be by today."

Bick ignored the outstretched hand. "When was that?" he asked in a weak, gravelly voice.

"She would probably have spoken to you yesterday or the day before."

Bick squinted up at Dante, as if that would focus his attention along with his eyes. "What kinda doctor?"

"I'm a psychologist, Mr. Bick."

The squint faded, the misty look in the eyes cleared. "Oh, yeah, she said somebody'd be by. What'd you say your name was again?"

"Dr. DiMarchese. Is this a bad time? I don't want to intrude."

"You said you were a psychiatrist, right?"

"Psychologist."

The voice, still gravelly, no longer sounded feeble. "Then intrudin' is what you do for a livin', isn't it? Might as well have a seat; I got nothin' but time."

Dante grabbed one of the chairs scattered around the solarium and sat near Bick, keeping an unthreatening four feet or so between them. "Did your daughter explain why I'd be speaking with you?"

Bick shrugged and looked away, uncaring.

"Mr. Bick, if you don't want to speak with me, that's fine. Just say so, I'll leave and save us both a bother. But if you care about your daughter –"

Bick turned sharply back to Dante, his eyes now laser focused. "I care about both my kids, mister."

"Then just a few minutes of your time. As you said: you have it to spare."

Bick weighed it, then nodded.

"So, again, did your daughter explain why I'd be coming to see you?"

"Since you're a head doctor, I guess it's to see if I'm off my nut."

"Well, there's more to it —"

Bick's head bobbed as if startled: "Oh, yeah! The will!"

"Yes. Are you aware that your son has engaged legal counsel to have you declared mentally incompetent and your current will voided?"

"Harlan's not too happy, I guess."

"That shouldn't come as any surprise to you, should it? Mr. Bick, you should know that my report on this interview will not be confidential and will be available to both your daughter's attorney as well as those representing your son. Your participation is strictly voluntary, and you don't have to answer any question you don't wish to. Do you understand?"

Bick shook his head helplessly. "I lost you after, 'Mr. Bick.'"

Dante blinked, a little lost as to how to proceed, then the long, deep furrows of Harlan Bick's face slowly pulled upward into a smile.

"Just kiddin', Doc. So, you're sayin' I can tell you to kiss my patoot at any time."

"It's your patoot to do with as you will."

Bick resettled himself in his wheelchair and nodded at Dante to proceed.

Dante reached inside his jacket for his reading glasses, pen, and a small notebook. "Some of these questions are going to seem terribly basic, but please bear with me. Do you know where you are?"

"Old folks home. I forget the name. I'm not sure I ever knew the name. My daughter picked it out. West-Somethin', Wood-Somethin'."

"West Essex, actually."

"Close enough."

"Your daughter says it was your decision to move out of your house and into a facility."

"Girl's been playin' house for me since my wife died. Figured she deserved a break."

"Is that why you told her to pick a place this far from New York?"

Bick frowned. "She tell you that?"

"No."

Bick nodded in the affirmative.

"And then you told her not to visit you as much, didn't you?"

Bick's head cocked rearward in a narrow-eyed appraisal of Dante. "That another one you figured out by yourself?"

"I have my moments. Do you like it here?"

"'S'ok. I guess." Bick huffed impatiently. "You want to keep talkin' to me, Doctor What's-Your-Puss, then I'm gonna want a favor from you."

"If I can."

The favor was to wheel Bick through the grounds. The old man let his head loll back, eyes closed, basking in the sun. The summer heat hadn't abated, but there was a steady breeze ruffling through the bordering trees which made the day almost pleasant.

"Seems a nice enough place," Dante said. "Are they taking good care of you?"

"Hm?" Bick seemed unhappy at the break in the quiet.

"We had a deal, Mr. Bick."

Bick let out a resigned moan. "Food's hot and they fluff the pillows. At this point, what else do I need?"

"Do you mind if we discuss your son?"

The old man's head came upright and sank back between his shoulders, the same slumped posture Dante had found him in in the solarium. "I can think a hundred other things I'd rather talk about, but ..."

Dante had steered Bick's chair into an isolated circle of hedges. Though well out on the complex's open grounds, he felt it would give the illusion of isolation ... and privacy. Like a confessional.

"Do you mind?" Dante said, pretending to breathe heavily. "I wouldn't mind stopping for a bit."

"Maybe you're gettin' old," Harlan Bick said dryly. "Want me to see about gettin' you a room?"

Dante grinned good naturedly, took off his jacket and neatly laid it across the back of an iron and wood bench, then took a seat on the bench, neatly crossed his legs. He did not take out his notebook.

Keep it conversational.

Bick eyed him from his Italian loafers to razor-sharp shirt collar. "Emeline musta cracked the piggy bank on you."

"Her lawyer is paying me. We were talking about your son."

"*You* were talking about my son."

Dante gave the old man a gently reprimanding look.

"Right. We had a deal. Guess it comes down to one question, doesn't it? *Why.*"

"Your daughter says you don't love your son any longer."

Bick shook his head over that. "Well, not bein' a parent, she'd say that. Ya know, you never read 'bout Alexander the Great *Junior*, or Napoleon *Junior*. Why is that?"

"Actually, Alexander the Great was a junior, but I get your point. The same need that often drives the fathers isn't always in the sons. Nor is ability necessarily an inherited trait."

Bick looked up past the tops of the hedges, his eyes lost in the wind-ruffled leaves of the trees surrounding the grounds. "I wasn't lookin' to get rich, Doc. All I ever wanted to do was take care a my family. I just got lucky. Well," and he smiled ruefully, "up until now, I thought I was lucky."

This is what he's been holding in; once the damn cracks, it crumbles.

"Mr. Bick, do you know how much you're worth?"

The question took him off guard. "Hm?"

"Do you know your financial worth?"

Bick shrugged. "I never cared. I wasn't keeping score. We were comfortable, didn't have to go overboard. It wasn't 'bout bein' cheap. We lived nice. What we didn't need, I put away. It wasn't gonna be for me. It was always gonna be for them. That's what a father does, right? Leastways that's how my dad did for me, and it seemed the right thing for me to do for mine."

"'Sure as I ever earned a guinea, that guinea should go to you. I swore afterwards, sure as ever I speculated and got rich, you should get rich. I lived rough, that you should live smooth; I worked hard, that you should be above work.'"

"You got some way with words, Doc."

"They're not my words. Dickens. *Great Expectations*."

"Well, as much of it as I understood, yeah. That was the idea."

"Which doesn't explain –"

"He's a good boy, Doc. Maybe not the sharpest pencil in the box. But a good heart."

"Still?"

Bick shrugged helplessly, but then his face went hard. "What's her name: Dorothea."

"His wife."

"In the beginning, I thought she might be good for him, give him a little push. Like you said; he didn't have the same need. Me, I had a family to take care of. Harlan – and Emeline, for that matter – they always had what they needed. Maybe not everything they *wanted*, but what they *needed*. So … What's the word? Sometimes I can't find it. Damnedest thing. *Ambition*. That was never Harlan's strong suit."

"I'm guessing Dorothea was too much of a good thing."

"That's a nice way a puttin' it. Harlan doesn't have enough push in him –"

"And she has too much."

"And it doesn't even out. Still, you put up with a lot 'cause he's your son. And then you have a grandson to consider." Now his face grew soft, wistful. "I miss seein' him. The hell's that kid's name? Isn't that a damned shame I don't remember?"

"Harlan Bick … III."

"You're kiddin'." The old man smiled. "Maybe that's why I was blockin' it out. Wasn't my idea to name Harlan Harlan, but my wife, she liked the idea of a junior. Hell, *I* don't like the name Harlan!"

"You remember your wife's name?"

"Petey."

"Your wife's name was Petey?"

Bick smiled at Dante's reaction. "Murial. She hated that name; Murial. She always said it sounded like an ol' lady's name: Murial.

"Petey ...?"

Now the smile turned nostalgic. "Stupid little thing. First apartment we had, a little walk-up, we didn't have much money so we had to do the movin'-in ourselves, us, some friends, you know. She walked into a doorsill and gave herself a black eye. Don't know why, but it reminded me of that dog from what was it? The Rascals?"

"*The Little Rascals*."

"Yeah. Petey."

"The break between you and your son? What instigated that?"

Bick's smile faded instantly. "They didn't want to wait for me to kick off to get their half. They wanted me to sign over stuff now. That didn't sound like Harlan at all. That was *her*. His mouth, her words. So I told him; you want some big money? I'm not stoppin' you; go earn it."

"And that's when you told him you were re-writing the will and –"

Bick shook his head. "I never told him, Doc. I'll be damned if I know how he found out."

"You're sure you didn't tell him?"

"Meanin' maybe this foggy head forgot?" Bick grinned.

"Maybe you inadvertently hinted –"

"Doc, I'm 79 and after a coupla strokes I don't pretend everything between my ears works the way it's supposed to but I'm not stupid. You think I'd ever be off my nut enough to want to go through this? I was supposed to be dead and gone when he got the news."

Dante nodded. He stood, paced around the small hedged space, processing it all. Then: "Mr. Bick, do you love your son?"

"Well, Doc, I may not *like* him much these days, but he's my son. You might not understand this, and I don't know how to explain it, but I cut him out a the will 'cause ..." Bick paused as he searched for the words.

97

"Yes?"

"What it was is I was tryin' to do somethin' for him. If that makes sense."

Dante draped his jacket over his arm and began to push Bick's chair back toward the complex.

"You have kids, Doc?"

"There's a boy."

Harlan Bick cocked his head. "That's a damn funny way a puttin' it."

"Funny?"

"I woulda said, 'I got a son.'"

9

Dante could've picked up Route 3 just ten minutes from Dr. Singh's facility, and that would've taken him straight back to the entrance of the Lincoln Tunnel in a half-hour; less if the traffic wasn't too bad. But he didn't do that.

He didn't quite follow the route toward Newark his father used to take to the Essex County Airport because driving by the old homestead would've been too much of a nostalgia cliché for him to bear. Besides, he knew it was no longer there; it had been razed years ago for a development of townhouses, another in Newark's endless attempts to resuscitate itself a neighborhood at a time.

Instead, he vaguely angled himself west of the old route, passing through the barrier towns until he hit Newark; poor, tired Newark, its windows barred, its streets filled with double-parked cars and blaring Spanish music and people who also looked poor and tired. He slipped down to Route 21 which was the east border of the city, paralleling the green-gray band of the Passaic River. Then, ahead, he saw the girder latticework of the lift towers of the Belleville Turnpike Bridge, and passed over the river. The pike ran uphill into North Arlington, a town of tidy little blue collar homes crowded together on the heights above the river. At the crest ran the main boulevard, Ridge Road, and that took him to the solemn stone pillars marking the gate to Holy Cross Cemetery.

He stopped the car at the gateway.

What the fuck are you doing?

He was still trying to come up with an answer when an irritated horn honk behind him made the question moot.

He still knew the way, followed the narrow cemetery roadways to one of the older, shaded parts of the grounds, and stopped. He sat in the car for a moment, the engine still running, listening to the whir of the air conditioner.

If you sit another minute, you won't get out, and that might not be a bad thing.

This sounded too much like cowardice for him to abide. He killed the engine and stepped out.

There was only one other car on this stretch of road, parked not far from his. Other than that, this part of the cemetery was empty, comfortable under a broad, shady umbrella of elms, quiet except for the birds chirping and tweeting unseen from the cool interior of the trees. He began to wind his way between the headstones. Before long, he saw ahead of him the hunched back of someone kneeling on the ground tending to one of the graves, then saw a familiar burst of long, red hair streaked with gray.

Turn now and she'll never know.

Yeah, but I'll know.

"Aunt Connie."

She had been pulling up dead blooms from in front of the headstone and planting a cluster of bright pinkish-purple peonies with a garden trowel. She looked up at Dante, her elfin face not quite frowning, not quite smiling, then turned back to her work. "Yeah, surprise,

I'm not dead yet, but thanks for checking up on me. What's dead are these flowers. *Long* dead. And I was the one who put them there. Back in early spring."

Which was her way of saying she could tell he hadn't been around in at least that long. "Finished?"

"It's not the zing you think it is. I'm just wondering why you're showing up *now*."

"I was doing some work out in the Caldwells."

"This is not on the route back to the City."

"Frankly, Aunt Connie, I'm not sure myself why I'm here."

"I thought that was your job; to know that kind of stuff about people."

"Physician heal thyself."

She grunted herself to her feet, short and huggably stout, and brushed at the dirt on her jeans and on her untucked denim shirt. "Well, yeah, that's always a good place to start." She tapped the blade of the trowel on the headstone to clear it of earthen clods. "You hungry? I could do with a sangwich or something. There's a great diner not far from here."

"A diner."

"You like foreign food; it's a Greek diner."

"Oh, well, then, by all means."

But he didn't turn toward his car right away. He stood there for a moment at the foot of the grave, looking at the stone.

Ok, now you're here. What do you feel?

It was a plain square of a stone, no fancy carving, no trumpet-blowing angels or Jesus with welcoming arms etched into the granite. Plain because they liked plain … and plain because, at the time, plain was all anyone could pay for.

Across the upper part of the stone was carved the name PIGNATELLO.

Beneath it, side by side:

ANGELO

1942   1983

Loving Husband and Father

What do I feel? Alone.

SYLVIA

1945   1983

Loving Wife and Mother

* * *

The diner was a big, bright box of silver and red aluminum down by the river, crowded for lunch, noisy with conversation and the clatter of dishes and cutlery. It irritated the hell out of Dante but Aunt Connie seemed quite comfy and at home there, munching her way through an oozy grilled cheese sandwich. Dante had ordered a dry toasted bagel and a cup of coffee assuming those were safe choices. He'd been right about the bagel; not so much the coffee.

"You look fine," his Aunt Connie said between bites. Then, with a frowning smile and her deep-water blue eyes fixed at the crown of his head: "Except for that shag carpet you got on the roof."

He had worn his loose, relaxed hair for his interview with Harlan Bick. "I've got a whole shelf of them at home. Something for every occasion. Silly, I suppose."

Aunt Connie shrugged. "Oh, I don't know. If I had the money, I might do the same thing. Get a bunch of 'em all without gray." She studied him for a moment. "How are you, Danny?"

"Things are going well."

"I know that. That's not what I asked."

She should be the shrink.

"Sometimes it all seems to fit. Everything is just the way I want it to be."

"Sometimes."

Dante pushed his bagel around on its little plate with his butter knife. "Are you happy, Connie? I mean, with your life."

She laughed. "Who's happy? My dog's happy. She has a brain the size of a walnut. You have good days, you have bad days. Any day my knees work well enough I can get off the toilet on my own I call a good day."

He laughed. Then, when he stopped laughing: "I'm sorry."

"For what?"

"I have this feeling … they'd be disappointed. And you're the only one left I can apologize to for that."

She reached across the table, took the butter knife out of his hand and set it down on the table, then took his empty hand in hers. "Well, I won't lie to you, Danny, I think you've done some things that woulda made 'em sad. They woulda liked Edie, ya know."

"I know."

"And maybe a couple things you've done woulda got 'em teed off. Like how you don't come for Christmas anymore!"

"I have my own Christmas, Aunt Connie."

She nodded skeptically, then squeezed his hand. "But not disappointed. They could never be disappointed in you, Danny. Look, if you think you got something to be sorry for, apologizing to me doesn't get you off the hook. And they're gone so you're stuck living with it. I think maybe the one who's disappointed is at this table. And it's not me." She gave his hand a last squeeze and reached for her coffee. "Ya know, they never got a chance to tell you, but they only wanted for you what every parent wants, what I want for my kids, for my grandkids. All a parent wants is their child gets to be happy. We just don't know how to tell you how to get there."

Dante thought it over. "Evidently, having a brain the size of a walnut helps."

"Works for me."

* * *

Per arrangements, the car service driver paged Dante as the town car turned onto his street so he could be waiting at the curb to open the rear door for Rachel Blume when the car pulled up at his brownstone. She held out a hand in mock elegance, and in equally mock gallantry Dante took her hand and helped her from the car. It was too warm, even in the evening, for anything more than a gossamer wrap which capped the precise simplicity of her never-fail black dress, set off by a simple string of pearls and matching earrings. Dante deftly passed a $20 bill to the driver as a tip and led her up the front stairs to the main floor.

"I see what you mean about your hair," she said as he took her wrap in the vestibule, noting the full, sweeping piece on his head. "Is that just for me?"

"It's one of my best. Do you like it?"

"I'm curious …"

"Yes?"

"*I* know it's not real. You told me it's not real. So, as long as we *both* know …" She smiled and shook her head in amused puzzlement. "I suppose what I mean is, just how vain are you?"

"A fair bit, but it's not vanity. Well, not completely."

"No?"

"It's what, in the tongue of my people, we call *bella figura;* making a good impression."

She laughed. "Do you ever …?"

"Go *au natural?* Play your cards right, madam, and you'll see."

Along with his private sanctum sanctorum, the main floor hosted a dining room slightly squeezed to one side by the kitchen, and then a living room overlooking the backyard. He escorted her to the living room. "Drink?" He gestured to the pitcher on the English-made oak liquor cabinet by the fireplace. "I have a pitcher of martinis ready, glasses chilling in the freezer, but I can make something else if you'd like."

"Martini's fine." As he got the glasses and poured, she stood at the picture window looking down at the yard. "Pretty." Then, "You said you were taking me *out* to dinner."

"I'm surprised at you! An attorney with your reputation, but with such a loose command of language. Shame! What I said was, 'How would you feel about dinner?'"

"And that you'd pick me up –"

"Again, I just gave you a time and sent a car. I said nothing about *my* picking you up, or a restaurant."

"Because you remember exactly what you said."

He handed her an icy glass, raised his own in salute, staring over the vapor-wreathed rim. "I should. I chose my words very carefully. I don't think you'll be disappointed." They clinked glasses and took their first sip.

"Well," she purred, "if this martini is any indication … And that smell from the kitchen …"

"That's not a smell, my dear," he said, setting his glass down and slipping off his suit jacket, draping it neatly across the back of one of the Spanish leather sofas. "That's an *aroma*. ."

The kitchen, as most brownstone kitchens tend to be, was a bit on the cramped side, a circumstance certainly not helped by Dante's having equipped it with a chef-caliber stove and oversized stainless steel refrigerator/freezer. He took a cooking smock from a hook by the doorway and slipped it over his head. "The fish is done. Do you like seafood? You'll like this, I think. I found some lovely Chilean sea bass at a little market I know." He gave her a peek at some golden-seared pieces in a lidded pan on the back of the stove, then turned to a sauté pan on a front burner. "And that goes on a bed of broccoli rabe which I just need to stir up a bit. If you don't mind, I have a salad in the fridge; could I get you to put that on the table? Just a simple green salad; hope that's to your taste. And if you can manage it, uncork the bottle on the table. It's a very nice, light chenin blanc, should go quite well with the fish."

He was showing off, she knew it, he knew she knew and could tell she knew he knew … and that seemed perfectly fine with all concerned.

She was back in the kitchen about the time he was plating their dinners.

"Anyone can take you to a restaurant," he said as set the rabe in a pool of red pepper sauce, then lay the fish down on the tangle of soft green leaves. "Someone with taste can take you to a particularly good restaurant. But only someone exceptional can make you a dinner as good as what you'd get at a *fine* restaurant."

"You're pretty sure of yourself."

"Usually." He scraped a fork along the edge of one of the pieces of sea bass and offered it up to her.

That same dainty little tongue he'd seen her use to scoop up blueberries the day before slowly licked the fish off the fork. She smiled, impressed. "I can see why."

The conversation over dinner was kept light; despite what she had threatened the day before, Dante was pleased to see they fell into a tacit agreement not to mention or refer to anything concerning Abel Gant or his case.

Dante kept the talk focused on Rachel: her family (mom, deceased; dad a history teacher at Syracuse), her career. When she attempted to ask Dante about himself, he always answered with some deflecting maneuver: "I want to know about *you*. You can find out everything you need to know about me under 'About the Author' on the jacket flap of one of my books" – which was patently untrue. And then he'd redirect the conversation with something like, "Now tell me more about this contract law professor on whom you had this torrid crush." She seemed, as he'd calculated she would, flattered by the attention, enough so that she missed his ploy for the evasion it was.

After dinner, he escorted her to the backyard, sat beside her in the gazebo and poured Remy Martin into crystal snifters, served from a silver salver and a carafe of Italian hand-blown glass.

It was late enough that the evening had cooled comfortably. The protective wall of town houses around them was haloed by the glow of street lamps. The distance from the avenues at either end of Dante's block was enough to mute the sounds of traffic to a near silence.

"You could almost forget it's New York," Rachel Blume said, settling a little deeper into the cushion of the wicker settee.

Then, distantly, the irritated whoop-whoop of a police siren.

"Well, almost," Dante said wryly and they both chuckled and sipped their cognac.

"Can I ask you something?"

"Certainly."

"There was something you said yesterday ..."

"Yes?"

A pause, then, "Why don't you treat patients anymore?"

He looked into the deep bowl of his snifter, the cognac looking dark and oily in the shadows of the yard. "I don't really have the time or the schedule that allows for the kind of –"

"I'm not a shrink, but I'm pretty good at detecting a dodge."

"So you are," he smiled.

"It's as much a part of my job as it is yours. So why?"

"I don't like it."

"That simple?"

"That simple." He turned to her, leaning toward her slightly: "If I had regular patients, when would I have had the time to become a master of culinary arts so I could present you with an extraordinary repast?"

"That's another evasion, you know," but she was leaning towards him.

And then Dante winced as he heard the sound of his front door chimes. He took a quick glance at his watch: too late for casual visitors. "I should see who that is."

* * *

He heard her heels on the living room's parquet floor behind him just as he was hanging up the phone. He forced a smile but could tell it was a transparent mask from the look on her face.

107

"I've called you a car. It should be here in a few minutes."

"Are you alright?" she asked, and he could see she knew he wasn't. Then she saw the open Fed Ex mailer on the floor, a ragged piece of notebook paper in Dante's hand. Now, more pointedly: "Are you alright?"

He forced a bad imitation of a reassuring nod, shoved the piece of paper in his trouser pocket, and led her to the vestibule to retrieve her wrap. "I'm sorry," he muttered as he settled the wrap on her shoulders.

"I'm not angry. Just worried."

"Thank you."

"I shouldn't have asked … what I asked. It's none of my –"

"Had nothing to do with it, believe me."

"Is there anything I can –"

He was already shaking his head. "Your car's here."

He walked her down the steps to the car. The driver was already holding the rear door open. She turned, gave Dante a light kiss on the lips, and stepped into the car.

Back in his study, he sat at his desk, a tumbler of scotch at his elbow, the wrinkled piece of paper spread on the blotter before him. The ragged edge told him it had been torn from a small composition book. The letters were all caps, written in the bold red ink of a felt tip pen because that's all that would have been allowed:

> DEARIE –
> IT WOULD BE SUCH FUN.
> XOX

10

Dante had hired a town car for the day's reconnaissance. Having a driver would allow him to sit in the back making preliminary notes for his assessment reports on Harlan Bick and Abel Gant. He wanted to be busy, wanted his head filled with *stuff* because when it wasn't it was filled with the image of that ragged-edged piece of paper and its bold letters declared in bleeding red felt tip ink. That same image had kept appearing in his head all the previous night as he'd closed his eyes and tried, with little success, to sleep, even after two more tumblers of scotch, and it had still been there in his head when he'd woken up that morning.

That mental picture was also why Dante had dodged Rachel Blume's phone calls all morning. When'd he'd headed past Checkpoint Charlie telling Esther Froelich he'd be out all day, not to call but he'd call in, she told him that Rachel Blume had, having given up on his home and cell phone, tried calling the office number asking if he was alright.

"Is there something I should know that would make you not be alright?" Mrs. Froelich asked.

"If she calls back, tell her I'm fine and I'll call her."

"And when she tells me that sounds like a load of crap – because it does – what do you want me to tell her?"

By that point, Dante was already halfway out the door and pretending he hadn't heard.

Normally, other than writing up his evaluation of Harlan Bick, Dante wouldn't have had much else to do for Dominick Castellano until the deposition of Bick Junior and his wife, but Dante had called Dominick at home that morning offering him – at no charge which brought a droll, "Hold on, I gotta sit down" from the other end of the line – to help him with some of the pre-trial preliminaries. Part of it was he needed something to do: stuff to fill his head, distract him, occupy him.

But he had told Dominick, "Something doesn't figure and now I'm curious," and that was true, too. The something that didn't figure was Harlan Junior's finding out about his father's will. If the father was remembering correctly, he hadn't told his son about the contents of his will, and it made no sense for Emeline to have told him, which left only Harlan Senior's lawyer who should've been bound by confidentiality.

Harlan Bick, Jr. and his family lived in one of the Nyacks, a cluster of cozy villages gathered around the western end of the Tappan Zee Bridge. The Nyacks were pleasant enough places, sitting in a comfy interstitial cushion between suburbs and countryside. Nice as they were, Dante calculated it was nearly a 30-mile one-way commute to the supermarket in Brooklyn where Harlan Jr. was manager.

The driver found Harlan Jr.'s house with his GPS; a sprawling ranch in a development Dante dated to the post-WW II suburban rollout. At one time, it would've been an attractive house, even striking with its sleek, expansive lines, but its white aluminum siding had faded to a dull gray broken up here and there by streaks of green and rusty brown from leaks in the gutters. The house's appearance was certainly not helped by the half-dozen half-finished improvements like the addition on the back end, its exposed stud skeleton more or less covered in flapping blue tarps; or the half-dug new flower beds along the front of the house and bordering the front walk; the re-sodded lawn only partially re-sodded, the rest an ugly scar of bare earth; or the torn-up driveway with only a few feet filled in with new paving stones, pallets of unused stones sitting nearby. Parked on the short stretch of finished driveway was a fairly new white Escalade, and an older – *much* older and looking it – Suburu station wagon.

Dante doubted Harlan Bick, Jr. had so many projects ongoing because he was an avid do-it-yourselfer. He could see Harlan Jr. on his knees in the unfinished driveway, setting the stones himself. Judging by the arm-waving and could-hear-her-from-the-street critiquing he was getting from the bleached blonde woman in a bathrobe with her hair up in curlers standing over him – as well as from what Dante could see of the quality of his work – do-it-yourselfing was definitely not Harlan Jr.'s forte.

Escalade, hers, he guessed. *Subaru, his,* and as far as Dante was concerned, that said it all.

Dante had had the driver slow as they passed the house, then told him to head on to their next stop.

"You sure you've seen everything?" the driver asked. "I could go around again."

"I've seen plenty, thank you."

* * *

It was nearly an hour drive to the Bick's Foods in Brooklyn where Harlan Junior worked. It had been Harlan Bick, Sr.'s first store, begun as a small neighborhood market which had done well enough to expand into the store first on one side, then punch into the one on the other, until finally it had just made more sense to tear down a half-dozen store fronts and put up a single market. Still, it was not some overbearing blocky monstrosity; Harlan Sr. had called for a façade that would blend in with the storefronts of the neighborhood.

Back when Harlan Sr. had been working out of that little grocery, the neighborhood had been primarily working class Italian and Irish. It had since gone mostly struggling Spanish, but Bick had kept the store up inside and out, kept it friendly. For every sign that read "Hey, Friends and Neighbors: Make Sure You Check Out Today's Sales!" there was another that read, *"Hola, Amigos y Vecinos, Asegurate de Comprobar a Cabo Ventas de Hoy!"* There were plantains next to the bananas, boxes of Goya yellow rice stacked next to the Uncle Ben's.

The staff, from what Dante could see, was a mix of white old-timers he guessed went back to the days when Harlan Sr. had been running the place, and young Latinos and Latinas. When Dante asked to see the person in charge, he was greeted by the assistant manager, Ramon Osuna, a goateed, moon-faced young man Dante guessed couldn't have been more than 30.

After Dante introduced himself, Osuna nodded gravely, shook his head and gave Dante a look with his large, dark eyes that said, "Damned shame it's come to this." Dante asked Osuna to show him around the store. *Keep the interview comfortable, let the man walk his home ground.*

"I gotta tell ya, I'm a little bias'," Osuna apologized to Dante. "The ol' man, he gimme this job. My mama was comin' here when it was still a small place. She brought me here since I'm a baby. 'A's how the ol' man knew me. Then Mama, her legs go bad, I gotta do the shoppin'. Mr. Bick, he see me here, he see the food stamps, he say, 'Hey, kid, you wanna job?' He start me in the back luggin' boxes, 'n' now …" Osuna held out his hands as if to say, *Voila!*

"Was he like that with everybody here?"

"Is like this: you do your job, the ol' man love you."

"And if you didn't …"

"You gone."

As Dante let Osuna lead him up and down the aisles, he noted the store was immaculately clean, bright. By the bakery counter, there were free samples on a plate, and an easel announcing the "Birthday of the Day/*Cumpleanos del Dio*" which, this day, belonged to a gap-toothed five-year-old cutie (blow-up photo provided) named Sammi.

"Did Mr. Bick ever seem forgetful?"

Osuna shrugged. "No more 'n' anybody else. Look around; this business is a lotta details, it's easy for somethin' to get by you. But the ol' man, he been doin' this a long time, 'n' once you got a way for things to work, a lotta day to day pretty much takes care a itself. You could forget your name 'n' things still get done."

As they passed the deli counter, Dante noticed the counter people seemed to recognize most of the customers. On the counter, a sub sandwich had been cut into sample sizes and left on a plate for passers-by under a sign that read, "Have a Nice Day ... and a Bite!/ *Que Tengan un Buen Dia ... Y un Bocado!*".

"Did he ever seem moody?" Dante asked. "Unusually combative or aggressive? Ever seem disoriented?"

"Not even after he got sick the firs' time."

"He was still managing the store after his first stroke?" Dante asked, surprised.

"Well, like I said, a lotta stuff takes care a itself. So, yeah, he come back, seemed fine. He only started to back off after the second time, 'n' only 'cause the doctors tol' him to. He liked comin' to the store. This is what he did. Damned that ol' man know half the people come through that door by name!"

"Did you have any dealings with Mr. Bick's son?"

"Junior? Sure, course." But there was a change in Osuna's tone, the slightest air of tension. "He been assistant manager here since he got outta school, 'n' when the docs make the ol' man cut back, he makes Junior to manager." Osuna shook his head as if not quite believing himself what he was about to say: "He's *still* manager."

Which Dante had an equally hard time believing. "Wait a minute; you're telling me —"

But Osuna had seen something up ahead, excused himself and hustled up to the produce displays. Osuna frowned and poked at a rack of peaches. There was an older, gray-templed gent unpacking another case of the fruit nearby who didn't look any happier about the peaches than Osuna.

"*Que es esto,* Ricky? This stuff got more bruises 'n' the loser in a cage match. Who's the supplier? This from Lew Aldo? Get on the phone with him, Ricky, you know what you gotta say. We're not payin' for this mush. He give you a headache, come get me. When you're done, toss the bad ones, then get Gladys down here to do some a her display magic so it won't look so bald after you thin out the shelves."

"This is what I'm talking about," Osuna explained to Dante. "Ricky knows what to say, I prolly won't even have to get on the phone, 'n' once he taps Gladys, she'll know what she's gotta do here."

Osuna led Dante to a small break room off the main floor. There was a platter of bagels and a variety of spreads for the employees by a coffee machine, pictures from staff birthdays, anniversaries and so on covering a good bit of the walls. Osuna poured himself a cup of coffee, offered Dante one, then they sat across from each other at one of the Formica tables.

"You were saying Bick Junior still works here? Even after this business with the will?"

Osuna responded with a can-you-believe-it? nod. "He happen to call out today. I t'ought 'a's why you picked today to come in, 'cause you knew he wasn't gonna be here."

"No, I didn't know. And Bick Senior is aware of this? That his son is still working here?"

Osuna grinned. "Aware? Doc, right after this whole mess started, he tell me the son would still be comin' to work 'n' for everybody at the store to treat him the way they always did, just go on like always."

"Tell me about the son."

That slight tweaking of tone again. "Nice fella, easy-goin'. Ya gotta like him. Not always the guy gonna make quick decisions, though."

"Good at his job?"

"Hey, Doc, you don' gotta be a atomic scientist, you know? Like you just saw, we got a good way it works here, a lotta good people. Junior was ok and we all worked together pretty good."

Dante smiled slightly, knowingly, and it made Osuna fidget. "But something changed. He started coming in with ... ideas."

Osuna looked down into his coffee, shrugged. "Look, the old man never had nothin' 'gainst nobody comin' to him sayin', Hey, I think I know a better way to do this, or, I found a better supplier. His door was always open."

"You've left a rather large 'but' hanging in the air, Mr. Osuna."

Osuna sighed at being caught out. He pointed at some place beyond the break room walls. "Over there, Junior says we should put a goor-may coffee bar." Osuna rolled his eyes at "goor-may." "Rip all what's there out 'n' put in a bee-stro, he says. The ol' man says, If people wanna sit around drinkin' coffee all day, let 'em buy a can 'n' go home 'n' put a pot on. You lose all this retail space, you got the cost a construction, all your bee-stro hardware, and whaddaya get for that? Look around, Doc. This look like the latte 'n' cappuccino crowd?" Osuna's face clouded. "Ya know somethin'? 'A's not Harlan Junior, neither."

"This happened several times?" Dante guessed. "Bick Junior has an idea, Bick Senior kills it?"

"Coupla times."

"Then it stopped."

Osuna shrugged prosaically. "How long you gonna bang your head against the wall, right?"

"At some point I would think the son would feel he'd do better elsewhere. He ever discuss his possible leaving?"

It was Osuna's turn to smile slightly, knowingly. "Where's he gonna go, Doc? This is all he knows."

* * *

115

Back when Harlan Bick and his wife had lived in four cramped rooms over his one, small grocery story, Leo Schilling had had a one-man law practice a few blocks away in equally cramped office space over a barber shop. Schilling's practice now filled a converted townhouse in Greenpoint where his several younger partners did most of the work and Schilling's role was, as he described it to Dante, "A kind of semi-retirement. When the oldies show up, I put in an appearance to give them a familiar face to talk to. Other than that …" and he gave a not-my-job shrug.

Which was probably why Schilling's office seemed more a den than a place of business, cluttered with family photos, misshapen porcelain mugs with "World's Best Grandpa" hand-painted on them, and the like. As for Schilling himself, he was a tall, lanky gent with a bit of a stoop and a sagging basset hound face which combined to give the impression that forty-odd years of dealing with people bitching/picking/digging at each other didn't leave one with the best impression of the human race. Talking about the Bicks seemed only to hunch him over a bit more.

"How long were you Mr. Bick's attorney, Mr. Schilling?" Dante asked.

The faint flicker of a nostalgic smile: "Back to when he had the first store."

"You know him well?"

"I've known Harlan most of my adult life, Doctor. He wasn't just a client. He was – is – a friend."

"Have you been out to see him since he moved out of the house?"

"You mean out to that place over in Jersey? A few times. Can I ask you something? You've seen him? You're the doctor, Doctor, but in my opinion, I don't think he should be there. I'll grant, maybe he's a little fuzzy around the edges, maybe it sometimes takes him a moment to place things …"

"What're you saying, Mr. Schilling?"

Schilling leaned forward on his desk. His jowly face hardened into concern for his friend. "Harlan Bick wasn't like that until he moved out there. He's vegetating in that place. And I think if he stays there long enough, it'll kill him."

"Emeline says him moving there was his idea."

"It was. But I can't fathom it."

"Were you upset about being replaced as the family attorney by Emeline?"

Schilling relaxed back in his chair, his face resuming its air of aggrieved bemusement at what people were willing to do to each other. "Upset, yes. I've been upset since this whole mess started. But about being replaced? No. If Emeline hadn't brought someone in, I would've stepped aside. Like I said; Harlan is my friend. And I've known Harlan Junior and Emeline since they were babies. How could I take sides in that?"

"That's why you were upset?"

"Was and *am*," Schilling sighed. "I *hate* seeing this. I advised Harlan not to redraw his will because I knew this would happen."

"What made you so certain?"

"Because I've been doing this a long, long time, and that's what always always *always* happens."

"But he didn't listen, obviously. Did he ever explain his thinking to you?"

Schilling smiled apologetically. "You know I can't reveal any attorney–client communications, Doctor," though he sounded like he wished he could.

"I understand that, Mr. Schilling, but is there anything you *can* tell me to help me get a picture of Mr. Bick's state of mind?"

"If you want to know if he ever seemed confused? Agitated? No. Did he know what he was doing?" Schilling smiled grimly. "He knew *exactly* what he was doing, and he pretty much anticipated the consequences. He just didn't anticipate them coming while he was still alive."

"Which wouldn't have happened if his children hadn't found out about the will." Dante said it pointedly, looking for some reaction in Schilling, but saw only glum agreement. "Did you tell Harlan Junior about the redrawn will?"

"Doctor, I wouldn't violate Harlan's confidence with you, why would I with anyone else?"

"You were close to all of them. Maybe out of concern for Harlan Junior ..."

"I never told him. I never told *anyone*. Not even Emeline."

And with that, Schilling had finally said something to surprise Dante. "You didn't tell Emeline?"

Schilling shook his head.

"Then how did all this –"

Schilling cut him off with a shrug. "That's *the* question, isn't it? I assumed she found out from her father somehow. Maybe he told her –"

"He says he didn't precisely because he was afraid of, well, all *this*."

They both considered the problem for a moment, then Schilling tapped at his desk blotter as if to emphasize that what was coming needed to be especially noted: "I'll tell you this, Doctor: he wasn't trying to hurt his kids. He knew it *would* hurt them, but that wasn't his aim. He did it because he was worried about them. About their ability to be their own people."

"Even Emeline."

"*Especially* Emeline. Harlan and Murial – Harlan's wife –"

"Murial? He told me he called her Petey."

Schilling laughed. "He told you about that? Yeah. She pretended it bothered her, but it was really one of those things ... I don't know how to explain it. It was fun for them."

"That's a good explanation."

"Anyway, Harlan and Murial – Petey – when they sent Emeline to college, they practically had to push her out the door. Penn State. For a while, I think it was working the way they hoped. She met a boy;

nice fella, I met him once when he came out with Emeline for one of the holidays."

Dante remembered photos of the Bicks from the file Dominick had given him; a young man with glasses on Emeline's arm at some of the family get-togethers. And then he was gone.

"But she came home after Mr. Bick's first stroke," Dante said.

Schilling smiled ruefully. "Oh, she was back before that, Doctor. When her mother first fell ill. After that, she was home to stay."

"I get the impression things grew more fractious between father and son after Harlan Junior got married?"

"Ah, you've heard about Dorothea."

"I presume you've met."

"Just a few times," sounding like that was more than enough, "Early on."

"Didn't like her?"

"She seemed to like herself well enough without anybody else having to like her, too, which is good since she put so little effort into being liked. After a while, Harlan didn't like what he thought she was turning his son into."

"Which was?"

"Another Dorothea."

* * *

It was about four by the time Dante came through the door to Checkpoint Charlie. It had been too many hours in the town car, and he was already looking forward to a shower and a drink. He stood in front of Mrs. Froelich and tiredly dropped his notes on her desk.

"The notes for Mr. Castellano — I have those flagged so you know which ones they are — need to be done first, before you leave tonight, I'm afraid. Email them to him as soon as they're done; he'll be waiting for them. He'll need those before he deposes the Bicks. I'll be sitting in with him on that. The material on Abel Gant can wait for tomorrow."

"Um –"

"Did Ms. Blume call? Never mind; if she did, tell me about it tomorrow. I'm too –"

"Um."

He'd been so tired, so lost in making sure he'd forgotten nothing in his instructions, he hadn't noticed until that second "um" that Mrs. Froelich was looking to a corner of the waiting room behind him. Dante followed her eye-line to a short, spongy young man, maybe 30, reeking of "wannabe" with his expensive if shoddily tailored suit in an unnatural shade of blue intended to look stylish but coming off cheap. He had a round, doughy face, and thin hair which, in another miscalculated attempt to be stylish, he'd moussed into a sparse forest of short spikes which only emphasized how prematurely balding he was. He flashed a too wide smile and Dante instantly didn't like him.

"Who is this?" Dante asked Mrs. Froelich.

"This," said Mrs. Froelich, "is Eldon Stewart. Esquire."

"Why is Mr. Eldon Stewart, Esquire in my waiting room?"

"He wants to see you. He wants to see you bad enough to sit there for an hour and a half keeping me from getting my work done waiting for you to show up."

"Is that true, Mr. Stewart? You've been keeping Mrs. Froelich from getting her work done?"

"Maybe it's different in your line of work, Doc," Stewart said in a thin, scratchy voice, "but I usually start off with a hello," and he held out his hand.

Dante didn't take it.

Stewart's smile flickered a bit. "So you know who I am."

"Anybody want to let me in on it?" Mrs. Froelich asked.

"This," Dante said flatly, "is Joss Lee's new attorney."

"You want me to throw him out?"

Eldon Stewart started to laugh but then Esther Froelich's cold face had him thinking maybe she wasn't joking. "Doc, I really think we should talk. Really."

Dante took a moment, then nodded Stewart through the door leading to the lounge. As he followed, he turned to Mrs. Froelich, holding one hand up to his head pantomiming a phone, then holding up five fingers, a long-ago agreed upon rescue signal.

Dante followed Stewart into the lounge, crossed behind the bar and mixed himself a scotch and soda.

"I wouldn't mind one of those, too," Stewart said.

"Then I hope your bartender has one waiting for you when you leave."

Stewart nodded an oh-so-it's-gonna-be-like-that nod. "Can I at least sit?"

Remaining behind the bar, Dante nodded at him to help himself to a seat.

Stewart plopped into the leather sofa and looked admiringly around the room. "Nice."

"You waited an hour and a half to comment on my interior décor?"

"Your editor, Moffitt, she passed on a proposal to you from Mr. Lee, didn't she?"

"She mentioned it."

"I only talked to her on the phone. She as cute as she sounds? She sounds worth meeting."

"Get on her wrong side and she'll cut off your testicles and force-feed them to you. I think you *should* meet."

"Ahh, feisty!"

"What do you want, Mr. Stewart?"

"It's obvious. We're waiting to hear what you think about the proposal —"

"I haven't thought about it. At all."

"Really?"

"Mr. Stewart, I have things to do, people are waiting for me."

"And for you, they'll wait." The forced, salesman's smile twisted slightly; a touch of … cruelty? "I believe you may have received a communication from my client recently?"

"From your client? I wasn't aware one could Fed Ex from the cell block of a state penitentiary. So it would have had to come from you."

"I just, how do you want to say it? *Facilitated.* Mr. Lee thought maybe a personal plea might persuade you."

"It only persuaded me that Mr. Lee is where he belongs, and the less anyone hears from him the better."

"Listen, Doc, just talk to the man. Hear him out. What can it hurt?"

"Are you Joss Lee's attorney? Or his agent?"

Stewart chuckled. "Kinda both."

"Wherever did he find you?"

"We kinda found each other. His old lawyer, Castin, he didn't want to handle this deal."

"I always had a good deal of respect for Mr. Castin."

"Respect is great, Doc, but it doesn't buy plane tickets to the Bahamas."

"Castin referred this to you?"

"I heard the slot was open, let's say. So I went for it."

"From where?"

"William Morris."

"You're an agent for William Morris?"

"I was doing contracts for them."

"Ah. And this 'opportunity' arose –"

"They didn't want to touch it either. So I'm going rogue, you might say."

Dante's cell phone in his inside jacket pocket let out a few bars of Vivaldi's "Summer." He excused himself to Eldon Stewart as he put the phone to his ear.

"Hello, Beautiful," said Esther Froelich.

"Yes, I'm on my way," Dante said, looking apologetically toward Stewart without bothering to make it particularly convincing. "I'll be leaving in a few minutes." He disconnected. "I'm afraid, Mr. Stewart, this will have to wait for another day."

Stewart made no move off the sofa. "I don't know how many days it's gonna wait, Doc." He made a show of looking around the room, again. "Not that it's any of my business, but what pays for this? The books? You still got patients?" Then his eyes and that unpleasantly twisted smile settled back on Dante. "Or is it the name you made off my client?"

Dante began to mix himself another drink. "You're right, Mr. Stewart; none of my business is any of your business. Toodles."

"Ok," Stewart said and grunted himself to his feet, but then stopped at the lounge door. "You should talk to him, Doc. What he's told me about you? It's in your interest. It really, really is. You talk to him, or he's gonna talk … and talk and talk and talk. About *you*. This thing's gonna happen, Doc, one way or the other."

"If you don't mind my saying, I don't much care for you, Mr. Stewart."

Stewart shrugged, unimpressed.

"But I presume you hear that a lot."

"I have ears for chirping birds and cash registers, Doc, and nothing else," and with that Eldon Stewart left.

11

If for nothing else, Dante thought Shanahan & Shanahan deserved some measure of respect for having had the good taste to hold a suite of offices in the Flatiron Building, a wedge of vintage Beaux-Arts elegance in an otherwise drab bit of downtown.

For a moment, standing on the sidewalk in front of the entrance, looking up at the terra cotta lions and Grecian faces adorning the palazzo-styled crown, a moment of nostalgia plucked at Dante. "I used to sit in the park there," Dante said to Dominick, pointing across thronging traffic to the far side of Madison Square, "just to look at this place."

Dominick grunted as he settled accounts with the car service driver. "I'm sorry I missed when you were such a cheap date. Ya know, a cab woulda got us here just the same and cost less."

"Yes," Dante said, heading for the Flatiron's doors, "it would have."

The Shanahans were waiting for them in the 17th floor lobby. Although they were several years apart, the Shanahans could almost pass for twins: they had the same, long-limbed physique, the same little pot belly, even the same receding hairlines. But Sean was colored traditionally Irish, with fierce green eyes and a blaze of red hair (though flecked with gray), while Terry ran Black Irish with sad, dark eyes and coal black hair (though flecked with gray). The coloring seemed appropriate enough; Sean, Dante recalled, was the fiery courtroom warrior, while the soft-spoken Terry was the quiet strategist and peace-making mediator.

"I don't know if you remember," Terry began as they shook hands.

"Corley *v.* Lyle," Dante said, "About seven years ago. You were one of my first trial cases."

"I'm flattered you still remember after all this time."

"I always remember talent, Terry." Dante nodded at Dominick. "You can just ask what's-his-name here." He nodded questioningly at the empty offices on the floor; the Shanahan & Shanahan suite seemed to be the only occupied space.

"Some Italian outfit bought the building a few years ago," Sean said. "Soon's our lease is up, we're out like the rest. I think they're supposed to turn it into some kind of fancy hotel."

"Are you going to be able to stay in Manhattan?"

Sean and Terry looked to each other and then back to Dante with the same who-knows shrug.

The brothers led Dante and Dominick through their small cluster of offices to a narrow conference room running along the Fifth Avenue side of the building.

"I'm afraid the Bicks are running a bit late," Terry said, which Sean followed with an irritated grunt. Dante sensed this was not the first time the Bicks had irked their attorneys. "Help yourself," and Terry nodded to a Saran-wrapped deli tray of bagels and spreads and a box of Dunkin' Donuts coffee and creamers on a sideboard. "I'm going to try their cell phones and see if I can find out where they are."

Terry left and Sean dropped into a chair at the conference table with a part-tired, part-unhappy sigh.

"Not the easiest of clients?" Dante guessed.

Sean smiled at being caught out. "If they were always easy, where would the fun be?"

"Jesus, what is it with this stuff?" Dominick was wrestling with the Saran wrap. "It's like you gotta be Houdini to get into this thing."

While Sean helped Dominick tear his way through to the bagels, Dante parked himself at one of the windows, looking down at Fifth Avenue. It wasn't long before a familiar white Escalade pulled up at the curb.

"I think your clients are here," Dante said.

Sean took a quick look out the window, drew a long breath as if to steel himself. "I better go corral 'em," and he left.

Dante watched Harlan Bick, Jr. jump out on the driver's side to scurry around and open the door for his wife. It was a replay of what Dante had seen at their house in Nyack; Mrs. Bick, Jr. evidently giving a lot of instructions, a stoop-shouldered Harlan nodding meekly before climbing back into the Escalade. Then Sean was on the sidewalk getting the same treatment from the woman while trying to guide her into the building while she resisted, evidently wanting to wait for her husband.

"She's a bit of a bitch on wheels," Dominick said through a mouthful of bagel and cream cheese. "Where's the mister?"

"I imagine he's off parking the car. You'll want to depose him first."

"Some gentleman you are. What happened to ladies first?"

"If she goes first, she'll call for a break when she's done and she'll prep Harlan."

"You don't think the Lucky Charms already prepped him?"

"Not like she will."

They were set up in the conference room thusly: Dominick sat at the midpoint on one long side of the table, a pad of yellow foolscap

126

at his elbow, his laptop open in front of him with two screens showing: notes on the case, and a window for texts. A few chairs down
from him were seats for the Shanahans, and, at the far end of the
table, a court reporter. The deponent would sit directly across from
Dominick. Dante sat at the other end of the table, his cell phone in
his lap, his notebook and gleaming Meisterstuck on the table in front
of him.

Sean escorted the Bicks into the room.

Dorothea was a not unattractive mid-30ish or so, but her heavily
applied make-up, bleached blonde hair, a dress designed for someone
ten years younger, and overstated jewelry suggested to Dante that, at
some level, she didn't believe it. She had a permanent furrow between
blue eyes so pale they almost seemed transparent. She studied everything – Dominick, Dante, her own attorneys, the room – with a hard
suspicious look which never relaxed. As Terry made the introduc-
tions, Dorothea made no pretense that she was anything other than
an adversary, not offering her hand, ignoring Dominick completely.
But when Terry introduced Dante …

"You said 'doctor'?"

"Yes, Mr. Castellano's firm has engaged Dr. DiMarchese to examine your father-in-law."

"To see if he's competent?"

"As I'm sure your attorneys explained, Mrs. Bick," Dante said,
"'competency' is a legal determination. My job is just to assess his
'capacity'."

She made no acknowledgment she'd heard anything Dante said,
turning back to Terry: "But why is he here *today?*"

"He'll be consulting with Mr. Castellano during the deposition."

"It's fine, Dorothea," Sean put in. "Routine."

She huffed and Dante got the impression she didn't trust anything
her own attorneys said any more than what Dante had to say.

If Dorothea was a picture of carefully composed antagonism,
Harlan Bick, Jr. was not much of a carefully composed anything. He

seemed uncomfortable in his suit, fidgeted with his poorly knotted tie, nervously ran his fingertips through thinning hair that had resisted the comb. But he was, to his credit, the kind of fellow who couldn't help but be pleasant.

"How you guys doing?" he said, sticking out his hand as the Shanahans introduced him. He took Dante's hand and his head bobbed in an odd blend of apology and philosophical resignation; a mimed message of, "Sorry we gotta do this, but what're you gonna do?"

Dorothea was clearly unhappy when told Harlan would be deposed first.

"It's *his* father, Mrs. Bick," Dominick explained with – if Dante wasn't mistaken – a taunting edge. "And your husband's the plaintiff. Isn't he?"

Sometimes, Dante thought, trying to tamp down a smile, *I forget Dominick's actually good at this.*

Dante, Dominick, and the Shanahans took their places around the table while the court reporter swore in Harlan Jr.

As he took the oath, Harlan Jr. grinned nervously, turned to the others when it was over: "Wow, I didn't know it was gonna be serious like this."

Dominick beckoned Harlan Jr. to the deponent's seat, and asked him, for the record, for his name.

"My name?" Harlan Jr. cleared his throat nervously. "Harlan Bick. Well, I guess you want the whole, the formal, you know, the whole thing, right? Harlan Joshua Bick, Jr. The Joshua was my grandmother's thing, my mom's mom, she was kinda into the whole Bible thing –"

Dominick nodded that that was more than enough, and Harlan Jr., suddenly aware of his chattiness, nodded apologetically in return.

GO SOFT, Dante typed on his phone's keyboard and the message came up on Dominick's laptop screen.

"Mr. Bick – . Well, hey, would you mind if I called you Harlan?"

Which seemed to relieve Harlan Jr. "Actually, I think I'd kinda pre-fer that."

"Good," Dominick smiled. 'Ok, then, Harlan, let's get down to it, ok?"

Harlan Jr. gave a go-ahead nod.

"So, when did you meet your wife?"

"My wife?" Harlan Jr. seemed thrown by the question, looked over at the Shanahans, Sean made a motion with his hand that it was ok. "Oh, wow, she'll kill me I don't get this right on the button. That's the kinda thing you're supposed to remember right on the button, right? I mean, the husband, everybody jokes they don't remember –"

"I know, I know," Dominick said, nodding sympathetically. "Mine gives me grief about that stuff all the time. Birthdays, anniversaries. So, when was it, Harlan?"

"Oh, sorry, I was just going off there, wasn't I? Well, ok, I guess that would be ..." Dante could see Harlan Jr. counting off the years in his head. " ... like fourteen years and change. Yeah, that's about right. Gimme a second, I could do the math and get it –"

"That's fine, Harlan, that's good. Where did you two meet?"

"Oh, hey, that's a funny story –"

"I don't need the whole story, just, you know ..."

"Yeah, sure. Party at a friend's house."

"A friend of yours?"

"Yeah, one of my college buds."

Dante typed: GET THE FRIEND'S NAME.

"See, Dorothea was a friend of his girl," Harlan Jr. went on.

"Do you remember your friend's name?"

"Oh, yeah, sure, he was one of my buds, like I said. Freddy Elway. We used to hang all the time. . . "

Dante noted the name.

"Yeah, I get it. You working these days, Harlan? Have a job?"

"Well, yeah, you know."

"Gotta have it for the record, Harlan."

"Oh, yeah, sure. I manage my father's store. Well, one of 'em, the one in Brooklyn."

Dominick put on a look of faint surprise. "And you're still there?"

Harlan Jr. fidgeted around in his seat, plucked at some unseen lint on his pants. "Yeah, why wouldn't I be?"

"I just figured, well, I mean your father didn't ask you to leave when all this trouble started?"

Harlan Jr. frowned at the invisible lint. "No."

Dante typed: HE DIDN'T BUY THAT HOUSE ON HIS OWN.

"I have to ask you, Harlan, and I understand you might be uncomfortable with this because nobody likes talking about money, but how much do you make managing the store?"

"How much?"

"I'm sorry, I just remembered," as Dominick scrolled through his laptop notes, "I have your financial records here. Hm, I see your father co-signed for your mortgage."

Harlan Jr. frowned at something on the ceiling. "Oh, yeah, well, yeah, he did, yeah."

"I'm looking at your monthly payments. Man, I wish mine were that small! That would mean there must've been a fairly hefty down payment."

"You said you have his records," Sean Shanahan said. "You know how much he put down."

"Son of a gun, Sean, you're right, I do. I'm just wondering where Harlan came up with that much money on his salary. How'd you swing that, Harlan?"

Harlan Jr.'s mouth made a small, unhappy "o."

"You were going to say something?" Dominick prodded.

"Yeah, well …" Harlan Jr. winced. "I guess this kinda makes us look kinda ungrateful, right?"

Dominick worked at looking confused. "I'm sorry, what makes you look ungrateful?"

"But, see, he didn't do that for us, that wasn't for us."

Dominick smiled patiently. "*What* wasn't for *who?*"

Harlan Jr. moved around in his seat again. "See, like, the house was kinda like a gift after little Harlan – my son – after he was born. My dad wanted his grandson to have a nice home, so ..."

"So."

"Yeah, well ..."

Dominick paused, smiled at Harlan Jr.

"Now," Dominick continued, "you say you manage one of your father's supermarkets."

"Right, yeah, the old one, that was his first one."

"He's the owner, but you're the manager. You run the shop."

Harlan Jr. shrugged, then shrugged again ... and a third time. "Yeah, I guess."

"You're the *boss*. So if you have an idea for something you want to do at the store, if there's something at the store you want to change, you can just go ahead and do it. You can snap your fingers and go, 'Hey, gang! Hop to it!'"

Harlan Jr. took a deep breath. "Welllll ..."

"Because you do manage the store, right? That's your job?"

"Well, you know, Dad always took an interest. 'Cause, like I said, this was his first store. He has, like, an attachment, if you know what I mean."

Dominick nodded understandingly. "So you have to run ideas past him, I get it."

"Well, yeah, kinda. I mean, that makes sense, right? 'Cause this was his first store?"

"Sure. That's his baby."

"Yeah, like that."

"Does your dad always like your ideas?"

Harlan Jr. went back to studying the ceiling. "Well, sometimes, a coupla times, we didn't agree. You know, like I said, see, he has this *attachment –*"

"When you disagree, is he particularly combative?"

"Wow, 'combative'? That sounds like an awful strong word. 'Combative.'"

"How about 'argumentative'? Does that work better?"

Harlan Jr. frowned, still reluctant. "I dunno, that's still kinda strong. I mean, we don't always agree, ya know? You don't agree, you say stuff."

"So sometimes maybe you've had a few words."

"Well, words, I dunno …"

"Was he always like that? Or did this mark a change in his behavior?"

And then a change came over Harlan Jr. He sat up in his chair, his fumbling was gone, he tapped on the table to accent each syllable: "Yeah, it was different, his behavior was different."

That's the question he's been waiting for, Dante thought. *He's been looking for that cue.*

"Was he like that with everyone?" Dominick asked.

Harlan Jr. went back into his slouch, more shrugging. "I dunno how he was with other people. I wasn't with him all the time, ya know. Before he went into that home place, that facility thing over in Jersey, he was always moving around all the stores. But with us," and now he was upright, again, "like you said, he was changing, arguing, like you said."

"Did you notice any other changes in his behavior?"

"Oh, yeah!" Another cued response. "He started forgetting things."

"What kind of things?"

"All kinds of stuff. You know; like he was losing it, like that."

Dominick nodded gravely, took another of his strategic pauses. Then he set his forearms on the table, folded his hands together, and put on a bulldog-drooping face of sadness …

Damn, Dominick, if I didn't despise you so much I'd nominate you for an Academy Award.

"Harlan …" Dominick took a deep breath as if it was hard to go on. "Harlan, do you care about your father?"

Priceless.

"What?" The question threw Harlan Jr.

"It's a simple question. With everything that's going on, do you still care about your dad?"

Harlan Jr.'s mouth worked this way and that, trying to form one word then another.

He's fighting between what he's supposed to say and what he wants to say.

Dominick mercifully ended Harlan Jr.'s agony saying, "That's ok, Harlan. Never mind." He turned to the Shanahans who didn't seem particularly happy with Harlan Bick, Jr.'s performance. "If you fellas don't have anything to add, why don't we take a few minutes for a pee break and then get Mrs. Bick in here. With luck, we could be done in time for lunch."

* * *

Dorothea Bick didn't flinch or fumble, she didn't squirm in her seat or pick at lint or dance her eyes around the room. She sat as still as if she'd been poured into a concrete mold, and she kept those eerily pale eyes fixed steadily on Dominick Castellano.

Dominick didn't ask if he could call her Dorothea.

Dominick asked her her name for the record, and she replied, "Dorothea Meader Bick."

Dante typed: MEADER-BICK?

"Is that with a hyphen, Mrs. Bick? Or should I say Mrs. Meader-Bick?"

"No hyphen. I just wanted to, you know, be official. Formal."

Dante typed: NOBODY NAMES THEIR KID DOROTHEA.

"If we do a records search – and that would be purely routine – that's what we'd look under? Dorothea Meader Bick?"

There was a slight movement of her head.

She knows he's after something.

"Actually, it's Dorothy. That's my given name."

"When did you change it?"

She looked to the Shanhans, willing them to step in, Dante guessed, but they didn't. "I never legally changed it."

"Just didn't want everybody calling you 'Dotty' all the time? I can understand that. When I was younger, I got tired of everybody always calling me 'Dom.' Dom Dom Dom." Dominick shook his head at the recollection. "I wanted to change my name to Hawthorne. God knows why."

Dante typed: HAWTHORNE?

"Seriously, Dominick?" Sean Shanahan made a motion with his hand to move on.

"When did you and your husband meet?"

"It was a party, I was friends with this girl, her boyfriend was friends with Harlan. That would be fourteen years, five months ago when he first said hello."

"That's nice you remember."

The slightest of shrugs as if to say, Why wouldn't I?

"Your husband has only ever worked at his father's store, am I right?"

"He wanted to be a good son, and a good son works for his father."

"My father had a gas station. He didn't seem bothered I didn't want to work there."

A peevish "Really?" from Sean Shanahan.

"Harlan could've done anything he wanted to," Dorothea said. "But he wanted to be a good son." She punctuated it with a hard knock of knuckles on the table.

"I find it curious that his father didn't ask him to leave when this business started. Or that Harlan would even want to stay at the store."

"Why should he leave? Just because his father's getting senile? My husband's worked his whole life in that place! He's entitled!"

134

Dante looked down at Sean and Terry who were both avoiding looking back.

"Mrs. Bick, I understand your father-in-law helped quite a bit with the buying of your house."

"Of course he helped us! Harlan's his son; why wouldn't he help us? If he paid his son a decent salary —"

Dominick held up a finger to stop her as he scrolled through his laptop notes with his other hand. "Actually, your son's pay is market comparable."

"Excuse me?"

"It's typical for a supermarket manager. It's even a bit over the average."

"It's his *son!*"

Dominick shrugged; what difference does that make?

"You have to understand," Dorothea said, "he did that for us back when things were better. Between them. I mean between all of us. But don't think for a second he was doing it because he was a saint or something! What he wanted — what he *always* wants — is to remind everybody whose ass needs to be kissed." She turned to the court reporter with an apologetic nod. "Excuse me."

Sean Shanahan made some kind of low noise in his throat and Dante could see him flashing messages through his glaring green eyes at Dorothea Bick to get her tongue on a leash. Terry was hastily scribbling notes which he pushed in front of Sean and which Sean irritably pushed away, and Dante was sure he heard Sean mutter, "I *know!*"

"Have you noticed any change in the behavior of your husband's father recently?"

"Yes! Yes!" Emphasizing each "yes" with a pile-driving tap of her finger on the table. "He used to be a sweetheart, took me into the family like you would've thought I was his own daughter. And when little Harlan was born — I mean we named him after the old man as much as for his father — when he came along, every day was Christmas."

"You mean in a way that wasn't just him reminding you whose ass to kiss." Dominick turned to the court reporter. "Excuse me."

Dorothea smiled a that's-one-for-you smile. "Yes, not in that way."

"But then he changed."

"He got so unbearable we stopped spending time with him."

"He was like that with everyone? There are no similar complaints from other employees —"

"Of course they're going to talk the old man up! Even if he stood naked in the aisles howling at the moon! Some of those people have been working for that man all their lives! He signs their paychecks; what're they going to say?"

"Did you notice any other changes in his behavior?"

Dorothea nodded emphatically. "Intermittent amnesia, irritability, paranoia."

Dante typed: SHE'S BEEN READING UP.

Dominick started jotting on his foolscap pad. "I'm sorry, I didn't get all that. It was intermittent amnesia, irritability, and what else?"

"Paranoia."

"Growing progressively worse as time went on?" Dominick pushed.

"Yes, progressive."

Dominick allowed himself the slightest of mocking grins as he turned toward the flinching Shanahans: "Intermittent amnesia, irritability, paranoia, growing progressively worse. Oh, I forgot to ask earlier, Mrs. Bick, where did you go to college?"

"College?"

"It's obvious you're an articulate, well-educated woman. I just assumed you have a college degree."

That furrow between her eyes deepened a bit. Again, she sensed Dominick was after something. "I only managed a year at county. We didn't have money for much more."

"And your major? Pre-med? Public health?"

Dorothea held herself a little higher in her chair as she proudly declared, "Business."

Dante watched both Shanahans – as if on cue – slowly close their eyes, pained.

Dante typed: YOU HAVE SOMETHING HANGING FROM YOUR NOSE.

Dominick took an inconspicuous swipe at his nose as he asked, "Your husband stayed at the store, even though your father-in-law's amnesia, irritability and paranoia were growing progressively worse."

"He's entitled."

STILL THERE.

"I understand one of the big supermarket chains made an offer on your father-in-law's stores. They approached your father-in-law?"

"Actually, Harlan – *my* Harlan – went to them."

"It was his idea to seek them out?"

"We're a couple, we talk about everything, but it was his idea, yes."

"And if the deal went through, your husband would be kept on as manager?"

"For all three stores. Which'd give him a chance to clean out that dead wood that's been hanging around those places for years."

STILL THERE.

Dominick called for a break and sped off to the men's room.

Dante caught Dominick in the bathroom, his head tilted back as he tried to search his nostrils in the mirror.

"Made you look."

"You're an asshole," Dominick said.

"Praise from Caesar. And I was going to compliment you on the job you're doing in there."

"Ok, you're an asshole with discerning tastes. I see what you mean about taking Harlan first. That was a good call. Thanks. And that business about Dotty's name; that was sharp, too. I guess you picked up on it because – funny thing – you and Dotty have that in common."

What made it sting so much was the element of truth to it, but Dante was satisfied he gave no sign the remark had registered. "You think you could finish up the missus on your own?"

"Why?"

"Could you?"

"Where're you gonna –" Then the light went on for Dominick. "*Mr.* Dorothea."

Dante looked for Harlan Jr. in the Shanahans' waiting room, but their receptionist told him he was outside. Dante found him pacing the corridor past the shuttered offices on the floor.

"It's over?" Harlan Jr. asked.

"Soon."

Harlan Jr. pulled a pack of gum from his jacket, shook a stick loose for himself. He held the pack out to Dante. "Gum?"

"I don't chew gum, thank you."

"I gotta sneak in some chew time. Dorothea doesn't like me to chew gum in front of people. She says it makes me look like a dumb cow. I mean, don't get me wrong, she tries to look out for me like that. You know, making the right impression for business purposes and stuff."

Dante nodded.

"I know she can come off a little, you know …"

Dante nodded.

"It's 'cause she really wants us to, you know, she's just trying to, well, it's kinda hard to explain."

Dante nodded.

Harlan Jr. stopped in front of one of the empty office suites, a view through the glass doors of barren desks shadowy in the light coming through the pulled blinds of the windows overlooking Broadway. "Can I ask you something, Doc?"

"Sure."

"I mean it won't violate anything legal, would it?"

"Depends on what you ask."

"How's my dad?"

"That's why we're here, Mr. Bick, isn't it?"

"I mean …" A hand reached out to the office door, fingers drummed restlessly on the glass. "How's he doing out at that place?"

"He's all right. A little lonely. He misses his grandson."

Harlan Jr. nodded. "Well … yeah."

"Mr. Bick, do you love your father?"

He turned to Dante with a sad smile. "Yeah. Believe it or not, even with all this crap, yeah."

"I believe you."

"It kills me to have to do this –"

"I believe he still loves you, too, Mr. Bick." Dante stepped close. "I'm overstepping my bounds here, but I'm asking you not to continue on with this. It'll open a wound that will never heal. Your father is alive, he's capable. You should be enjoying these years with him. And he should be enjoying them with you … and your son."

They could hear voices coming out of the Shanahan & Shanahan conference room. Harlan Jr. sighed. "It's gone too far, Doc." He held out his hand to Dante. "But thanks." He saw his wife looking for him, waved to catch her attention.

"One last thing, Mr. Bick. How did you find out your father changed his will?"

Harlan Jr. seemed surprised. "Didn't she tell you?"

"Who?"

"Emeline. She told me."

* * *

The Bicks were gone, the court reporter was gone, and in the conference room a rather unhappy Terry Shanahan was pouring coffee for himself and his brother as Dominick packed up his notes and laptop.

"So we done for today?" Sean said.

"For today," Dominick answered. "I'll confer, you'll confer –"

"How're the rents in the neighborhood?" Dante asked from his resumed place at the far end of the table. The other three men turned to him.

"The what?" Sean asked.

"I imagine you're looking to try to stay in the same general area once your lease is up here," Dante said.

Sean gave Terry a what-the-hell's-he-talking-about look, and then Sean and Terry both gave the same look to Dominick, and then all three turned it on Dante.

"Just wondering," Dante said. "Must be a very difficult situation for you. Losing this place after so many years here, having to find something affordable without leaving Manhattan. And with today's rental market being what it is …" Dante gave his head a very theatrical shake of sympathy. "Very difficult situation. Do you mind if I ask you if the Bicks are paying you on contingency or retainer?"

"With all respect, Doctor," Sean said, "do you mind if I tell you to fuck off? You know that's confidential –"

Dante nodded. "Retainer."

Terry set a soothing hand on his brother's arm. "Can I ask you why you're interested?"

Dante sat back in his chair, carefully crossed his legs, and smiled. "Because if you're being paid by retainer, that would explain why we're here … and we shouldn't be. I know you gentlemen. Not just from seven years ago, but I know your reputation. You're not ambulance chasers, you're not vultures, and you're certainly not stupid. You've seen my preliminary report, you've got reports from his doctors, hospital reports, reports from the facility where he's living. No observed periods of agitation, no serious disorientation or confusion."

"Doc, you were with him for what?" barked Sean. "An hour?"

"True, and maybe I caught him on a good day. And maybe today was just a bad day – a *very* bad day – for the Bicks. I've seen better performances at community theater."

Sean was about to say something more, but Terry held up a hand to hold him quiet. "My brother and I have already had a conversation along these lines, Doctor. And we've discussed the tenability of their position with the Bicks. But we are here, now, acting on the instructions of our clients as we are obliged to."

"If you care at all about the well-being of your client, gentlemen, you would do well to talk him out of pursuing this issue any further."

Terry and Sean exchanged a helpless look. Then Terry turned back to Dante. "The thing is, Doctor, we have *two* clients."

* * *

As soon as Dante came through the downstairs entrance of his brownstone, he turned to Mrs. Froelich at Checkpoint Charlie as he flipped through his notebook. "Mrs. Froelich, look in the Bick file, see where Harlan Jr. went to college. Try to run down a school chum of his , a Freddy Elway. It might be Alfred, it might be Frederick —"

"It might also just be plain old Fred."

Dante looked up from his notebook to Mrs. Froelich who was making a pistol of one of her hands and pointing Dante's gaze toward Rachel Blume rising from the sofa against the far wall.

"Hello," she said.

"Anybody ever tell you you're as observant as a mole?" Mrs. Froelich said.

"Relax," Rachel said. "I'm here on business."

Dante beckoned to the door that led to the lounge. "Would you like to come inside?"

"No."

She was wearing the same severe pantsuit and glasses she'd worn to The Tombs. "You've been to see Abel Gant."

She smiled over his recognizing her prison visit uniform. "Yes." Then no more smile. "I've been looking over your prelim. It's not enough."

"It's a standard assessment for a case like this."

"Did you ever handle a case like this?"

"Not per se –"

"Then put your per se away. It's not enough. There's an old lawyer's axiom which I'm sure you know: never ask a question –"

"– unless you already know the answer."

"There's a corollary to that. You don't want the other side asking questions you don't know the answers to either."

"Such as?"

"You said the way Abel acted out on that ball field was very specific. He didn't just lose it; it was like he was reliving a moment."

"That's my sense, yes."

"But he doesn't remember it."

"No."

"I want to know what he was reliving. If this gets to court, and if I can show that this was something he'd gone through back in Iraq coming back to life for him –"

"Yes, I see. I'll do what I can."

She started past him for the door.

"Rachel –"

"Don't bother."

He set a hand lightly on her arm which was enough to stop her at the door. "You could've done this on the phone," he said. "You could've left a message."

"I was worried about you. I wanted to make sure you were all right. And, evidently, you are."

He started to speak.

"Before you say anything, let me tell you what *my* sense is. I spent that whole next day calling you. That would've been your time to tell me what was going on. *My* sense is you weren't ready then, and you're not ready now. So anything else you have to say about that night would be, as we lawyers like to say, irrelevant. And also, after the fact. If you're that set on dealing with your demons on your own, then good luck to you." And at that, she turned and left Dante staring at the door slowly closing behind her.

Mrs. Froelich watched the door close. "Gee, a master of romance like you should teach a class."

12

"Why here?" Stavros was standing across from Dante on the far side of the atrium, on the broad, shallow stairs of polished dark brick which led from the 42nd Street entrance of the Ford Foundation Building up nearly a full story to the doors facing 43rd Street.

Dante was sitting on an iron bench on the upper deck of the tiered garden. "You don't like it?" Their voices sounded small in the great space.

Stavros shrugged noncommittally. "I've lived in this city all my life. Funny I've never been in here."

"I hardly ever see anybody here," Dante said. "I don't think most people know about it. That's what I like about it."

The summer sun cast a bright light through the two 12-story-high glass walls, one fronting 42nd, the other facing Tudor City. The spiky leaves of the subtropical greenery glowed with the light. Dante had been sitting there for … Actually, he wasn't quite sure. The quiet, the stillness of the place was lulling, hypnotic; always had been for him. The other two sides of the atrium were the glass fourth walls of the offices of the Foundation; a 12-story mime show of the city at work – people at their desks, typing, phoning, meeting, walking here and there, chatting, arguing, flirting, making copies, eating lunch at their desks. He found it all soothing, like watching the silent movements of fish fluttering this way and that around the castles and sunken ships in an aquarium.

Dante got to his feet with a sigh, reluctant to give up the pleasant stillness for business. He made his way down the tiers, along the black brick paths between the rows of shrubs and bushes to the small, square, concrete-decked lily pond sitting at the deep heart of the atrium. Stavros met him there.

"You didn't answer me," Stavros said. "Why here?"

"You chose the last place. It was my turn. I was feeling nostalgic."

"Why? You used to live in a cave in here or something?"

Dante sat on a small bench by the pond. "I've found myself in a rather nostalgic mood all week. I keep finding myself at places that remind me of earlier days."

"Sentiment." Stavros nodded, impressed.

"'If you prick us, do we not bleed?'"

Stavros looked puzzled.

"I'm as human as anyone else, Lieutenant."

"I was never quite sure. I always figured you were born just the way you are, walked out of your mother's womb in a three-piece suit asking for a glass of something snooty."

"Not quite. I did my internship at Bellevue."

"You were at Bellevue? Hard for me to picture."

"From such humble acorns do mighty oak trees grow. Do you know Bellevue?"

"Not as a guest, but I doubt there's a cop in Manhattan who hasn't ferried a Looney Tune over there at one time or another."

"Every shift I had at Bellevue always put me in mind of a lecture from one of my first psych professors. The Manhattan Study."

"Never heard of it."

"It was conducted by Cornell University back in 1950. My professor's interpretation of the study was that if you extrapolated the study subjects out into the general population, and you added up all the people who were receiving some sort of therapy – that could mean anything from seeing a professional to pouring your heart out to an understanding friend – then you added in all the people who *should* be seeing somebody, you came out close to 100%. There were times at Bellevue, when the cases piled up, new ones coming in every day, that it was easy to believe that; that everyone in this city was at least a little crazy."

"In my job you get those days, too. You get a *lotta* those days. Does that go for high-priced shrinks? They ever go crazy?"

Dante smiled. "The last study I saw said one in sixteen psychiatrists have attempted suicide. So …" Dante watched the lily pads bob on the small eddies in the pond. "I didn't have much money back then. My pleasures were simple. You can walk here from Bellevue in about 20 minutes. I would come up here with my lunch."

"You brown bagged it? *You?*"

"Is it that hard to believe?"

"I'd believe it if you brown bagged caviar and champagne."

Dante laughed quietly. "It was more like a couple of Sabretts and a Yoo-Hoo."

Stavros walked around the lily pond, standing across the water from Dante, then looking up past the tops of the spindly trees to the skylight 130 feet up and the clear blue sky beyond. The only sound was the gurgling of the re-circulating pond water. "It is pretty."

"Better than that. It's sane."

For a moment, Stavros smiled in agreement, but then the word seemed to bring him unhappily back to the probable reason for the meeting. "So why am I here, Doctor?"

Dante slipped on his reading glasses, reached for the notebook in his inside jacket pocket. "Abel Gant served in your platoon."

"Yeah."

"Does that mean he served directly under you?"

"I had three rifle squads under me. Abel was in one of them."

He calls him Abel. Vance is obligation. This is personal.

"Sometimes they worked independently," Stavros went on, "sometimes together. Depending on the mission, I might be in the field with them. I'd worked with them all close enough and long enough that I knew my people on sight, by name."

Dante flipped through his notes. "There was an action for which you recommended Gant for the Silver Star. You're also listed as a witness, so, obviously, you were there."

"I was there."

"He also won the Purple Heart for the same action."

"You say that like it's a prize. That's a prize you don't want to win."

"When I spoke with Gant, he alluded to an incident where he was part of a convoy escort involving an IED. That was the occasion that won him his decorations, correct? Could you tell me about that incident?"

"It should all be in the citation."

"It is, but I'd like to hear it without the grandiloquent prose."

Stavros looked around at the atrium greenery again. "I can see why you like this place."

"You don't want to go back to that day, do you?"

"Who would?"

"Nobody. Including Gant. That's why I need someone else to tell me about it."

Stavros turned to him. "It's important?"

"It's important."

Stavros let out a deep, resigned breath. "It wasn't anything spectacular. No Battle of Hue or anything. It was the kind of thing that happened all the time. Sad to say, it was almost routine.

"I was in a Humvee at the head of the column. Six trucks. There'd been a mix-up at the assembly point. Abel was supposed to have been in the lead truck, but he wound up in the No. 2. They let me pass, but the IED took out the lead truck."

"What should have been Gant's truck."

Stavros nodded. "Lit off the gas tank. The driver and his escort were trapped in the cab. We started taking sniper fire. Not much, just enough to keep us away from the truck."

"But not Gant."

"He got them both out. Didn't matter. They were in such bad shape they never made it. That's when he got hit. I don't think he knew it. Sometimes, when the juice is going you don't feel it, not until later."

"There were some Iraquis in the immediate area, yes?"

Stavros paused for a moment, and Dante could see he was wondering how he knew that bit of information hadn't been in the citation. It had been nothing more than a fair guess on Dante's part, but if it were true, it was, to Dante, the thing that would make Abel Gant's actions in the park make a certain amount of sense.

"Yeah," Stavros said. "This one guy, and an old guy with him. I was never sure what the deal was; the old guy was his father, his uncle, I never found out. Abel saw them, he ordered them down on the ground. The one, the young one I think it was, he didn't like the way Abel was pushing the old guy around.

"See, there's something you have to understand. You don't speak Arabic and they don't speak English. You're paranoid; they're afraid. That's a bad combination on a good day. But right then and there, some buddy of yours … the way they looked after Abel pulled them out … You're hit, there's rounds coming in, the juice is going …" Dante could see he was trying to find the words that would do it all justice, but there weren't any.

"What happened?" Dante prodded gently.

Stavros came around the pond, sat on the iron bench with Dante. "Abel kept telling the guy to stay put, the guy wouldn't. Abel laid him out. Butt stroked him."

"And?"

Another long, sad breath. "Put him into a coma. He died three days later. There was no ID on him so we never found out who he was. And the old guy, he lit out when it happened. The dead guy was unarmed which, over there, doesn't mean much one way or the other. They could've just been two guys in the wrong place at the wrong time, or … Who knows?"

"And then they gave Gant a medal."

"I recommended him and they gave it to him for pulling those two guys out of the burning truck under fire."

"The truck that should have been his."

"Yeah. And as for that other thing … Well, everybody figured it was just the kind of shit that happens."

Dante put his glasses and notebook away. "Is that how you saw it?"

Stavros' eyes were lost in the silent little ripples of the lily pond. Then he shrugged. "Like I said: that's how everybody figured it. What is it you're looking for you couldn't get from the citation or the after-action report?"

It was Dante's turn to shrug. "I'm just trying to learn as much about that day as I can. What someone can't – or won't – remember can sometimes tell you a great deal about them." And then, as Dante knew they sometimes did, the one thought caromed into another, and he sat up a little straighter on the bench. "And what someone lies about will also tell you a great deal about them."

* * *

As Dominick Castellano had told him, Emeline Bick's house wasn't far from Dominick's home; they were maybe only a 10 to 15 minute ride apart. It was a neighborhood of wide streets, spacious colonials and split levels, but, unlike Dominick's street, had the feel of a place that had outgrown rumbling Big Wheels and street hockey, replacing it with an empty nest sedateness. Dante recognized the Bick house immediately from the photographs Dominick had given him; a well-kept split level fronted by an immaculately groomed lawn – the kind of place Dorothea and Harlan Bick, Jr. seemed to be straining to have.

Dante instructed his cab driver to wait, walked up to the front door. The screen door was closed, the inner door open. Dante tried the bell, knocked, called out, but there was no answer. He tried the screen door, found it unlocked, stuck his head into the entry hall and called out to Emeline again, but there was still no answer.

He stepped into the central hall, let his eyes adjust from the bright sun outside. He could see down the hall and out through sliding glass doors at the back of the house leading from the kitchen to the backyard where Emeline was hanging laundry on a pair of lines running to a pole some yards from the house. Dante turned to the living room through an archway on his left.

The furniture was heavy, durable, but styleless. Practical; very Harlan Bick, Sr. Dante ran his fingers along woodwork; not a speck of dust anywhere. He ran his fingers along the upholstery; thin but not worn through. Dante could almost imagine the conversation between Harlan Bick and his wife – "You wanted the nice house? I got you the nice house, but let's not go crazy with it" – and then he furnished it with what would last and to hell with how it looked.

The many pictures on the walls were family photos, an endless variety of combinations of the elder Bicks, little Emeline and Harlan, Jr., Emeline and Harlan, Jr. growing up, Emeline and Harlan, Jr. and Mom and Dad. But the progression of photos stopped long before Dorothea Bick née Dorothy Meader showed up, and even before Emeline's mother showed signs of being sick.

The living room led into the dining room. There was a large, heavy breakfront against one wall; another piece built to last, not to impress. The dishware and cups on display in the breakfront were all one set, heavily flowered in the attractively uneven way that told Dante the blossoms and twining vines had been hand-painted. Dante opened one of the glass doors and examined some of the plates. Made in

Dresden, according to the manufacturer's stamp on the undersides, and, by style, Dante guessed pre-WW I. Another guess: the one decent thing owned by the parents of either Harlan Bick or his wife, passed down from one generation to the next, and now preserved by Emeline Bick.

Dante took in the quiet, still living room with its unchanging furniture, the dining room and its old showcased and no doubt unused dishware, and the photos on the walls with their truncated timeline.

Emeline Bick had stopped the clock.

"Hello!" Dante called to Emeline as he stepped out onto the redwood deck.

She had been startled by the glass door opening, had almost dropped the sheet she was trying to pin to the line. "Oh, Doctor! You almost gave me a heart attack!"

"I'm sorry. I tried the bell, I even called out. The door was open. I hope you don't mind."

"I'll be fine as soon as my heart stops racing!" She patted at her chest as if that would soothe it. "Just give me a second to finish up."

"No rush."

He'd studied her from the dark of the house for a few moments before coming out. She was different here. In jeans and an oversized men's T-shirt, out in the sun, a slight breeze flicking at her hair, she didn't seem the hunched over, worn, cowed-by-life woman he'd met at Dominick's house. Even handling a bit of household drudgery like hanging out the laundry, she seemed more vital.

"The neighbors hate this," she said, obviously enjoying that they did. "They think hanging your laundry out is too, I don't know, old-fashioned or something. Can you believe one of them even said something to me once? 'Emeline, dear, we don't do that here!'" She shrugged the remembered neighbor off. "H-J —"

"Your brother."

"He used to laugh at me because I didn't use the dryer. We have one, you know. My mom didn't believe in it."

"The dryer? Was she Amish?"

Emeline laughed. "She liked the way the sheets smelled when they dried outside. I do, too."

"I'll wager every time you do this it reminds you of her."

"Yeah, it does." Then she stopped, looked at Dante as if he'd performed some feat of magic. "Say, you're as good as Mr. Castellano says you are!"

Dante looked at the lines of linens flapping like signal flags; all bed linens. "There must be a month's worth of sheets here."

"Oh, I change all the beds every day."

"Do you have guests?"

She shook her head. "Just a habit. I guess that sounds ... What's the word? Would that be phobic?"

"Not really."

"I'm not used to the house being so empty," and she pinned her last pillow case to the line. "Taking care of Dad used to keep me occupied. This helps fill the time. Maybe you should be examining me instead of my father!" She picked up the empty laundry basket and headed for the house. "Can I get you something cool to drink? I could use something. We can sit out here on the deck if you like."

Dante agreed, took a seat at an umbrella-shaded table as she puttered around inside, then returned carrying a tray with two ice-filled glasses, a pitcher of iced tea, a bowl of sugar packets. She poured them each a glass, and Dante took a sip. "You brewed this yourself?"

"Dad was always bringing home the mix from the store, but Mom hated that. He liked it was so sweet, but she thought it never tasted right, so she always made a second pitcher from scratch, just for herself."

"You kept doing that after she passed."

She smiled, a little embarrassed. "Well, I liked it, too."

"And you kept making another pitcher for your father the way he liked it."

The assumption impressed her – no play-acting this time – but she didn't deny it. She reached for the sugar and emptied two packets into her glass. "I have to be honest; I always wind up sweetening this a little bit. Feel free," and she nodded at the bowl of packets. "I won't be offended.

"I'm fine, thank you."

Deep back in the yard – Dante hadn't seen it at first, buried in the shade of a small copse of elm trees – was a cedar play set, the kind with things for kids to swing and slide and climb on. "Was that yours?"

Emeline smiled and nodded. "Dad used to say, 'They want to go on swings, that's why they have parks.' But that was one luxury Mom managed to talk him into."

"I'm sure you and your brother spent many a summer's day – a day like this – climbing all over that thing."

Her eyes fixed on the play set. "We did."

"It would've been nice if H-J's boy could've played on it when your brother's family came to visit. Sort of a passing on the tradition thing."

"It's all rotted out now. I'm surprised it doesn't collapse when the birds sit on it."

Yet it's still here.

"Well, as I'm sure you know, I've been out to see your father."

Her eyes swung from the play set to Dante, very sharp. "And?"

"Have you been out to see him since he moved into that facility?"

She watched her iced tea as she swirled it around the ice cubes. "I was going out there pretty regular at first, but he told me that was ridiculous. He said he moved out there to give me a break. What was the point if I was out there all the time?"

"How did he seem to you when you saw him last? Compared to when he was living here?"

"I don't know. Ok, I guess."

"The reason I ask, Ms. Bick –"

"Emeline, please."

"All right, Emeline. I've spoken with your father, I've examined his medical records. He's recovered exceptionally well from the strokes. There's some mild physical impairments, quite minor, actually. If he'd be a bit more cooperative, with some physical therapy he could live independently." Dante could see something flicker in her eyes at "independently" – like some inward flinch. "In fact," he continued, "if your brother is foolish enough to take this all the way to court, I don't foresee any problems for your case. Is he that foolish?"

"I don't know. I don't really know him anymore."

"His wife's influence?"

"Who knows?" but she gave too grand a shrug.

"In fact, Ms. Bick – Emeline – I'm wondering why your father's in that facility at all."

"I told you; it was his choice."

"How did you feel when he moved out there?"

"It was like when Mom ... Like this big hole opened up inside me. I felt ... like, what do I do now?"

"Your father is in reasonably good health, all things considered. But I'm sure what's happened has made you consider the possibility ... Well, Emeline, not to be indelicate, but you know that inevitably your father will pass."

She frowned into her glass. "I try not to think about it."

"But you have thought about it."

A reluctant nod.

"When the time comes, what're you going to do?"

"I don't know. Like I said; I try not to think about it."

"You could always go back to school."

Her shoulders started to slump, her voice become more plaintive; the role she'd played in Dominick's home office. "I'd feel silly at my age."

"Nonsense. You'd be surprised how many older students are in college these days. They're usually the only ones who can afford it.

You could take up whatever it was you were studying – . Where was it? Penn State?"

She nodded. "It's been so long … I can't even remember what I was studying."

"There was a boy, wasn't there?"

She flushed. "Ben."

"Ben – ?"

"LeVoi."

"I'm sorry, I didn't mean to overstep. It's just that I believe I saw him in some of the family photos Mr. Castellano showed me. If you don't mind my asking, was it serious between you two?"

"A college thing, that's all."

Bullshit.

"Didn't matter," she said, "I had to come home."

"Mr. Castellano is under the impression you came home after your father had his first stroke. But you came back earlier than that, didn't you?"

And now a different cast to her face; studying, guarded. "When Mom got sick. I must've remembered it wrong when I was talking to Mr. Castellano."

Dante smiled. "Talking to Mr. Castellano often confuses me, too. Your father asked you to come home?"

"Is this important to the case?"

"Just curious."

"Dad wouldn't put something on me like that. But I knew he needed help with Mom."

Dante's cell phone tinkled its way through Vivaldi's "Spring." "Excuse me." He gave the text a quick glance. It was from Mrs. Froelich:

ITS GOOD OL FRED ELWAY

And then there were instructions on how to find him through Elway Contracting in Queens.

"Ah, my apologies, Emeline. I have to run. But I must be keeping you; I'm sure you have things to do."

"There's always a hundred things to do around here, but I don't mind the company." If she'd been wary about Dante's questions, she still didn't look happy at his leaving.

"Walk me out?"

When she saw the cab, she said, "You had him wait for you? That's going to be expensive, isn't it?"

"I'm sure Mr. Castellano will think so. Emeline, why did you tell your brother about the new will? That couldn't have been your father's wish."

She stopped on the walk, surprised, then he saw her eyes re-fix as she calculated a response. "Oh, we were arguing about some damn thing and I guess it slipped out."

Dante smiled and nodded. "A Dad-likes-me-best sort of thing?"

"It sounds so childish when you put it that way. But I suppose it was."

"Siblings fight. Whether they're four or forty. And the fights don't seem much different as they get older; it's just the weapons get sharper. Well," and he started down the walk again toward the cab, "Mr. Castellano will keep you apprised of where things are at. I'll probably be seeing you –" Dante froze; he thought it was a very nicely executed performance of a sudden realization. "I just thought … ."

"What?"

"I'm a little confused."

"About?"

"You said you were fighting. I thought you two hadn't been talking?"

"Oh, well, we weren't, not really, but he had called, something about the store. I don't remember what it was. I didn't want him bothering Dad, so we got into a fight about it, and, you know …"

"And one thing led to another …"

"You know how it goes."

"Of course. Well, Emeline, until next time." He got as far as the cab door this time before he pulled off another one of those one-more-thing pivots. "It just occurred to me. I mean, I understand how your brother found out about the will. What I don't understand is how *you* found out about the new will?"

"Me?"

"Mr. Schilling says he didn't tell anybody. And your father says he didn't tell anybody. Unless he did and he can't recall in which case maybe your brother does have some ammunition –"

"Oh, no, Dad didn't tell me! I came across it when I was cleaning. Dad has a desk in the den, I just, you know, there it was … Why? Does it matter?"

"No. Like I said; just curious. Thank you for the tea. You keep a nice house, Emeline. Your parents would be proud."

Which seemed to make Emeline Bick surprisingly happy. "Thank you, Doctor! That was a really nice thing to say."

While the cabbie programmed his GPS with the directions to the Queens location Mrs. Froelich had sent for Elway Contracting, Dante watched Emeline Bick return to the house, stand on the front step and give him a wave. She looked small against the large, empty house where she found a hundred meaningless things to do to pass each day. Dante thought of her trapped in that house, lost in it, buried in it, and felt an unwanted, unpleasant pang in his chest.

It occurred to him, then, with an irony he was sure neither woman would appreciate, that Emeline Bick and Dorothea Bick nee Dotty Meader were quite alike.

No, not alike. Two sides of the same coin.

Emeline was trying to trap a fading past inside a shell she was building one memory at a time. And Dorothea was trying to trap a dreamed-of future with a shell built out of one *House Beautiful* fantasy after another.

They were both empty shells. No meat inside. No heart.

Dominick had been right in what he'd said at the deposition, and that realization gave Dante another pang, different this time, like that cold queasiness one gets when the doctor calls to say, "I'm seeing something in your test results I don't like. You better come in."

You and Dotty have that in common, Dominick had told him. Dante wasn't sure what part of that disturbed him most; that it was true, or that it had come from Dominick.

* * *

As Dante climbed out of his cab, he picked out Elway immediately; he was the only Anglo on the crew pouring a new cement driveway, giving directions the skilled team didn't need. Fred Elway was the picture of disappointment and surrender: a beer-bloated face, beer-bloated belly tenting his sweat-stained plaid shirt out past his twill work pants, beer-bleary eyes.

Elway saw Dante coming his way, red-rimmed eyes wincing at the tailored suit, then his shoulders rose and fell in a philosophical here-we-go-again shrug as he came down to the curb to meet him. "Listen, friend, I got all my permits," he said with a boozy carelessness, "'n' every one a my boys here is legal, so –"

"I'm not with the city, Mr. Elway, or Immigration, or anybody else you have to worry about. I'm harmless."

"Nobody's harmless, mister." Then, barely interested: "Ya wanna talk 'bout a job?"

"I want to talk about your old college friend, Harlan Bick, Jr. Have you talked to him lately?"

"I haven't seen Harl in a while. Who're you?"

Dante introduced himself as he handed over a business card, gave a quick sketch of the case, but as soon as he mentioned the lawsuit – .

"Jesus, that's got Dotty all over it," Elway said, shaking his head and walking around in a small circle.

Dante made sure to point out that he was working for Emeline's lawyer, and that if Elway wasn't comfortable speaking with him, he quite –.

"I haven't seen Harl in a coupla years 'n' that's all her, so fuck it, right? Pardon my French. Prolly be more comfortable talkin' in my office."

"Office?"

Elway nodded across the quiet Bayside street to a mud-splattered Elway Contracting pick-up truck, its cargo bed cluttered with cement crusted tools of the construction trade. At the truck – "Hey, ya wanna cold one?" – Elway reached into a cooler jammed in back among the tools and wheelbarrows and pulled out what was certainly not his first can of beer of the day. Dante nodded a no-thanks when Elway held up the can, offering, then they climbed in the cab, Elway kicked over the engine and turned the air conditioner up full blast. "Jesus, I can't take the heat no more," he said, wiping his sleeve across his sweat-streaked face and back over his matted, prematurely graying hair. "Gettin' old I guess. Hey, just kick that crap outta the way." He meant the litter of fast food bags and beer cans on the passenger side floor.

"You said something about not seeing Harlan for several years and that that was Dorothea's –"

"Dorothea!" Elway chuckled. He ran the cold beer can along his forehead, then flipped the opener tab and took a swig. "I *never* called her that. I knew it drove her crazy I didn't. That's why I did it. I mean, Jesus: *Dorothea!*" He burped.

"You were saying that she was –"

"Well, yeah, I mean, all the way back to school she was like that."

"I'm curious, then, as to why you introduced them. It's my under-standing you did introduce them, didn't you?"

"First off, it ain't my fault they hooked up –" a quick *huh* of a laugh "– 'n' second, I don't know I'd use the word 'introduce.' There was this girl I was datin' back then, Dotty – 'n' it's *always* gonna be

Dotty for me, ok? – Dotty was a friend a hers, always hangin' 'round when my girl came to see me at school. So, my girl comes over, I think the first time was some campus beer bust or somethin', I'm hangin' with Harl, Dotty's hangin' with my girl, Dotty and Harl bump into each other, they *keep* bumpin' into each other, bump, bump, bump –"

"And they hit it off."

"Whatever you wanna call it. After the first couple times I got the feelin' she kept comin' over with my girl *hopin'* she was gonna see Harl again. Then we're not *hangin'*, we're all *datin'* together and there you go. Hey, you mind?" He didn't wait – or seem to care – for Dante's answer as he pulled a crushed box of White Owl plastic-tipped cherry-flavored cigars from his breast pocket. He clamped one in his mouth, found a cheap Bic lighter under a carpet of coffee-ringed paperwork on the dashboard and lit up. He cracked his window but it didn't help; mixed with the smell of canned beer and sweat, Dante hadn't smelled anything so vile since his Bellevue days handling homeless psychotics fresh from the streets.

"So then obviously you must've spent some time with both of them."

"Well, yeah, for a while," Elway sighed. "Then once they got seein' each other regular, she seemed to kinda wanna keep Harl to herself. I always got the feelin' she, well, I don't wanna make her sound too bitchy or nothin' – . Ah, fuck it, it used to piss me off; she *was* bitchy 'bout it. Pardon my French."

"About what?"

"I don't think she thought much of us. Ya know, me, our other pals. I mean, granted, we weren't the kind a college kids ya see in the bro*choor*. The only reason most of us was there was our parents made us go. Ya know; go, get a college education, *be* somethin'. Thing is, when it came to me 'n' Harl, neither of us had an idea what we wanted to be. We mostly majored in beer 'n' parties 'til our folks got tired a payin' tuition. I think we both always figgered things was gonna wind up where they wound up which was each of us workin' for our dads."

"So this is your father's company?"

Elway took a deep pull on his beer. "I'm supposed to get it when he croaks 'cept he's never gonna croak. The old bastid's had one heart attack, a triple bypass, lost three a his toes 'cause a the diabetes, he still smokes like a chimney, drinks like a sailor, 'n' he's still here. He don't do nothin' no more 'cept schmooze people at the office, flirt with the seckerterries and watch ball games on that big-ass TV he's got in his office. I'll bet the sonofabitch buries me."

Dante considered the rank cigar, the beer empties clanking on the floor as he shifted in his seat, and calculated Elway's prediction had a good chance of coming true.

"I did try to do somethin' different," Elway said, his rubbery face wrinkling into a rueful frown. "When we got outta school, I mean when our folks figgered out that tuition money was money down the terlet, Harl went to work at one a his ol' man's stores 'n' he offered me a job."

"Working for him at the store?"

"Yeah, but I don't think Dotty liked that. I was one a his ol' party pals from school 'n' she, ya know …"

"Wanted to sever all those past associations."

Elway grinned bitterly. "That's prolly how she'd say it, too." Nose in the air, a bad English accent: "'We must sevah those pahst associations!' So then Harl sits me down, we have a conversation, somethin' like him sayin' I don't think this is workin' out, 'n' I don't know what the fuck he's talkin' 'bout 'cause, man, you know, it's a grocery store, it's not runnin' a nookalar reactor or nothin'. But that was Dotty; I could tell. So, fine, I leave, I wind up workin' for my ol' man, me 'n' Harl get on the phone 'n' bullshit once in a while, but then even that –" Elway made a motion with his hand – *poof!*

"And you think that was his wife's doing as well?"

Elway gave Dante a what-the-hell-do-you-think look. He drained the last of his beer, let out a foul cherry-smoke-and-beer burp that filled the cab. Dante blinked; his eyes were beginning to water, the full-tilt air conditioner notwithstanding.

"It just seemed kinda sucky," Elway went on. "I mean me 'n' him were friends. He's *still* my friend even if I haven't seen him in a while. 'N' I guess the thing *really* pisses me off is it's not like ol' Dot's a member a the royal family or nothin', ya know?"

"You knew her family?"

"Well, not personally, 'n' maybe I'm not 'memberin' it right, but the way I 'member it is her ol' man, he cut grass in the parks, 'n' her mom worked the counter at some local bakery. I 'member walkin' in there one time – I didn't know this was where her mom worked – I had to get a cake or somethin' for some goddamn thing, 'n' I go in there 'n' there's Dotty helpin' out Ma behind the counter."

"She was embarrassed."

"Jesus, I thought she was gonna crawl under the counter or somethin'. It was no big deal to me. I mean, lookit me; who'm I gonna look down on? I mean, seriously, right?"

"You seem to be doing alright for yourself."

"You're a sweetheart, Doc. Let's face it; if my dad wasn't the boss, I'd be out on my ass."

Dante made a polite if-you-say-so smile.

"So, what I'm sayin' is as far as we were concerned, Dotty's family was workin' stiffs like the rest of us. She was the only one didn't seem ok with that. She made it seem like there was somethin' wrong with that. I mean, really, Doc, what's wrong with that?"

And, again, Dante smiled his agreeable, empty smile, feeling all the while that same pang in his chest he'd felt when he'd left Emeline Bick alone in front of her big, empty house.

13

During the half-hour ride back to Manhattan, Dante had his gleaming pen in his hand and little leather-bound pad in his lap, meaning to noodle over some notes on the day's interviews. But the logical analysis and neat ordering of notable points kept getting pushed aside by items less logical and certainly far less neat.

Like Harlan Jr. and Fred Elway. Another pair like Emeline and Dorothea; different but the same. Harlan seemed to have acquired a lot of his father's decency, but none of his ambition, while Fred had taken on all of his father's self-destructive habits and none of his ambition.

Emeline and Dorothea. Harlan Jr. and Fred.

Like moon rockets, the launch calculations off just a fraction of a fraction at lift-off, the error amplifying over distance to a miss of the moon by a million miles. These were all damaged children on years-long trajectories to ending as massively damaged adults.

It was so easy to get it wrong as a parent, *so* easy Dante wondered how anyone ever got it right.

But then he thought of Tom Vance, still hurting over what had happened to his son in Afghanistan, so much so he'd gone behind his son's back to Dante to try to keep his son from being hurt again.

There was George Stavros, who so loved his own kids that he couldn't help but love the kids of others, even when they were grown.

And that brought Dante's thinking to Abel Gant. Except for Tommy Vance III's sense of honorable obligation and George Stavros' overspilling paternalism, Abel Gant was alone. In his own, broken, roundabout way, he'd looked to Dante for help, hinted around after it, but Dante had told him that wasn't his job. Dante would not bleed for him.

In his days at Bellevue, one of the psych ward veterans had warned Dante, "You can't bleed for them. If you bleed for each one of them, you'll be bled out in a week." It was, after all, a city in which there were days, as Dante'd told George Stavros, when it seemed like everyone who lived in it was at least a little crazy. If you bled for even a fraction of them … It was good advice, particularly since Dante hadn't signed on with the idea of bleeding for anybody.

And then thinking of Able Gant got him thinking of his own son and wondering who was there for him.

Stick to business.

Business business business.

He pulled out his cell phone and began texting Mrs. Froelich:

> CALL DOMINICK
> CASTELLANO HAVE HIM
> MEET ME AT THE HOUSE
> ASAP

A few seconds letter, a message from Mrs. Froelich:

> MSGE FRM D MOFFITT
> SAYS TICK TICK TICK U
> SPPOSED TO KNOW
> WHAT THAT MEANS

Dante sat with that for a few seconds, then sent:

PREHEAT OVEN TO 350

Business business business, and he made his pen move across the clean white pages of his notepad.

* * *

By the time he'd reached his town house, Dante felt like Dante again, forcing intruding thoughts back into their sealed-tight boxes allowing the mental machinery to, again, purr along smoothly. But then his cab pulled up to the curb and there was Eldon Stewart in his bad blue suit (was it the only dress-to-impress ensemble he had in his arsenal?) using his on-end attaché case as a wobbly stool by Dante's front gate.

"Your lady in there wouldn't let me in," Stewart explained getting to his feet. "I don't think she likes me."

"Impossible. Mrs. Froelich likes everybody." Dante tried to step by him, reaching for the entry keypad. Stewart grabbed him by the arm, then quickly let go, nodding an apology.

"Listen, Doc, I'm *really* sorry about the other day. I tried to bully you into something, I should've known better, my bad, ok? I'm the first one to admit I can be a bit of a dick. You know agents; it's an occupational hazard. Give me a chance to reboot the process."

"All right, Mr. Stewart; talk."

"It's kinda hot out here. Could we do this inside?"

"We *could*." Which was Dante's way of saying they wouldn't.

Dante enjoyed – without showing it – watching Eldon Stewart fight like hell not to show his irritation, to keep forcing a look of repentance and appeal on his face which he wore as well as his baggy suit. "I don't blame you for being mad, Doc. I would be, too. And I know I'm not your favorite person. But, ok, just listen for a minute."

"I am all ears, Mr. Stewart."

"We're not as far apart on this as you think."

"Then we're using incredibly different scales of measurement."

A forced smile. "That's good, Doc, you keep busting my balls, I owe you a couple free shots, fine. But I'm with you; Joss Lee is right where he belongs. That psycho bastard should never see the light of day. Never mind prison; that nutbar should be in a cage on some island somewhere. We're agreed on that, right?"

"All right."

"Good, good." Stewart evidently thought he was making headway and Dante could see him getting less defensive and more excited. "I'm gonna be perfectly straight with you, Doc. I want you to be clear in your head: no way I can make a dime on this. *Nada.* No matter what happens, I walk away with empty pockets. Son of Sam laws and all that. Lee can't make any money, I'm his rep, and fifteen percent of nothing is nothing. You're clear on that, right?"

Dante nodded for him to continue.

"The only one – and, goddammit, Doc, I mean the goddamned, God blessed *only* one – who stands to walk out of this deal with a dollar in his pocket ... is *you*."

By which point Dante was honestly curious. "Then why are you bothering with this?"

Stewart waved his finger in a glad-you-asked swish. "Like I said, Doc, I'll be honest. It'll *make* me. I pull this off and no more drafting contracts for *other* people's deals. *I* get to make the deals; *my* deals. This puts me in the majors as a rep instead of a paper-pusher. I figured if I come clean about what I'm after, well, maybe you'd be, what do they call it; *simpatico.*"

"Me?"

Stewart seemed puzzled by the response. "C'mon, Doc, what am I doing that's different from what you did? And I don't blame you! The guy's a psycho, we're both agreed, nobody's going to cry he got milked a bit. You got yours, I just want to get mine."

Dante turned away, as if pondering the idea, but the truth was it was hard for him to look Eldon Stewart in the eye just then.

"You need a book for next year, right, Doc?" There was an edge to Stewart's voice, now, and he was no longer wheedling and pleading. He was poking a sore spot with precise aim.

He's talked to Dolly. Which also explained the message from her. They'd worked it out between them; a squeeze play with Dante in the middle.

"I'm handing you a bestseller on a silver platter. And the advance – *all* of it, and it would be a goddamn *monster!* – goes in *your* pocket. Nobody's letting that loon out of his cage, so all the talk show stuff, all the interviews, that's all *you* getting to promote your brand again. So; what's the problem?"

Dante turned to his front gate, began punching in his entry code.

"Ok, I gave you a lot to think about," Stewart said, and Dante could hear a slight, grating sense of I-know-I've-got-you-hooked in his voice. "Talk it over with your cutie editor, and maybe you should talk to the guy yourself. He's expecting a visit. Tomorrow."

The gate buzzed open. Dante grabbed hold of the wrought iron bars, turned, and saw Eldon Stewart heading down the street. "Remember, Doc," Stewart called over his shoulder: "Tomorrow. The man'll be waiting for you."

* * *

Dante liked to think his occasional baking binges were some form of Zen-like exercise, clearing his mind by focusing his frontal lobe on a mindless activity in order to free the deeper centers of his intellect for more mindful cogitating. Dante liked to think this because he liked that vision of himself better than acknowledging he suffered the common affliction of stress eating, and Dante never liked to admit to anything common. So, rather than plow through a package of Oreos or a pint of Haagen Dazs or something from Dunkin'

Donuts drenched in pink icing and confetti sprinkles, none of which could be camouflaged as a Zen anything, Dante baked, and his baking favorite was chocolate chunk cookies, and he persuaded himself the exercise wasn't about the cookies but about baking as a mindless Zen-like activity.

There wasn't a lot Dante could do to make chocolate chunk cookies less plebian, but he fancified them as well as he could, cutting the chocolate chunks himself from sheets of imported Swiss chocolate, and dosing the batter with espresso powder and kahlua. It still might not have been French pastry, but he had the satisfaction of knowing the end product was nevertheless more than a few notches above Chips Ahoy!

By the time Dominick Castellano had arrived at Dante's townhouse, Dante had the first two trays of finished cookies laid out on wooden cutting boards on his kitchen counter to cool, and was waiting on the next two trays in his oven.

With Mrs. Froelich in one corner, Dominick squeezed in another, the small kitchen grew even more cramped as Dante flitted around them from batter bowl to prepping the next pair of trays to checking on the cookies in the oven.

"I could've stayed home and watched Rachel Ray do this on TV," Dominick said. "Bonus: she's cuter."

Dante shushed him, then, "Mrs. Froelich, that cabinet right behind your head. Three plates, please." Dante kept a stash of decorative plates picked up at garage sales and junk shops; not collectible quality, certainly disposable, but offering a better presentation than Dixie plates.

Dante turned from prepping trays to see Dominick reaching for one of the cookies on the cooling boards. "They're hot!" Dante barked, rapping Dominick across the knuckles with his spatula. He threw the spatula into the sink – "I'm going to have to have that one sterilized." – and reached for a fresh one from an urn of kitchen utensils by the stove.

While Dante's back was turned, Dominick grabbed a cookie anyway and popped it in his mouth. Dante was gratified to hear him *Ooof*ing and *Ahhh*ing because the cookie was, indeed, still hot.

"Are you just naturally contrary?" Dante asked, enjoying the sight of the red-faced Dominick fanning his open mouth, "or is it just me you won't listen to?"

"Li'l bi' a bofe," Dominick gasped out.

Mrs. Froelich poured Dominick a glass of milk. "I don't know which of you is more pig-headed."

Dante pointed at Dominick. Dominick pointed at Dante.

"Children," Mrs. Froelich muttered and retreated to her corner of the kitchen.

"I called you here, Dominick, because I've recently become aware that something about this business is *askew!*"

"I know," Dominick said. "Too many chocolate chips."

"You can never have too many chocolate chips," Mrs. Froelich said.

"Not with the cookies, you ass," Dante said to Dominick, "which, if you had any taste at all, you'd realize are perfect. I mean with this matter of Emeline Bick."

"Uh-oh."

"Don't get your bowels in a knot. Your case – your *legal* case – is fine, at least as far as I can tell."

"So then what's the problem?"

Dante began dividing the now cool cookies among the three plates. "Let's consider Harlan Senior for a moment."

"Please don't tell me the old guy really is nuts."

"I told you to relax. But think about this: you have a man who has worked his entire life at something he seems to have enjoyed doing."

Dominick blew a curt raspberry. "What enjoy? He ran a grocery store!"

"And you're an attorney. Frankly, I'd rate him higher on the evolutionary scale. He enjoyed it, Dominick. He was engaged, he interacted with his staff, with the customers. My point is he doesn't need to be in that facility."

"The strokes –"

"Minor impairments easily addressable with physical therapy."

"Maybe the guy didn't get off on being a supermarket tycoon as much as you think. Maybe he got tired of playing with the potatoes."

"All right, then, let's put Mr. Bick aside for the moment and discuss Emeline."

"Emeline? What's the matter with Emeline?"

"Well, for one thing, she's told you a lot of little lies."

Dominick had been, again, taking advantage of having Dante's back to reach for a cookie but froze with it halfway to his mouth. "Emeline?" Dominick's heavy brows flagged up and down signaling that he thought Dante had had some momentary loss of sanity. "Listen, that poor lady –"

"That poor lady has a bit of the barracuda about her. She's been telling you one manipulative fib after another."

"We talking about the same Emeline?"

Dante pulled out the trays in the oven, slipped in the newly loaded trays, and began laying out the freshly done cookies on the cooling boards.

Mrs. Froelich took a deep, sighing breath of the aroma in the kitchen. "If that was a drug, I'd be a junkie."

"That doesn't make any sense," Dominick said, getting back to Emeline Bick. "Her brother and that bleached blonde Tasmanian devil he's hooked up with don't have a leg to stand on and Emeline knows it. She's got no reason to lie."

"I know. A high school nurse could spend five minutes with her father and know Harlan Junior has no case. And you saw them in that deposition. You wouldn't even have to present a defense. Just let them talk and they'll talk themselves and their case into the toilet. That's what's so *askew*."

"You really like that word."

"He does that," Mrs. Froelich said. "One week it was 'untenable.' Everything was untenable. After a while I wanted to hit him with my stapler every time he said untenable."

"So," Dante continued, ignoring Mrs. Froelich and her commentary, "why should Emeline lie with a slam-dunk case like this?"

"Do you even know what a slam-dunk is?"

"Something about football?"

"He's precious, isn't he?" Mrs. Froelich said.

"Number One," pronounced Dante, "She told you she came home to help her father after his first stroke."

"So?"

"A lie. She'd come back much earlier, when her mother fell ill, and then she never left. Did she tell you *she* was how Harlan Junior found out about the re-drawn will?"

Dominick's caterpillar brows were coming together in an angry frown. "No, she didn't."

"She told me it came up in a phone argument with her brother over something having to do with his store."

"Another lie?"

"I believe there was an argument, but I don't believe her brother called her which is what she says. When you and I sat with her at your house, she told us they hadn't been talking for some time before the issue of the will had come up. And as for that business about trouble at the store, Harlan Junior had been keeping a low profile there."

"So you think she called him?"

"And she says she found the new will accidentally, and I'm having a problem swallowing that as well. Mrs. Froelich. Hypothetical."

"Oh, God," Mrs. Froelich said, "I'm getting to hate these."

"You discover your father's will leaves everything to you but nothing to your brother, and please don't bother to mention that you don't have a brother."

"Ok, so this is my father killed by one of my homicidal kids for the money he doesn't have? Which goes to me instead of split with my non-existent brother?"

Dominick looked dazed. "Do you guys talk like this all the time?"

"If you knew beforehand your brother was to get nothing, why would you tell him? It could only stir up trouble for no good reason, provoke a drawn-out legal case, etc."

"So there's already bad blood between me and my pretend brother?"

"A bit."

"How come you never hypothetical something nice?"

"Please …"

Mrs. Froelich thought a moment. "I don't know. Maybe to hurt him. Really stick it to him. *Twiiiiist* the knife –"

"You're already not on speaking terms. Your father is already not speaking to him. And you get to look forward to the pleasure of seeing the look on his face –"

"And his cow of a wife," Dominick added.

"Oh, I have a pretend sister-in-law, too?"

Dante continued: "– when the will is read and they get –"

"Bupkus," Dominick said.

"So, what could you gain? You know if you tell your brother he's only going to make trouble for your father; his wife'll see to that. And it'll reveal you to your father as something of a snoop. Why make a painful situation even more painful?"

"Sounds like picking at a scab."

"A lovely image, but yes it …" Dante froze, his cookie-laden spatula frozen in air as an idea began to jell for him; sometimes the baking did do what he pretended it did. He set the cookie down on the cooling board, turned to Dominick and smiled.

"What?" asked Dominick.

"Call Emeline. Use the phone in my den."

"And tell her …?"

"Tell her the Shanahans have approached you with a settlement offer from Harlan Junior. Make up the kind of particulars that would make it attractive. See what she says."

"And I do what if she says yes? What do I tell my *firm* if she says yes?"

The corners of Mrs. Froelich's mouth flicked upwards a fraction; as much of a smile as she ever showed. "She won't."

Dante turned his smile toward Mrs. Froelich. "She won't."

"She won't," Mrs. Froelich said.

"She won't?" Dominick said.

Dante and Mrs. Froelich shook their heads together. After Dominick, looking slightly perplexed, left to make his call, Dante had instructions for Mrs. Froelich: "While he's busy with that, I want you to contact the alumni office at Penn State. See if they have any contact information for a Ben LeVoi. Maybe Benjamin. I don't know if it's a capital 'V' or not. He was a student the same time as Emeline. Posthaste."

"God, I hate when you say posthaste," she said as she headed out the door.

When the cookies cooled, Dante stacked them on two of the dishes so that each plate carried two dozen. He wrapped each plate in a sheet of yellow gift-wrapping cellophane, then took three strands of curling ribbon – red, blue, and green – twined them into a single, rainbowed strand and used it to tie off the sheet, raking the ribbon ends with a scissors to produce a multi-colored bouquet of tight curls.

Then Dominick was back, his frown now flavored with confusion. "I just got nervous. Tell me again this doesn't have anything to do with the case."

"What'd she say?"

"Not only did she refuse the settlement offer, but now she's talking about a countersuit. I told her I didn't see any grounds for one, but she still wants me to look into it. She's got a sure win here. All a countersuit will do –"

"Is drag this nasty little mess out."

"Yeah. Why would she do that?"

"To drag this nasty little mess out," Mrs. Froelich said, reappearing in the kitchen doorway.

Dominick shook his head. "I'm missing something."

"To which I am unsurprised. Even Mrs. Froelich, despite her normally limited perception, has picked up on it."

"Was that a compliment?" Mrs. Froelich said. "I might've missed it."

"Dominick, Emaline's mother is dead. Her father has removed himself from her life as much as he can. The only member of the family she's still in contact with is her brother, even if it's through attorneys."

"Because he's suing her! Well, him and his wife."

"And I guarantee you, that at any point when this case seems likely to resolve itself, she'll change course. Get it to court and before the judge can render a decision, she'll say, 'I've changed my mind; let's talk settlement.' And as soon as you're close to a settlement, she'll have you back in court."

"Just to keep a connection with her brother? Isn't that a little sick?"

"What it is, Dominick, is it's either that or she has nothing." Dante held out one of the wrapped cookie plates.

"For me?"

"No, for your wife and your children. *You* don't get any. They're counted. I'll check with Sylvia to make sure you didn't touch them. I'm done with you now. You may leave. Mrs. Froelich, would you please have a seat in the living room?"

Dante walked Dominick out onto the front stoop.

"You know I don't give a shit and a half what you say," Dominick said, "I'm eating these on the train. Now; what do you want? You never walk me out. It's always, 'Scram, Dominick, you know where the door is.'"

"I never say scram."

"Whatever hoity-toity thing you say, that's what it means."

And now, when it came to it, Dante felt awkward and silly, feelings he hated, like someone locked out of his house in his underwear. But he could not find his way out of the awkwardness and silliness.

Just ask him, you ass!

"Dominick, the other day, at your house, with Emeline Bick –"

"Jesus, you got more to drop on me about Emeline?"

"Would you shut up, please? That was no accident; I mean, Edie's showing up there when she did."

"My dear sir!" Dominick took a step down the front stairs, held a splayed hand to his chest protectively like some threatened Victorian melodramatic maiden. "Are you making an *accusation?*"

"I know you never liked me, Dominick. And I'm not surprised that you'd pull something underhanded like that just for the fun of making me uncomfortable. But I never thought you'd use your sister like that."

Dominick smiled, but it was a small, sad, almost pitying smile. "Well, you're right, I never liked you, Danny. Even before all this –" and he gestured at the townhouse behind them "– I thought you were a pretentious prick. But the rest of it ..." He shook his head and started down the steps, stopped at the sidewalk and turned. "You know, back there in the kitchen, and at the deposition, too, I hate to admit it but you start looking like you're every bit as smart as you think you are. And then you come up with this and I have to think, 'Jesus, what a fucking moron.'"

* * *

Dante found Mrs. Froelich sitting in the middle of the living room sofa, her small, slim frame looking ready to disappear into the billowy cushions. Dante set the other wrapped plate on the coffee table in front of her.

"For me?"

Dante nodded.

"Jesus, I hope that's not what I'm getting instead of a Christmas bonus."

"For you and your family. A token of my appreciation."

"Despite my usual lack of perception? Thanks," and she shrugged the puzzled shrug of someone not used to such niceties.

Dante pulled a chair in from the dining room to sit close to her. "I just want to ask you something, Mrs. Froelich, and I hope you'll be frank with me. Not that you're ever anything less."

"Another hypothetical?"

"No." That awkward, silly feeling was back. Dante found himself clearing his throat, then irritated with himself at such a cliché. "Do you ... Well, do you think of me as a doctor?"

She blinked once, then a second time, then she shifted her glasses on her nose as if she needed to adjust her focus. "What?"

"Do you think of me as ... a doctor?"

"I can't think of you as anything else. Every piece of paper and email that comes into me calls you 'Doctor.'"

More awkward; sillier. "That's not what I mean. I mean ... Do you think of me as doing any good for people?"

Her little eyes narrowed in concentration. "You mean like helping people?"

"Yes."

She shrugged. "Well, back when you had patients –"

"No, I mean *now*."

"Now?" Another shrug. "Maybe somebody who reads that new book, the one about going senile, they might get something out of that."

Dante sighed impatiently which drew a what-do-you-want-from-me look from Mrs. Froelich. "I suppose what I'm asking is do you ever think of me as a ... as a *healer?*" He winced at the ostentation of the word.

"A healer? When do you heal anybody?" She said it without an edge, without sarcasm; a simple statement of fact. "That serial killer book didn't do anything but give people nightmares. Are you saying you want to be a healer now? Maybe if you got a TV show like Dr. Phil. Then you could heal a whole family in an hour on national TV, five days a week." Then, an uncharacteristic softness to her usually implacable face; something between sympathy and pity. "It's a little late to be worried about this kind of thing, isn't it?"

To which he had no answer.

They sat quietly for a moment, then Mrs. Froelich reached for the dish of cookies to leave.

"Why do you keep working for me?"

"You pay well. It's not spectacular, but –"

"That's it?"

She settled deep in the cushions and fixed him with a gaze. For a moment, a stray beam of sunlight coming through the picture window flashed across the lenses of her glasses. "I don't want to get myself fired."

"You think I'm that thin-skinned?"

"You threw a conniption the other day because you thought that TV lady came off prettier than you."

"You won't get fired."

She sat still for a moment. "I don't know. I mean, I never thought about it. I got used to it. Maybe ..."

"Yes?"

"Well, maybe it's a kind of hangover."

"Hangover?"

"I keep remembering when you weren't a total jerk."

"You're fired."

"Not funny."

"I'll see you tomorrow, Mrs. Froelich."

She looked at her watch. "It's still –"

"I won't be needing you for the rest of the day."

177

She sat for a moment, then gave a so-be-it shrug and started out of the room.

"Before you leave," Dante called after her, "could you please call a car for me."

Dante was still sitting in his chair, alone in the living room, when he heard the downstairs door close behind Mrs. Froelich some minutes later.

* * *

Dante had never been out into the northwestern part of New Jersey, but he remembered his father talking about it. "You don't even believe it's New Jersey," his dad would say. "It's like another *country!*"

Young Dante had always hoped that one day they'd take that ride. It never happened.

Dante's driver followed Route 80 away from the cities crammed along the lower Hudson, past the belt of suburbs, and up into the Highlands; farms, forests, towns that were no more than a dozen stores, a bar, and a gas station. Then even those meager settlements thinned to nothing as the interstate fell into a parallel with the Delaware River. Out on the wide swath of water, Dante could see canoers and tubers lazily floating downriver, picnickers and fishermen along each bank waving to them as they bobbed by. Then through the cut in the Kittatinney Ridge – the Delaware Water Gap – and they were in Pennsylvania.

Stroudsburg was just a few miles over the border, and Dante's driver followed the GPS' directions to a work crew finishing up its day's work installing a new playground in one of the parks; one of those tangled piles of tubes and slides and monkey bars. Ben LeVoi, according Mrs. Froelich's information, was a city engineer, and Dante guessed that was him consulting with the crew's foreman over blueprints spread across the hood of a car carrying the emblem of the Stroudsburg Public Works Department on its door.

178

Closer, Dante recognized LeVoi from the photos Dominick had given him. He was older, of course, his hair thinner, his middle thicker, and he'd traded in his blocky horn-rimmed glasses for moderately more stylish wire rims, but he was still the same soft-featured, pleasant-faced man from the photos. There was another difference between then and now; the gold band on his left ring finger.

"Mr. LeVoi?" Dante asked, stepping up. "Sorry to interrupt. Your office said I might catch you here before you went home for the day. My name is Dante DiMarchese." Dante handed him his business card.

Reading the card, LeVoi's face quickly went from curious to a bit alarmed: "Doctor?"

"I'd like to speak with you about Emeline Bick."

"Emeline?" A ripple of concern passed over his face.

"You remember her?"

"Sure I remember her! Is she all right?"

"She's perfectly fine, Mr. LeVoi. Can we talk?"

LeVoi looked back to the business card, still curious, still concerned. "Sure, sure. Just a second." LeVoi gave the foreman some last instructions for the following day, reached into the car, came out with a brown lunch bag, and led Dante to a bench facing the half-finished playground. "I hope you don't mind, but I haven't had anything to eat since this morning! We had a sewer break across town just as I was sitting down to lunch. I had to run from here to there, then back —"

"Please, feel free."

LeVoi again looked back at the business card. "So, um, what kind of doctor exactly?"

"A forensic psychologist."

"Forensic? Isn't that when people are dead?"

"I wouldn't have much to psychoanalyze in that case, would I?"

LeVoi laughed at himself, took a bite of his sandwich and immediately spit it out into his bag. "Ooof! That's what happens when you let bologna sit in a hot car all day. Want a Snackwell? They don't go bad. I got the ones that are like Oreos only it's supposed to be better for you." He patted the slight roll around his middle. "My wife says I should watch."

"No, thank you. Enjoy yourself."

"So you're here about Emeline?" He looked at the card, again, and shook his head. "Somehow I'm not surprised."

"No?"

"Well, Em was … Well, there was always something about her … As we engineers might say, she had a load-bearing deficiency."

"She was fragile?"

"You didn't see it right away. You didn't see much right away. I mean, that was back in college. Maybe she's different now."

"She was shy back then?"

LeVoi took a moment to look for the words. "It was more like, I dunno, like she didn't want to connect with anybody, with anything. Not, like, shy. More like, why bother because she knew she wasn't going to be staying. Sure you don't want one of these?" He held out the small pack of cookies. "It's not *really* like an Oreo, but they're not bad."

Dante shook his head politely.

"You know where I'm from?" LeVoi asked. "Originally?"

"Some place in Indiana, isn't it?"

LeVoi nodded, impressed. "You've been studying up. I liked the program at Penn State, the engineering program, that's why I went there. After I graduated, this job came up. Em could never do that. She could never be that far from home. She didn't even like being at Penn and that was just a car ride from home."

"What was she studying?"

LeVoi chuckled. "As little as possible. At first, she was undecided. You only get a semester of that, then you have to pick something. She went for what everybody else goes for who has to pick a major but still doesn't know what they want to do."

"Liberal arts."

LeVoi nodded. "Thing is, she wasn't undecided. She just didn't care. Like I said, she didn't want to be there. She took a couple classes every semester, but she didn't work that hard at them. It didn't matter to her if she passed or failed, nothing interested her."

"Except getting back home."

"It was a shame. Emeline's no dummy, ya know."

"I'm coming to appreciate that."

"Ya know – and this is gonna sound really weird – but I think, well, when her mother got sick ..." Dante could see the reluctance in LeVoi to say something that might be construed as disparaging. "See ..."

"I'll bet when she got the news she was out of here like a shot."

LeVoi seemed surprised – and relieved – Dante had read the situation so clearly. "Yeah! Not like she was happy about her mom, don't get me wrong, she loved her mother, I don't think she ever let a couple days go by she wasn't on the phone with her passing some time talking about nothing. No, when she got the news about her mom, she was pretty upset about that. But that was the most energy I ever saw her put out about anything."

"I know it was a long time ago, Mr. LeVoi, but do you remember if anyone *asked* her to come home?"

"You mean like her dad?"

"Anyone."

"What I remember is her dad actually tried to talk her out of it. Said there was nothing she could do, she might as well stay in school."

"How long did you two know each other?"

"Oh, well, let me think. I guess it was, let me see ... I met her toward the end of my first semester, so almost two years, yeah, a little shy of two years."

"If you don't mind my asking, was it serious between you two? I mean –"

"I know what you mean," LeVoi said with a sad smile. He looked out at the unfinished playground and sighed. "*I* was serious."

"And she wasn't."

LeVoi shrugged. "I'll be honest, Doctor, I don't know *what* it was to her. I wanted to marry her, I really did. I know that kind of thing happens in college, you have your big freshman romance, maybe it even runs for a while, and then –" LeVoi punctuated it by blowing a raspberry. "But I can look back on it now and I can tell you, I, you know …" LeVoi looked sheepishly at the ground.

"You loved her."

"I did, I really did. It took me a long time to get over her. What sometimes bugs me, even now, is a part of me was picking up on things that I should've known it wasn't going to work out right. I just didn't want to see them, you know?"

"Like?"

"You know how a couple starts making plans? Kind of excited, talking about what it's going to be like together? I'd do that. She'd smile and nod, she never said anything that told you, 'This isn't gonna happen, Benny,' but the thing is she didn't say much at all. That should've red-flagged me. But when she started packing to go home to take care of her mother … It was all, 'First I have to do this, then I can set this up and do that' and on and on. *That* she was worked up about. All of a sudden, she's all plans and has a lot to say, and …"

There was a catch to LeVoi's voice and Dante let him have a moment. LeVoi settled back on the bench, watched the sun start to pass behind the trees on the far side of the playground clearing. There were sounds of birds hidden in the trees giving out their evening songs, the slow crunching of a remembering LeVoi chewing on the last bite of his cookies. "It's starting to cool off nice."

Dante took that as LeVoi's signal that he was ready to resume. "You didn't hear from her after she went home?"

"I tried to keep it up after she left. I really did. Calls, letters; people still wrote letters in those days. I would've come out for her mother's funeral but she didn't even tell me she'd passed."

"How'd you find out?"

"The brother told me."

"Harlan."

"Yeah. He called because he was wondering why I didn't come out since it seemed like Emeline and me were so tight, then he said he figured maybe she hadn't told me, so ..."

"You met Harlan?"

"I'd come out for a couple of holidays one year."

"What'd you think of him?"

LeVoi shrugged. "Nice guy. Didn't seem to have much going on, though. Kind of reminded me of Emeline; like they were both just coasting along."

"Did Emeline ever say anything about why she didn't come back to school afterwards?"

"I waited a couple of days after I got the call from Harlan to see if she'd pick up the phone, and when she didn't, I called her. She said she had to take care of her father, she couldn't see him alone in that house ... Maybe, she said, after she sees he's all right on his own. Every once in a while I'd call to see what was going on, but she always had a reason not to come back ... and then it just dried up."

LeVoi's face clouded; Dante could see recrimination there, the always asked question, *Did I do right?*

"It sounds like you gave her every chance," Dante said. "It was good that you were able to put it behind you," Dante said.

LeVoi shrugged as if unconvinced. "Like I said, it took a long time, but, like they say, life goes on, right? Then enough time goes by, you meet somebody, she's nice, it feels good ..." He nodded at the playground. "I have two kids, boys. Still in pre-K. When I'm on a job like this, I think of them. I know sewer lines are important and all that, but when I'm on one of these jobs it feels good knowing my kids are gonna be playing out there one day. It's nice when the job gets personal like that. I mean, in a good way."

"It's nice when you have a job that provides that for you," Dante said, and he ran that idea over in his head more than a few times.

They sat there quietly for a moment.

Then LeVoi said, "I wonder about Emeline sometimes. Don't get me wrong; I love my wife and all that, it's not like that. But she meant something to me and I worried about her. You show up and it hits me I guess I still do, kind of, in a way."

"Perfectly natural, Mr. LeVoi. Like you said; she meant something to you."

"Every once in a while, I would wonder: what about Emeline?"

"Yes," Dante said, "what about Emeline?"

* * *

Harlan Bick, Jr. stood in his front door a long, stunned moment at the sight of Dante on his porch in the deepening evening. When Dante figured Harlan wouldn't snap out of his trance on his own, he prodded him with, "I apologize for disturbing you at this hour, Mr. Bick. I probably interrupted your dinner."

"Hm?" Then Harlan seemed to gather himself. "Oh, yeah, no, it's ok, we're done. I mean, well, yeah, dinner, we were just finishing dessert."

"May I come in?"

Harlan shook off the rest of his daze. "Yeah, yeah, sorry, c'mon in. Hey, Dee! You'll never guess who it is."

Dante could see from the foyer through an archway into the living room and through another archway into the dining room where Dorothea was standing, her hands filled with dirty dessert plates, with what had been curiosity turning to suspicion at the sight of him.

"I apologize for the hour," Dante said.

Dorothea shrugged.

"I felt we should talk. The three of us."

Dorothea set the plates back down on the table. "Emeline sent you?"

"No."

"Her lawyer?"

"I'm here on my own account. Neither of them even knows I've come."

"Should you even be here?"

"I have a feeling that if either Emeline or Mr. Castellano knew I was here, they'd be quite unhappy."

"I don't know if I should be talking to you without our lawyers here."

"Call them. They'd probably tell you to show me the door."

Dorothea studied him with her pale, cold eyes for a moment, considering. Still wary: "We just finished dessert. Coffee and cake if you'd like some."

"Just coffee would be fine."

"Harlan, why don't you take care of this –" she nodded at the dirty plates behind her "– and heat up the coffee." She moved into the living room as Harlan did as he was told. She took a seat on the sofa and beckoned to a club chair across from her. "Have a seat, Doctor. Make yourself comfortable."

The house – what Dante could see of it – was expensively furnished but without much taste or cohesion. It reminded him of a department store display window; a jumble of attractive pieces that didn't go together butting up against each other. On the walls hung cheap copies of classics in overly ornate frames: Gainsborough's *The Blue Boy*, Van Gogh's *The Starry Night* – picked up for name value and the sense that a print was as good as a painting, hung in a clash of styles and colors.

Dante's eyes took it in in a quick scan, came back to Dorothea to find those unnerving icy eyes locked on him, studying. "I can see you've put a great deal of effort into your home, Mrs. Bick. Is this your first house? My compliments."

A barely perceptible nod, those eyes saying she didn't believe a word of it. "You drive all the way up here?"

"Car service."

"Who pays for that? Emeline? This is how she spends the old man's money?"

"I don't work for Emeline. I work for her attorney."

"Oh." She obviously didn't believe there was any difference. "Well, if this is how her lawyer spends her money, maybe somebody should be giving those two funny looks instead of us."

"Actually, tonight, I am, as the saying goes, on my own dime. I'm here for reasons of my own, Mrs. Bick. Where's your son? I was hoping I might meet him."

"In his room doing his homework. I don't want him disturbed when he's doing his homework."

"She keeps on him about that stuff," Harlan called from the kitchen. "Doesn't want him to wind up like his old man. Neither do I."

A slight frown on Dorothea. "Harlan always thinks less of himself then he should."

"He'd do better if his father wasn't in the way?"

"I'll say it: yes. Maybe we should get to the point about why you came all the way out here. On your dime."

"Of course. I'm sure that since the deposition, your attorneys have advised you as to what course of action you should take going forward. Unless I miss my guess, your attorneys have advised you to drop the suit."

"They told you that?"

"No. The Shanahans would never violate client confidentiality. But I've been doing this a while, Mrs. Bick. If I were in their position, that would be my advice."

"You've worked with them. Maybe that's the problem. All of you people are too buddy-buddy."

"I've worked with a number of the better law firms in the city, Mrs. Bick. It's not that big a universe. And this would not be the first time I've been on the other side from someone I've worked with in the past, and it hasn't compromised either of our abilities to do what we get paid to do."

"I'm thinking of changing attorneys."

"You are?" This seemed news to Harlan who was bringing in the coffee and a tray of cups. He set them down on the coffee table, poured out servings.

Dante took a sip. "This is good coffee."

"Just store bought," Dorothea said.

Jesus, she won't back off an inch.

"I don't think they're aggressive enough," Dorothea said. "Those Shanahans. I think you got them intimidated. See, I'm not as intimidated as they are. I guess they keep forgetting you're not really a doctor, right?"

"Sorry?"

"I mean, you're a psychologist, not a psychiatrist. You're not, like, a medical doctor."

Dante smiled. "No, I'm not a medical doctor,"

"In fact, if it wasn't for you writing that book about that maniac over in Jersey cutting up those hookers, you might not be such a big deal at all."

"It's clear you've been doing your homework."

"Despite what some people might think –"

"Some people" means me.

"– I'm not stupid."

"No, Mrs. Bick; you're certainly not. And you can always hire your own expert, but, in my humble, non-medical opinion, any honest mental health professional is going to tell you what I'm telling you."

Dorothea's cold eyes flicked away for a moment and Dante sensed that he was not the first one to tell her as much.

"Mrs. Bick, let's be clear about something. I work fee-for-service. I get paid the same amount whether or not the people who hire me win or lose. That means I have no vested interested in the outcome."

Now, honestly puzzled. "Then why are you here?"

Dante turned toward Harlan because he knew this would have no meaning, no value to Dorothea: "Whatever you believe about my credentials, believe I have the same obligations as a medical doctor, and that's an obligation that goes beyond what Mr. Castellano is hiring me to do for Emeline. I have an obligation to *everybody* who's involved in this case. That means your husband and you, and Emeline, and Harlan's father ... and your son."

"My son." A sneer, as if she thought the mention was a cheap shot.

"I believe there's room for reconciliation between Harlan and his father," Dante said. "Or at least the opportunity for a conversation. I sincerely believe that."

"I sincerely believe that's what you want us to believe," Dorothea said.

"It's Harlan's father. I think we should hear from him."

Dorothea reached out and took one of Harlan's hands from where they'd been sitting limply in his lap. "Harlan and I are a team, Mr. DiMarchese." A bit of a sting on the "Mr." "Now, considering your marriage track record, maybe you don't know how that works."

"Harlan, you're going to lose if this goes to court," Dante said flatly, ignoring the slight. "And not only will you lose, but both you and your wife are going to be embarrassed. You'll look like two vultures picking over your father without having the courtesy of waiting for him to die. And in the process, you'll hurt and embarrass both Emeline and your father as well. You'll go through all of that, Harlan, and you'll come out of it with nothing to show for it but a pile of legal bills. And then there's what your son is going to make out of all this."

Harlan's eyes flitted around the room as if he didn't know where to look, then he turned to Dorothea, but she'd kept that blue-ice gaze locked on Dante.

"You give a good speech" she said. "Emeline's getting her money's worth out of you."

She's not going to hear it. She can't hear it.

Dante looked from Dorothea to Harlan who sat there with a slack-faced helplessness. Dante gave Harlan a few moments to grow a spine, and when it didn't happen, he sighed, shrugged, and stood. "I hope you two will keep talking about it, keep thinking about it. I know you don't believe this, Mrs. Bick, " again, Dante looked pointedly at Harlan, "but right now I only have the best interests of all of you in mind; you, Harlan and his father, and your son, because if you don't think this will hurt him, too, I'm afraid that'd be the worst mistake you make in all this."

Harlan stood, Dorothea didn't, and Dante let himself out.

As he headed down the front walk to the car service LTD at the curb, a distorted rectangle of light splashed across the dark lawn and Dante turned to see a lit window at the far corner of the house and the silhouette of a child's head. Without thinking, Dante raised his hand in greeting, and the little backlit figure in the window raised a small hand in return.

* * *

The second floor of Dante's townhouse consisted of the master bedroom, and a smaller guestroom with an accompanying sitting room. Dante couldn't remember the last time he'd had a houseguest, let alone one who'd required separate sleeping accommodations.

The third floor was a loft. In one corner was some gym equipment, and scattered throughout the space were piles of stored business and case files, seasonal wardrobe, skis, luggage, and the like. In another corner sat a steamer trunk into which Dante had put whatever was left of his yesterdays.

He opened the trunk. A quick glance: a wedding dress, the lace slightly yellowed; a faded Army uniform with corporal's stripes on the

189

sleeves; a small, flat strongbox; a few ring boxes; and atop the wedding dress a leather-bound photo album, large and heavy in the old style, like a venerated family Bible.

Dante took the album with him downstairs, stopped by the kitchen for a mug of milk and a plate of chocolate chunk cookies, then went into his den and sat with the milk and cookies and the album on his roll-top desk.

The leather binding crackled as he opened the album. He turned the pages slowly, studying each cellophane-shielded image carefully, even the details of the backgrounds, wanting to know it all, reliving what he could remember, etching deeply in his mind what he couldn't. Sometimes he would turn back to an earlier image, already wanting to revisit some old, gone, but valued thing.

The pictures didn't look that much different than the ones Dominick Castellano had sent him of the Bicks. A young man and a woman, clearly in love, they marry, they have a child they love. There are birthdays and anniversaries, Christmases and Thanksgivings, getting sprayed by a backyard hose in the summer, floundering through snow in the winter. And happy. People in photos, Dante realized, are always happy.

He didn't know how long he sat with the album; the cookies were gone when he heard the front doorbell ring. He quickly glanced at his watch – it was after eleven – and hurried to the door.

It was Rachel. She looked like she'd dressed hurriedly – a wrinkled T-shirt, jeans, hair barely combed.

She said nothing. Her eyes were watery and red, she couldn't look at him. He took her by the arm to guide her inside, but then she pushed toward him, hugged him tightly, not in affection, but desperate to hold on to something, to someone. He could feel her breath against his chest, a stuttering breath, recovering from a good cry.

"Rachel …?"

"Abel Grant tried to kill himself tonight."

He led her into the living room, sat her down on the sofa, poured her a cognac. She downed it quickly and he poured her another.

"He's alive," she said, "He'll be ok. I mean, physically. Tried to hang himself with his bed sheet. They're transferring him to Bellevue, keep him on a watch. I … I've never had anyone …" She shook her head, lost.

After a moment, "You were right," she said. "He told me he wanted to plead guilty. I told him there was no need. I told him Tommy Vance, George Stavros, none of us would go for it because there was no need. I told him to sleep on it. Then I got the call … I screwed up, Dante."

We all did, sweetheart. I did.

"I came here …" Now she flushed. "I didn't want to be alone with this." She laughed caustically at herself. "God, what a cliché. 'I needed to tell someone, Dante.' I feel like an ass, like some goddamned soap opera queen." She downed the second cognac. Her eyes were growing misty, a combination of the liquor and emotional exhaustion. "I started to call my father, but I couldn't figure out what to say. I was trying to think who I could … My bosses said, 'Don't worry about it; it won't affect the case.'" She shook her head. "*'It won't affect the case'* … like that was my major concern. And then it occurred to me; I'm a typical 21st-century self-actualized high society urban professional, Doctor. I know a hundred people and there's not one I could go to when …" She put a hand to her head, her chest heaved and she seemed to be on the verge of crying, again.

"It's all right, Rachel. You should get some rest."

"I don't want to go home. It's too … empty."

"It's all right."

Dante thought he'd finally get some use out of his guest room.

14

Dante had been in a fair number of penal institutions in his time as a part of his job, but never to East Jersey State Prison. There was something particularly unsettling about this pile of brick he'd never felt before at any other institution. Maybe it was the man buried inside waiting for him who made the place feel more a dungeon than a prison.

In 1988, Rahway State Prison had had its name changed to East Jersey State Prison at the request of the city of Rahway. After almost sixty years, it had finally occurred to the locals that having their city's name incorporated into that of one of the state's most iconic prisons might not have offered the most positive sort of promotion for their municipality.

In its day, the original East Jersey structure had been state of the art in penal architecture, with four tiers of cells set in a Panopticon-like rotunda easily observed from a central guard station. Over the years, the prison had expanded with three three-story wings radiating out from the great domed hub. Seen across the empty fields from a distance, with the sun gleaming off the rotunda's massive metal dome, you might even think it was some kind of palace.

But East Jersey's day was long past; the oldest buildings, dating back to when the institution had been a boy's reformatory, were more than a century old, and the "newest" of the spokes dated to 1951. Towering above the grim, gray, soot-streaked wall around the prison yard, with its oppressively dark brick and cone-topped towers, there was something drearily medieval about the place.

Nor was it viewed across empty farmers' fields any longer. The space between the prison and Route 1 had filled in over the years with warehouses, rental storage, the county motor vehicle station, car lots, motels, fast food joints. In Dante's eyes, the prison seemed disturbingly non-isolated.

There was a guard captain waiting for Dante at the main entrance to escort him to the window visiting room.

"Ever made a prison visit?" the captain asked.

"A few. But never here."

"I'm surprised. I would've thought, well, you know ..."

"Actually, I've never met the man. Face to face."

"No kidding! Well, then," the captain said, "you're in for a treat. And I don't mean that in a good way."

Window visits were permitted every day; Dante should've been sharing the room. But Joss Lee was special. The room had been held empty.

At one end of the room, a guard sat in a windowed booth and handed Dante a plug-in phone. "I already checked it, sir, it works fine." He pointed halfway down the row of visitor bays. "You're in there, sir. I'll notify them you're here. They'll bring him up in a minute."

Dante took a seat in the booth in front of a sheet of smudged, shatter-proof glass. He plugged the phone into a jack in the wall and waited. The air in the booth was stale, clammy. He felt his forehead grow damp and dabbed at it with his handkerchief.

I don't want him to see me sweating.

A guard appeared on the other side of the glass, plugging in a hands-free phone. "Can you hear me ok, sir?" the guard asked and Dante nodded. "Let me hear you say something so I know it's working on this end."

"I hear you just fine," Dante said. He didn't like the strained, squeaky quality in his voice, the tightness in his throat, but he couldn't will it to relax.

"You have any problem – and I mean if *he* gives you any trouble – go straight to the visiting room officer," then the guard stepped back to let Joss Lee take his seat in the booth.

Dante had, of course, seen Lee as millions of others had: on TV, a strange little smile on his chipmunk face as he'd been escorted in and out of the Monmouth County Courthouse; grainy photos in the newspaper; that dramatically distorted grinning mug shot on the cover of *Time* under the crimson headline: "Madman!" That mute distance had given Lee the air of a menacing unknown, of horrible secrets hidden behind that incongruous little smile.

But that idea seemed almost laughable in the face of a slope-shouldered, round-cheeked, small-eyed balding man in his late 30s, his slight body lost in the folds of NJDOC coveralls that seemed a few sizes too big. On the street, in the flesh, he would've been utterly ignorable, invisible.

Somebody on the other side of the glass didn't think he was laughable; his handcuffed hands were shackled to a chain around his waist, and another chain ran from his waist to leather cuffs around his ankles which permitted him nothing more than a shuffle.

The chipmunk face opened in a wide smile. "So, at loooong last. Hello, Dearie!" The thin, nasal voice crackled in Dante's earpiece. "Nice to see you got my message." He took a moment to take Dante in. "Boy, you look even prettier than your cover picture. How've you been keeping? You're looking prosperous, quite prosperous. Doing well I trust? Sure you are, sure you are!"

Dante tried to force his throat open, smooth his voice. "What is it you want, Mr. Lee?"

Joss Lee smiled a little wider. "'Mr. Lee' is it? Keep it formal, right, keep the distance. Very smart, very shrewd. Well, that's good. I mean that you're prospering, that you're prosperous, that's good-good. Why not, right? But, c'mon, seriously; is it fair?"

"Is what fair?"

"I *made* you, Dearie! If it weren't for me, who would you be?"

"I was doing fine before we ... met."

Lee chuckled, cocked his head in a who-are-you-fooling way. "You were just another over-priced Manhattan shrink giving uptown types a place to hang out an hour a week. Give the menopausal biddies something to talk about with their menopausal biddy friends over cosmos and pinochle. Tell me: did any of your patients ever really swallow that slop you call advice? I doubt it. People don't want to change. They don't want to become better. They just want you to help them feel better about being fucked up. I mean, seriously, *seriously,* did any of them ever really get better? Seriously?"

Dante started to rise, to reach for the phone jack.

"You may have been bringing in the bucks, Dearie, but you weren't a *star! I* did that! And if you think that was gonna happen without me, then that's just *another* lie you're telling yourself."

Dante lowered himself back in the hard chair. "*Another* lie? What was the first one?"

That chuckle, again, sounding small, high-pitched, almost like a child's. "Well, I don't know, there's been so soooo many, *soooo* many. C'mon, Dearie, seriously, *seriously,* you're whole fucking *life* is one big lie! Made up of a million little ones."

"If you're talking about a little self-improvement, that hardly qualifies as —"

"'Little'? *'Little'!* Like Mount Rushmore was a 'little' patch and paste job; little like that. Ya know, I tried that self-improvement thing, too. Look where it got me."

"Maybe if mutilation murders were a socially accepted means of self-improvement, it might've worked out better for you."

Lee considered that and nodded. "True, true. Rather narrow-minded of society, dontcha think? Judgmental?"

"What do you want?"

Very business-like now: "I told you. Well, my new lawyer told you. What'd you think of him by the way? Of my Mr. Stewart?"

"Not much, really."

"But he's perfect for me."

"You deserve each other, I'll grant you that. I'm going to ask one last time, Mr. Lee, then I'm leaving: What. Do. You. Want."

"Like my Mr. Stewart said: to write a book with you. *My* side."

"Your side."

Lee grinned with excitement. "Think of it, Dearie; you get the Bailey Beach killer to talk. Inside the mind of a madman! There's your tagline right there! That's gotta have more heat than that estate planning horseshit you got out there now. I mean, Jesus, *seriously?*"

"Why?"

Lee shrugged. "Something to do. I have a bit of time on my hands, ya know."

"Why?"

"Boy, for a guy who tells a lotta lies, you're a bug about getting to the bottom of things."

"Goddammit, *why?*"

The small smile turned satisfied, and Dante hated himself for giving Lee what he knew Lee most wanted: to rattle the great Dante DiMarchese, to make the good doctor sweat, to make him afraid. Everything down to the "Dearie" was to get past the armor and go for the vitals … and he'd managed it.

"You think you know me, Dearie. And maybe you do. You're a smart guy, I'll give you that, so maybe, *maybe* you do. But I know you, too. You built yourself a castle and it's sitting on sand. I may be nuts, I may be totally in-fucking-sane, but I'm true to myself. *You* can't say that.

"I'm gonna write this book with or without you. Now; I write it without you, I'm gonna do the same thing for you you did for me: I'm gonna profile you. I'm gonna talk about where you came from, who you really are ... or, I guess you'd say, who you really *were*. But you work *with* me, you get to go on being Dante DiMarchese, fancy-ass uptown mentalist!"

What could he know? Locked up in here, what could he possibly know?
But he __does__ know! Look at him: he glows with it!

"None of that," said Dante, "answers the question: why?"

Lee sat back in his chair, studying Dante, pondering. "That's the annoying thing about your ilk. That's a great word, isn't it? Ilk? It suits you: *ilk*. 'Why?': that's your big question. You have no appreciation for mystery. Jesus, I know what I'm gonna be doing every minute of the day every day the rest of my fucking life. I could use a little mystery. But ok. Ok ok ok. It doesn't bother me I got caught, seriously. It doesn't, it really doesn't. It doesn't bother me I'll spend the rest of my life here. Know why?"

"Alright, why?"

Lee leaned forward, his voice dropping in self-directed awe. "Because they'll still be talking about me long after I'm dead and gone. I'll be in textbooks, I'll be in FBI training manuals. For-fucking-*ever!* Will you? One more turd like that last book of yours and you won't even be able to get a guest spot on public access. And that that *that's* what *really* bothers me; that I got brought down by a bullshit artist. A fucking *fake!* I may be crazy, but I'm *real!*

"Now, you write this book with me, and you'll be a bigger celebrity – and a bigger dick, if that's even possible – than you are now. And when that happens, it'll be stuck in your head that you'll owe it to *me!*" The chipmunk grin again, opening into a full, beaming smile. "And that'll kill you! That's a kick right in that fat, big-balled ego of yours! This book'll be everywhere! You'll be there on talk shows, maybe get a movie deal, and all the time you'll know it'll only be because I I *I* put you there!" Lee's face went ... not hard, but still. Cold. Not the slightest flicker of life in those small, barely-visible eyes. "I never hurt nobody like that'll hurt you! And here's the kicker, Dearie: the kicker is you can't afford to say no. You and me, we're fucking *married!* Till death, ya know? Kiss the bride, Dearie, because it's to have and to hold."

Lee lunged suddenly toward the glass, Dante flinched backward, almost fell over in his chair, but Lee stopped at the barrier, laughing, and ran his tongue in a long, slow stroke up the glass.

Then the guard was there, his hand on Lee's shoulder, setting him back down in his seat. "One more time outta that chair and you're done," Dante heard the guard say over the phone. "You know the rules."

Lee put on a face of mock contriteness. "Sorry, Mr. Mack, I forgot myself for a second. Won't happen again. I just got excited with my best buddy here. My soulmate."

The guard looked to Dante, Dante forced out a nod that he was ok, and the guard stepped away.

Lee leaned forward, close to the phone, his thin voice dropping into a purr, his lips twitching in an almost-smile. "You g'ahead and give it a good, long think, Dearie, but I'm not waiting forever. It's like that old soap opera, whatever the fuck it was, remember? The guy used to say, 'Like the sands in an hourglass ...' Well, Dearie, your sands are goin' down the hole, *sssssssss.*"

Dante stood, pulled the phone jack clear.

Joss Lee mouthed a coquettish *Bye-bye.*

Dante forced himself to walk slowly to the visiting room officer to turn in his phone, but he so badly wanted to run.

* * *

He didn't know how long he sat in his rented Lexus in the visitors' parking lot, the engine running, the air conditioning blasting. Yet his face still felt hot, he could feel himself swimming in sweat inside his suit.

From his inside jacket pocket, Vivaldi's "Spring" let him know he had a text. It was from Mrs. Froelich:

> D MOFFITT/E STEWART
> CALLED TO KNOW HOW
> MEETING WENT
> LOOKING TO HEAR
> FROM YOU ASAP

He turned off his phone, threw it in the back seat, then turned to the dashboard GPS to find a route to Bailey Beach.

15

Dante hadn't mentioned it in his book about the Bailey Beach murders, but he had a personal connection to the place; a faded, patchy childhood memory.

He didn't remember how young he was, just that he was very young when his father had taken the family on their only trip together to the shore. His father had picked Bailey Beach because it was the nearest and cheapest of the Jersey shore towns, and even at that it was a bit of an extravagance for them. He remembered being carried half-asleep to the car that morning so they could leave early enough to beat the southbound throngs that would clog the shore highways in just a few hours, and waking up in the car to the smell of the scrambled egg sandwiches his mother had gotten up extra early to make so they could have something for breakfast on the ride down.

His father took the old shore route, Route 35, so he could save a little money bypassing the Parkway tolls. Dante remembered sitting on his mother's lap, her arms around him, and that as they drove further south they passed farms with milk cows and horses; the kinds of things

Dante had only seen in picture books and which it had never occurred to his child's mind even existed in the same universe as Newark with its brick-topped streets and shoulder-to-shoulder tenements. He remembered his father leaning out the window and mooing at the cows, and them all laughing when one of the cows mooed back. His father stole a line from Bugs Bunny: "Wha'd I say? Wha'd I say?"

He'd never seen the ocean – the real-life ocean – before, and the tangy taste of the salt air and the constant rumble and hiss of the surf made him giddy with excitement, and a little bit afraid, too. His mom and dad staked out a small square on the mostly empty beach, spreading out an old, tattered bedroom blanket on the sand, anchoring it down with their shoes and a cooler filled with Cokes and the cellophane-wrapped cold cut sandwiches his mom had made the night before.

He remembered that he didn't know how to swim yet, and being tentative about even walking into the foamy surf, struck with a baseless fear that the ebbing waves would suck him out into that endless, bottomless sea. But he felt safe in the arms of his dad who boosted him up on his shoulders, walked him out past the breakers where, still with his son in his arms, he would jump and bob with the incoming waves. He remembered his mother on the beach, barely getting her painted toes wet, afraid of what the salty air would do to her lacquered hair, yelling at his father that they were out too far, to be careful, how the two of them were going to give her a heart attack.

Then it was later in the day, the beach now looked like a patchwork quilt of blankets and sun umbrellas and beach chairs. Roasted red and sweaty by the sun, they left the beach and headed off to the nearby amusement pier. His parents put him on the kiddy rides – a miniature Ferris wheel, little motor boats that moved in a circle with Dante yanking on a string that rang a small bell in the bow, a roller coaster shaped like a caterpillar. He remembered – and this he would never forget – seeing his father counting out change and asking his mother what she had in her purse so they could buy Dante one more ride on the pier.

Then it was still later, the hot midday was turning into a cool afternoon and the ocean breeze felt delicious on his sun-baked skin. His father had held back a few dollars to take them to Sam's which was little more than a shack on the boardwalk that his father swore made the best hotdogs in the world.

This all came back to Dante as he wound his way through Bailey Beach, around the barricaded stretches of road that still hadn't been repaired since Hurricane Sandy, past the empty lots where flood-collapsed houses had been cleared away.

Blissful ignorance, he thought because, as a boy, he hadn't been able to see that decades before Sandy had hit, even while he'd been riding the giant caterpillar through its little ups and downs, Bailey Beach had been dying. Like the other northern shore towns – Asbury Park, Long Branch, Keansburg – it had started withering when the state built the Garden State Parkway in the 1950s, giving people from the northern cities a fast shoot south to the more elaborate diversions of Seaside, Atlantic City, Wildwood. As a child, he couldn't see how cheap and tatty the whole town had been.

The police station was where he remembered it, and there were a few familiar faces still there who greeted him with a pleasing mix of welcome-back and celebrity fawning. They told him where he could find what he was after, and a few minutes later he found Sam's.

It was not the Sam's he remembered; that was gone, torn away along with much of the boardwalk by Sandy. This Sam's, Dante noted with a touch of melancholy, didn't look much different than any other metal and plastic Jersey diner.

Through the windows he immediately recognized the broad back of a black man in a Bailey Beach Police uniform sitting at the counter. When Dante had first met him, Reggie Ballantine had already had the figure of a high school footballer going soft, and it looked like he'd gone another twenty pounds softer since.

Dante entered Sam's quietly, stood behind the big man. "Officer Ballantine?" The large head, now with gray dusted through the close-cropped, spongy hair, picked up and slowly turned. Ballantine had a broad, jowly face, not fleshy like an aging, fattening man, but like a never-aging cherub. At the sight of Dante, the pudgy cheeks pulled up into a sunny smile. "Je-*sus!* How ya doin', Doc!" and Dante's hand disappeared between Ballantine's two massive paws.

"Hello, Reggie."

"Je-*sus!* Pull up a stool!"

Dante slid onto the vinyl-covered seat next to the cop. "I wasn't sure you'd remember me. It's been a couple of years."

Ballantine laughed. It rolled up slow and rich from deep inside. "Are you kidding? You're my only celebrity! How'm I gonna forget you?"

Dante pointed to the sergeant's stripes on Ballantine's sleeve. "Congratulations. When did that happen?"

"They put it through right after the bust."

"Well deserved."

But Ballantine shrugged it off. "Hey, you eat lunch? I know the joint's different, but trust me, the food's the same!" He pointed to the food in front of him: a pair of Sam's foot-long, crispy-grilled dogs, a plate of fries, a large Coke. "Hey, hon?" Ballantine called to the waitress. "See what my friend here wants. It's on my check."

"Reggie, I should be treating you," Dante said.

"Forget it. 'Sides, they got rules about that kind of thing. You'd just be getting me in trouble. You want to get me in trouble?"

"I don't want to get you in trouble."

"Ok, then. C'mon, Doc, tell the lady; whaddaya having?"

"Just coffee, thank you."

"Do you believe this guy?" a wide-eyed Ballantine said to the waitress. "He comes into Sam's for *coffee?* Who the hell comes into Sam's just to have coffee?"

"Never seen it," the waitress said. "Might even be a law against it."

"Well, if there isn't, there should be. Bring him what I got, hon. Bring him his coffee, too. Doc, you don't eat 'em, wrap 'em up and bring 'em home, but they'll throw you out you don't have a Sam's dog sitting in front of you."

"Ok, Reggie."

"So what're you doing here, Doc? Writing another book?"

"I was just in the neighborhood."

"Hey, you don't mind if I eat while we talk? I only got a half-hour meal break."

"Please ..." and Dante nodded at him to feel free.

The cop bit down, the brittle skin on the dog crackled and broke and Dante's nose filled with the smell of chargrilled meat. He remembered the old Sam's shack, how the smell of the hotdogs mixed with the smells of suntan oil and sweat and the salt air whiffling through the shack; with the smoke from the Kents his mom and dad took from the pack they shared and lit up after they'd finished eating.

"I miss the old place," Dante said.

"I know what you mean. I practically cried when it went, I really did. I mean, Je-*sus,* Sam's, right? That place was there forever. It's not the shore without Sam's. I mean it's good the food's the same, but ..."

"Yeah. I wished I'd known about this," and Dante tapped Ballantine's stripes. "I would've, I don't know ..."

Ballantine shrugged. "It's not like I did anything. Don't get me wrong; I'm not giving these stripes back. The extra bucks come in handy; my daughter started college last year. Did I ever show you a picture?"

"I didn't know you had a daughter."

Ballantine ran a napkin around his fingers to clean off the hotdog grease, then got out his wallet and slipped out a photo. "Here's my angel!" A high school graduation picture: a lanky, gawky black girl who, despite her braces, it was clear had her dad's ear-to-ear smile. "Renee."

"Very pretty."

"Gonna be a lot prettier when that metal comes off her teeth. Smart, too."

"She gets that from you."

"I dunno about –"

"You were a hero, Reggie."

Ballantine blinked a few times as if he wasn't sure he'd heard right, then he nodded it away as he carefully put the photo back in his wallet. "Doc, all I did was write a parking ticket."

"Reggie –"

"I wrote a parking ticket, that's all. Hey, it got me these stripes, I'm good, I'm happy."

And he is, Dante marveled. *He really is.*

"And it's not like I'm not famous. I see you on TV, I tell people, 'I know that guy! He mentioned me in his book!' I got a copy, ya know, I was down at the bookstore the day it came out. I'll bet I was the first guy in town to buy a copy! I show 'em that page, I say, 'Hey, this guy on TV, he mentioned me in his book!' Tell me that's not cool." Ballantine took a cheery bite out of his hot dog.

"It should've been you, Reggie."

"What should've been me?"

"The whole thing. The book. Talk shows. You know."

That deep rising laugh, finally detonating so hard Ballantine almost choked on his food. "Je-*sus,* Doc, are you kidding? I can't write a book!" He gasped, cleared his throat with a swig of his soda. "Hell, I don't even like to *read* 'em! Sports page and TV listings; that's about all the reading I'm good for." Ballantine leaned back a bit on his stool, let his eyes run up and down Dante's three-piece-suited figure. "You look good, Doc," he said, genuinely pleased for Dante. "I'm happy for you. Ya know, *you* were the guy, *you're* the hero! I don't know what we woulda done without you coming down to help."

Dante pretended to brush something off a trouser leg so he wouldn't have to look at Ballantine.

You would've done just what you did. You would've written your parking ticket, Joss Lee would've been caught. You did more good writing that ticket than I did in 302 pages.

The waitress was back, set the dogs and fries and coffee in front of Dante.

Something must've changed in Dante's face because Ballantine asked him, "You ok, Doc?"

Dante took a breath and let the aroma from the hotdogs fill his nostrils.

"You gonna stare at 'em or eat 'em?" Ballantine asked.

Dante picked one up and took a bite.

"Can I get you anything else?" the waitress asked.

Dante nodded. "Do you have Yoo-Hoo?"

* * *

On the way out of town, Dante stopped at the beach, climbed out of his car and went out onto the boardwalk ... the new boardwalk. Behind him, across the road, he remembered there had been a few hotels, grand old places dating back to the late 1800s when Bailey Beach had first become a summer haven. And there had been the mansions, just as old, summer homes for the moneyed set with candy-striped window canopies and broad porches for sitting and catching the evening breeze. His father had driven them slowly along the road, pretending to house shop. "What about this one, hon? Remember; you can only have one."

"Too showy," his mom would say. "Let's keep looking."

They were all gone, now, the hotels and the mansions, replaced by one condo village after another, each one looking much like another, Bailey Beach's attempt to revive itself.

Dante walked the boardwalk, the one that had replaced the board-walk Sandy had stolen away. He stopped where he thought the old Sam's shack had stood. To his left, that would've been where the amusement pier had been, lost even before Sandy, by a fire in the 1980s as he recalled. And over there to his right, the stretch of beach where they had picnicked and played and where his father had walked him for his first and only time into the ocean.

He felt a deep, welling up in his chest, refusing to recognize it for what it was, not believing in it because that was just rank sentimentality and he would have no part of that, but it wouldn't ease. Grief.

He took a deep pull on the salt air, felt his eyes sting and dampen.

Why would you deny all this? Why would you shit on this?

"Because," he said aloud, "Dominick's right. I'm a fucking moron."

16

Dante had the cab ferrying him home from the rental car drop-off drive slowly once around his block while he made sure there was no sign of Eldon Stewart before stopping outside his townhouse. Stewart wasn't there, but Mr. Froelich was sitting on his front steps. He struggled awkwardly to his feet, fumbling a smile as well as his greeting.

"As you were, Mr. Froelich," Dante said, breezing by him to key himself through the front gate.

Inside he found Mrs. Froelich locking up files.

"Your husband's waiting for you outside."

"I know. I think you got him afraid to come in here. On the desk; you got a message from your Aunt Connie. Something about some kid's birthday this weekend. It's at a Chuck E. Cheese."

"What's a Chuck E. Cheese?"

"You should go. Everyone should experience a Chuck E. Cheese. Once. It's like sticking your head inside a pinball machine."

Dante pushed the message around on Mrs. Froelich's desk with a finger.

"If you're wondering," Mrs. Froelich said, "your friend's still here."

He nodded.

"Your usual routine is to have me give you one of those bogus phone calls after you go in so you can say you've got to run off somewhere, and then you leave it to me to shoo them out."

"No shooing today, Mrs. Froelich. But if I need her shooed, I'll call."

She had her pocketbook – a massive, fire engine red monstrosity packed with rattling, clanking God-knows-what – in her hands, had it open and seemed to be going through some checklist of its contents. "Once I leave here, any shooing you do on your own." She closed the pocketbook with a satisfied snap. "Good."

"What's good?"

"No shooing. She seems different from your usual."

"In what way?"

"She's nice."

"Good night, Mrs. Froelich."

As she started for the door, Dante dropped heavily onto the waiting area couch.

"If you like her so much, why are you afraid to go in?"

"It's not that." He felt her studying him.

"I'm thinking you had quite a day."

"Good thinking."

"Are you alright?"

He shrugged.

"Where've you been?"

He didn't say it aloud because it sounded painfully melodramatic in his head, but the question resonated nonetheless: *That's the question, Mrs. Froelich; where have I been?*

"Do you want me to stay?"

"Mrs. Froelich, I want to put a circumstance to you."

"Oh, God, here we go." She hopped up on the edge of her desk and settled in for the duration. Her feet didn't reach the floor.

"A conflict of responsibilities."

"None of my hypothetical family is involved in this one, are they?"

"No, Mrs. Froelich, they are tucked away safely in their hypothetical haven off in the happy land of Hypothetica!"

"Ok, shoot."

"You have your obligation as a physician –"

"Oh, I'm a doctor now. Better than being the mother of my son the killer."

"–but you are also an officer of the court with an obligation to your client. And you cannot fulfill one obligation without slighting the other. How do you choose?"

"Ah, an ethical dilemma!"

"Yes, Mrs. Froelich, an ethical dilemma."

"Well, I always have a rule of thumb in these situations, Doctor."

"And that is?"

"I do whatever will let me sleep at night. Or keep me up the least." When he said nothing after a while, she asked, "Is that it?"

"You can go, Mrs. Froelich."

She slid off the desk and reached for the door.

"Mrs. Froelich?"

Impatiently: "Yes, Doctor?"

"Thank you."

Dante found Rachel Blume in his living room standing over the liquor cabinet stirring what appeared to be a pitcher of martinis. She was wearing the same clothes she'd shown up at his door in the night before, but she looked refreshed, her hair loosely knotted behind her head. He remembered how she'd looked that day they'd met with Abel Gant, afterward, when she'd shaken it loose.

"I heard you come in," she said. "I figure you for a drink-after-work type." She flashed him a quick glance. "You look like you could use one."

He nodded a thanks.

"I don't care what James Bond says, I'm stirring. I don't have the upper body strength for shaking." She poured two glasses. "I couldn't find olives. I don't presume these'll be as good as yours, but …"

She offered him a glass, then held her own up in a toast. They clinked glasses, he took a sip.

"Not bad," he said.

"Well, we can't all be Dante DiMarchese."

He turned away, stood at the window overlooking the yard. He knew she'd meant nothing by it, but it pricked at him: *Why would you want to be?* He looked down at the shadows sliding across the manicured sections of grass, the artfully curved path of white stones. *Getting late,* he thought tiredly.

He must've been standing there for some time because he suddenly became aware she was moving restlessly around the living room behind him. She must've taken his stillness as a dismissal: "Well, I … I just wanted to say thank you. You know, for, you know, last night, and, well …" And then she let it drop and he heard her heading for the stairs, going for her things.

"You don't have to go," he said. He turned, tried a smile but it wasn't in him. "It's not you."

"Long day?"

"Feels like." He appreciated that she didn't press, didn't try to insinuate herself. He saw the photo album on the coffee table. "I hope you weren't bored." He drained his glass, went to the liquor cabinet for a refill.

"I spent time with Mrs. Froelich."

"My sympathies."

"I found her … reassuring."

"Reassuring?"

"The phones get answered, letters go out, bills get paid, files get filed. Something about that made me feel no matter how big problems are, the world isn't going to stop. It'll go on, things'll get done. There's a comfort in that. Well, to me. Today."

"And that's how you spent your whole day? With the reassuring, world-spinning Mrs. Froelich?"

She sat on the sofa, reached out and touched the leather cover of the album. "I wasn't prying. I saw it open on your desk."

"I was looking at it last night. First time in ... I don't remember the last time."

"That's your family? Your mother and father?"

He nodded.

"The last pages are empty. Is there another –"

"They died," he said and took a deep pull on his drink. "When I was eleven."

She nodded as if that answered some puzzle. "They looked like fun people."

"They were. When they had the time. It was one of the few occasions they had the time – and the money – to indulge themselves. It was my mother's birthday. My father surprised her by taking her out to dinner. To a nice place. We usually couldn't afford nice places. It was late, they were coming back, a drunk driver ran a light ..."

He went back to the yard window. It was still summer out beyond the overlooking roofs, the sky still had that bright, warm glow, but the sun was low enough that the yard was now cast in an almost twilight, the white stone path now just a ghostly swirl, the gazebo at the far end an abstract of white bars floating in shadow.

Rachel's coming to him the night before had been carried by nothing more behind it than a few shreds of a pleasant evening, the fact that he had the title of "doctor," and that she'd had no one else to turn to. Dante thought this without any condescension because it now struck him that he had a seat in that very same boat, and in that kinship he felt a closeness with her.

"He was a mailman. My father. Well, that was one job. He had a second job working in a factory. My mother did the hair of the women in the neighborhood, did it in our kitchen. That was in Newark."

"New Jersey?" Genuinely surprised. "Newark, New Jersey? I thought you were a New York boy."

"An impression I have always made some effort to foster. It enhances the pedigree in a way saying one is from Newark, New Jersey does not."

"You were embarrassed? You shouldn't be; that's a hell of a climb up. You should be bragging about it, not hiding it."

"Yes, I should." He took another sip. "This is actually quite good."

"Maybe you're just getting sloshed."

He grinned. "Maybe." He finished the drink, poured himself another. "My mother and father spent whatever spare money they had putting me through a private Catholic school. They thought that would keep me from ending up a mailman."

"Or in a factory."

"Or in a factory. You're right; I shouldn't have been embarrassed. But I was. So ... I lied. To the other kids. About who my parents were. It was a stupid lie because my dad delivered mail to their houses." He shook his head at himself. "Stupid. Then ..." He turned away, his eyes wandering the walls, looking for something to set them on because he didn't want to look at her for this part: "It's horrible to say it, but I was almost relieved when they died. One of my aunts, my Aunt Connie –"

"The Chuck E. Cheese lady? I was there when Mrs. Froelich took the message."

"Yes, she took me in. New town, new school, no one to know the lies were lies. And by the time I was old enough to know how ridiculous I was being, well, it'd become a habit. I'd been lying so long I didn't know how to stop. I almost started believing the lies. I've spent the last twenty-odd years trying to make them true." And now he did turn to her. The photo album was open in her lap; she'd been leafing through it as he talked, but somehow he hadn't heard her flipping the cellophane-wrapped pages. "I want to apologize, Rachel. For the

213

other night. For ruining what was otherwise a delightful evening. And for not returning your calls. That was inexcusably rude."

"After last night, I've been figuring we're square." She closed the album with a quiet thud, like a clod of dirt on a grave. "It hurt. You closed me out."

"Because answering one question would have led to answering another and another … and I wasn't ready to do that."

"But you're doing it now."

He smiled. "Only partly." He turned for the martini pitcher.

"Why don't you try it without that."

She wasn't pushing, wasn't pressing. It was simply a suggestion.

He nodded and sank into one of the deep-cushioned chairs by the sofa. "There is no Dr. DiMarchese. He's a construct, a fiction. Nothing fraudulent, mind you, well, at least not in the legal sense. I am a licensed psychotherapist, and I legally changed my name some years ago."

She waited. She was very patient.

He huffed, almost a chuckle. "Danilo Guillermo Pignatello," he pronounced grandly, "That's the name on the birth certificate."

It was her turn to smile, but there was nothing mocking in it. "Well, that's not too bad."

"Yes it is. Still … It's silly. There was a person – a kind of person – I wanted to be, and I set about making myself that person. And I thought doing that meant having to, um …"

She nodded, understanding. "Erase the old stuff."

"As you said, it shouldn't have been embarrassing. That was my own –"

"I think the phrase you used the other night was *bella figura*?"

"*Sì.*"

"I still don't see the problem. People do this all the time; reinventing themselves."

He sank a little deeper in his chair. Like he wanted to hide. "The Bailey Beach case."

"Ok."

"I saw an opportunity. I knew it was a star-maker. I bulled my way into that case. Do you know that no criminal – no major criminal, anyway – has ever been caught because of a profile? Do you know how Joss Lee was caught? By some street cop doing his job. He remembered writing a parking ticket for a van that had been seen at one of the crime scenes. You'd never know that from my book. And that cop is still down at the Jersey Shore writing parking tickets, and I'm –"

"Dr. Dante DiMarchese. This cop is mad about that?"

Dante laughed. "Mad? He's happy for me. He's happy for *me!*"

"So, again; what's the problem?"

"Someone is threatening to air all that. About Bailey Beach. About everything else."

"You didn't do anything wrong."

He waved a finger. "I didn't do anything illegal. You can even argue I didn't do anything particularly unethical. But I think you'd have a hard time making a case it was *right*. Or that I've ever been anything other than a horse's ass about that case, about my whole life." Out loud, it sounded petty. Because – and this he knew – it was. But damned if Joss Lee didn't know his victim's vulnerable spots. "It's no more than talk show psychology to say it, but I suppose I never quite erased embarrassed little Danilo. He's still there, and he's still afraid of people finding out he ain't so much."

"And that would hurt you. You're afraid it might cost you this," and she nodded at the room around them.

"Yes. Petty."

"Human. Sometimes that's the same thing." She laid back deep in the soft cushions of the sofa, running it all over in her head, smiling at some points and he was relieved to see it was not in amusement, not mocking, but something between understanding and sympathy. "Well," she said with a resolved breath, "you *are* kind of a horse's ass."

"I know."

"Do you remember the other day when I came over here to talk about Abel Gant and we were discussing legal strategy. About not asking a question –"

"Unless you already knew the answer."

"There's another old courtroom axiom that comes close behind that one. Anything that could possibly be prejudicial to your client is always less damaging if you bring it up first." She sat up on the sofa, assumed a *faux* pose of rigid seriousness. "Well, Doctor, as you've explained the situation to me, in my professional opinion I must tell you that there's no way you don't come out of this looking like a horse's ass. But you have a choice. You can look like a horse's ass who realizes he's a horse's ass and decided to come clean about it …"

"Or?"

"You can look like a lying horse's ass."

"No third option, Counselor?"

"I know it'll offend your gourmet sensibilities to hear this, but it's almost always a short, crappy menu in situations like this."

Dante noticed he was still holding his empty glass. He grunted his way to his feet and started for the liquor cabinet.

"Seriously?" Rachel said.

He set his glass down on the polished wood, left it there while he returned to the yard window. There was nothing out there now but black night, some lit windows in the townhouses around him.

"Do you have a car?"

"Back at my apartment," she said.

"Could I borrow it?"

"Do you know how many drinks you belted down? New York insurance is high enough; I'm not letting you drive my car. *I'll* drive."

He turned and found her standing, a my-way-or-no-way grin on her face.

"It's a long drive," he warned.

"That'll give you time to let those martinis wear off so you can decide if you really want to do what you think you want to do. Shall we go?"

The Ellipse took them from the mouth of the Lincoln Tunnel upward, over Hoboken, gave them a brief view of the Manhattan panorama, the saw-tooth skyline aglow in the summer night haze, before the road curled again taking them deeper into Jersey. By the time Rachel Blume was pulling her car into the parking lot at the West Essex Assisted Living Village, Dante had had an hour to run his thinking by her several times, have her contribute her own legal opinion, and decide that even as the lubricating effects of the martinis eroded, this was still something he wanted – needed – to do.

Dr. Singh had left for the day but the place was still open to visitors and the shift supervisor told Dante they could find Harlan Bick in the wing where the cafeteria and the physical rehabilitation rooms were. The rehab rooms were dark, dinner hour had passed; the corridor was quiet and empty except for Harlan Bick shuffling toward the stairwell at one end in a walker.

"Good for you."

Dante hadn't realized he'd muttered it aloud until Rachel said, "What?" but he nodded it off.

Harlan Bick was not in pajamas and bathrobe, but in pants and shirt. His hair was combed, face shaven. And when he got to the end of the corridor, he turned and started back, and Dante realized the man was rehabbing himself. Bick saw them, stopped, squinted. "Is that you, Doc?"

Dante walked to meet him followed by Rachel. "Good evening, Mr. Bick."

Bick squinted again, this time in puzzlement. "What was it, again? Doc What? Like a king or queen or something? Something Italian, wasn't it?"

"Doctor –"

"DiMarchese." A flick of a grin. "I was messin' with you."

Dante turned to Rachel. "He does that." Dante gestured at Bick in his walker. "I'm impressed."

217

"I dunno, something clicked after we talked. Don't get too big-headed; wasn't anything *you* said. But you got me thinking. I dunno what's to do, Doc, but it hit me I'm not ready yet for them to start throwing on the dirt."

"Bravo, Mr. Bick."

"Who's this?" A nod at Rachel.

"A lawyer. A friend."

"My lawyer's a friend, too, but not nearly as easy on the eyes. No offense, miss."

Rachel nodded.

"Listen, Doc, this thing's a pain in the ass to walk with and I've been at this a half-hour. They leave the cafeteria open. They got coffee in there. You mind?"

They found a table, sat. Dante saw the row of hand-pump coffee urns, knew whatever was in them would be terrible, so took a gracious pass while Rachel got something for herself and Bick.

"Mr. Bick, I know what you were trying to do for your son and for Emeline. Right idea."

"Wrong strategy," Rachel said, setting a cup down in front of Bick.

"If it makes you feel any better," Dante said, "I think this mess between Harlan Junior and Emeline was inevitable. It wouldn't have come out any better if this had all happened after you passed."

"'Cept I wouldn'ta been here to have to see it."

"Well, yes, there's that. But more importantly, it wasn't going to have the effect you wanted. I think that should be obvious to you now."

Bick took a sip of his coffee and made a face. "Jesus, this musta been sittin' here since they invented coffee."

Dante congratulated himself on having dodged that particular culinary bullet. "I've been discussing the matter with Ms. Blume here, and, of course, you'd have to talk it over with Mr. Schilling since he's

218

your attorney, but, well, I think we've worked out something that does what you were trying to do with your will."

"So you got this all solved for me, Doc?"

Dante smiled sadly. "No, Mr. Bick. I can't do that. Neither can you."

"Then what good are either of us?"

"Emeline has to fix Emeline, and Harlan Junior has to fix Harlan Junior."

"How do I get 'em to do that, Doc? That's what I was tryin' –"

"Sink or swim," Rachel put in. "That's what you were trying to do. But they never learned to swim. What's been going on has been the flopping around of people afraid of drowning. What Dr. DeMarchese has in mind is something a little different."

"How so?" His eyes narrowed curiously at Dante.

"You're going to take them by the hand and slowly walk them into the deep end before you give them a gentle push off. Like a good father would." *Not that I would know.*

* * *

In the parking lot he heard an airplane, single engine, low, lining up on the airport not far away. Dante couldn't see it past the glare of the lights in the parking lot, just the blinking lights of the tail and wingtips. He wished it were daylight; he would like to have shown Rachel the airport, tell her about those summer days with his mom and dad watching the small planes flit in and out.

"What?" she said at his transfixed figure. "You thought that was the mother ship come to take you home?"

He smiled thinking he'd explain it to her another day. Then he stopped smiling. "I need another favor from you."

"Another ride?"

"No. Where's Abel Gant? You said they're holding him at Bellevue?"

"Under a suicide watch."

"I need to see him."

"What if he doesn't want to see you? The way you made it sound, he's no fan of yours. I'm not even sure he'll talk to *me*."

"I need to see him, Rachel."

She propped herself against the fender of her car, her head tilted meditatively, then she nodded to herself. "Whatever it is you're trying to make up for, you can't do it by fixing everything because you *can't* fix everything."

"I know. But I'm at least supposed to try." And now came the cocky, talk-show-book-cover grin and he was happy to welcome it back. It'd been a while and he'd missed it. "Horse's ass or not, lady, that's why they pay me the big bucks."

17

Dante showered and talced with perfumed powder. He shaved with hot foam and a straight razor. He used a straight razor not just because it gave him an exceptionally close shave, but because he knew guests were impressed when they saw the pearl-handled razor on his bathroom vanity (and he always left the razor out on his vanity).

He picked out a summery three-piece charcoal gray suit and a pair of light brown Italian-made quarter brogues to go with it. The shoes had such a hard shine on them they looked more like polished marble than leather. He wore a powder blue shirt with soft dark blue pinstripes, a white collar and white French cuffs, silver cuff links to play off the gray of the suit. For a day like this, normally he would've gone with a solid red tie; forceful strength. But not this time. Instead, he picked out something playful; a bright, solid yellow number. He strapped his heavy Breitling on his wrist, and ran the chain to his Phi Beta Kappa key across his flat, vested stomach

In his walk-in closet there was a wide cabinet where he kept his various toupes sitting on their white Styrofoam heads.

Bella figura.

And then it came back to him, what Rachel Blume had said to him the night before.

So, he put it to himself, *what kind of ass do you want to be?*

He stepped back from the cabinet, detached his Phi Beta Kappa chain and set it among the blank-faced white heads.

Standing before Checkpoint Charlie he asked Mrs. Froelich, "How do I look?"

"You always look –" At that point she looked up from her keyboard, her eyes hit his naked pate, and she froze.

He could not remember the last time he'd let her see that bare dome, and no doubt she was thinking the same thing.

She settled back in her chair, her usually stern body seemed to relax, and Dante could swear he saw the corner of her mouth twitch in that Mrs. Froelich excuse for a smile. And then finally, she took a deep breath, let it out in something like a pleased sigh, and said, "Resplendent."

"Ah, I see someone's been using their word-a-day calendar."

"I try to get some use out of it. Especially since that's what I get instead of a Christmas bonus. There's a phone message from your … 'guest.' I guess you did finally shoo her out."

"No shooing. She left of her own accord early this morning. Business. Which is, I presume, the nature of the message?"

"She says it's on with Abel Gant for ten this morning."

"Good. Mrs. Froelich, be a dear and call Vincent's. I need a reservation for, let's see, there'll be five of us. Make it for noon."

"Vincent's. Noon."

"Then call the Shanahans and Dominick Castellano, have them meet me there."

"Got it."

"Then call Dolly Moffitt. Tell her I'd like to meet with her and Eldon Stewart at three at her office."

"Do you want me to call Stewart?"

"Dolly'll do it. I'm sure she has his number."

Mrs. Froelich looked at the list of calls. Her eyes narrowed just the slightest bit. "Big day."

"Yes."

She looked from the list to Dante's unadorned scalp, then fixed him with a stare. "I'm getting a hint of Gunfight at the OK Corral."

He started for the door. "Mrs. Froelich, I'm not sure what the long-term upshot of the day's events will be. But you might want to update your resume."

That little twitch of the mouth again. "I think I got more faith in you than you do," she said.

"Yes," Dante said, "but that's not saying much," and he stepped out into the summer morning.

* * *

The tinted glass of the main entrance atrium of Bellevue Hospital took the warm yellows out of the sunlight, made the airy space feel cool, unwelcoming. As soon as he came through the revolving door, Dante saw Rachel Blume and George Stavros crossing the open floor toward him.

"Hello, Doctor," Stavros said.

Dante nodded, pointed a finger at Stavros and looked a question at Rachel.

"He's why you're getting in to see Abel," Rachel said. "I knew Abel wouldn't listen to me; he hasn't listened to me yet. But I thought ..."

"That was a shrewd call."

"Thank you for this, Doctor," Stavros said.

Dante remembered that afternoon looking at the children in the Tudor City playground, the look on Stavros' face, and saw the same look there now. He nodded, understanding, held out his hand. "Thank *you,* Lieutenant."

Rachel handed Dante his pass. "I can show you –"

"I know the way. I should go up alone. The Vances are on board with this?"

Rachel and Stavros exchanged a look. "It's up to Abel," she said. "He says yes, then Tommy Vance says yes."

Dante started toward the elevator bank.

He heard Stavros call out, "Good luck!"

As he walked through the mammoth complex, his days at Bellevue came back to him with a disturbing, unwanted clarity; the unending flow of the damaged, the disturbed, the psychotically frightened and/or angry. Breaking that flow was why he'd used to take those walks alone on his down time, had those brown bag lunches in the Ford Foundation garden; reminders that the whole world wasn't crazy.

But then he thought of Abel Gant, and George Stavros who bled for all children thinking of his own, and Tommy Vance who'd left a leg in Afghanistan and had only recently stopped screaming in his sleep, and Tommy Vance's father frightened the screaming would come back, and Harlan and Dorothea Bick and their son and Emeline, and their father haunted by what he'd failed to do for them all. And there was Leo Schilling who hurt for his friend and for Harlan Jr. and Emeline as if they were his own kids, and Freddy Elway dulling his disappointment in himself with a steady flow of beer, and Ben LeVoi who'd moved on from Emeline but couldn't lose his fear for her.

And there was Rachel Blume who looked around one night and found her life was a good deal emptier than she'd thought. And the son he'd left fatherless. And himself.

Maybe everyone wasn't crazy, but it did seem like everyone had been damaged in some way, everyone had scars.

He found himself at the end of a corridor, looking out a large window at the East River.

You could fill that river with the pain I've seen just in this building.

Which was why, those many years ago, he'd been in such a hurry to leave it.

Abel Gant was being kept in the maximum security ward. He had a room to himself, had one wrist handcuffed to the bedrail. A white-jacketed orderly sat in a corner of the room, texting or playing some damned thing on his cell phone, oblivious to Dante and even to the man he was supposed to make sure didn't try to kill himself again.

Dante wasn't surprised nor bothered.

That's how it is; you either stop caring or you cry all the time.

Abel Gant's eyes – red-rimmed, puffy, sleepless – had locked on him as soon as he'd come through the door, hard, studying, trying to decode. In gaps between the two ice bags on his throat, Dante could see the broad ligature mark circling Gant's neck. *Bed sheet*, Dante remembered.

Dante stood at the foot of Gant's bed. "Thank you for seeing me, Abel." He waved at Gant not to try to talk. "I know it hurts to speak, so don't try. Besides, I'm the only one who needs to say anything." Dante nodded at a spare chair in the room and indicated a space close to the head of Gant's bed. "May I ...?"

Gant shrugged.

Dante carried the chair over, sat upright, straightened his vest, looked around the room.

I've seen so many of these rooms. I hoped I'd never see another one.

Seated next to Gant, speaking through the bedrail, a flash came back to him from his Catholic childhood: *Bless me, Father, for I have sinned ...*

"You were right about me, Abel. I have been someone who let others deal with the messy end of this work. The hard end. The painful end." He gestured around the room. "I started here, you know. And after a year here, I said no more. No more.

"It wasn't even that I *couldn't* do it anymore. I just ... I just didn't *want* to."

There was nothing in Abel Gant's face, no reaction, no response. Just that hard, studying gaze.

225

"When I went into private practice, do you know who my patients were? People whose biggest problems were that they were bored and didn't know what to do with their money. Except pay my bill with it. There was nothing wrong with them, not really. They just wanted someone to tell them they were alright, that they were good people, that *other* people were the problem; not them. Essentially, I crapped on everything my profession is supposed to be about."

Dante moved his chair closer.

"Abel, I wouldn't blame you for sending me packing, but I'd be immensely appreciative if you'd let me try to help you, and be what I'm supposed to be. What I've been selling myself as."

Finally, something besides that stare: a question. A plea.

"I can't speak to what might happen if your case goes to trial, that's not my province. If it does, I will do everything I can to substantiate a plea of not guilty by reason of mental defect. But the prospect of a trial isn't what's keeping you up at nights, is it?"

That same plea in Abel Gant's eyes.

"What's done is done, Abel. You can't undo it. Not what happened in that ballpark, not what happened back in Iraq. And I can't erase it from your mind. It's a part of you now. It always will be. But maybe I can help you find a way to live with it. *Maybe.* That's all I can offer, and I can't even promise you that. The only promise I can make is that I'll try.

"But half of this is up to you. I can't do your part for you. But I'll stay with it for as long as you will. I'm in for the long haul."

Gant looked away, his eyes looked up. The question he was now asking he was asking himself.

"This all comes with a condition, Abel. If you say yes, no more of this. This kind of thing is off the table, no matter how long it takes or how hard it gets. Understand?" Dante stood, surprised his legs felt weak. He felt weak.

Then the weakness was gone and he looked down at Abel Gant, smiling. "If I take you on and you try another stunt like this, you little dumbass, it could be bad for my reputation."

And at that, Gant seemed to settle on something. He looked to Dante, held out his free hand, and Dante took it. Gant's eyes were moist. His lips moved silently, mouthing something.

Dante shook his head, he hadn't made it out.

Abel Gant repeated it, his lips moving slowly and carefully: *You're a prick.* His mouth twisted into a wry little smile.

Dante smiled back. "I've heard it said. More than once."

* * *

There was no sign for Vincent's, no indication above ground it even existed. In the past, Dante had, with a certain snooty sense of the cryptic and a practiced haughty sniff, explained to his guests that Vincent's was "known only to those who know."

An unmarked, innocuous stairway led off the marbled lobby of an uptown Bauhausian office tower, opening into a wide, carpeted swirl emptying into a low-ceilinged cellar lounge done in maroon and black, with a backlit bar and clusters of sleek chairs and love seats. At the far end of the lounge, a frost-blonde young woman with the slim elegance of a champagne flute stood by a maître d's podium.

"Ah, Doctor," she said as Dante approached. "It's been a long time."

"Busy busy busy, Ivette. Is my party …?"

"All but one."

"Older gentleman?"

"Not yet arrived."

"That'll be Mr. Schilling. Send him straight through as soon as he shows up."

"Of course. I've arranged for Michael as your server if that's alright?"

"Perfect."

She directed him to a corner of the low-lit dining room where several screens had been set up for privacy. Dante hesitated for a moment outside the screens.

227

Enjoy it, Danny. A year from now it'll be Sabretts and Yoo-hoo.

Inside the little *ad hoc* grotto, seated around a circular table, were Sean and Terry Shanahan, and, across from them, Dominick Castellano.

"Ahh, gentlemen!" Dante hailed them. "Sorry I'm late, I had a devil of a time trying to get a cab." He shook hands with the Shanahans. "Good to see you gentlemen again." A curt nod: "Dominick."

"You live a fifteen minute walk from here," Dominick said. "Why'd you need a cab?"

"I was on other business, Dominick – not that that's any of your business – so don't worry about getting billed for it. But even if I weren't, when on someone else's dime, why not spend a quarter?"

"Yeah," Dominick grunted, "why not?"

He knew they were all looking at his bare head and he took some pleasure in the way it puzzled them a bit.

Only Dominick was tactless enough to say anything. He nodded at Dante's head: "What's with the, uh …?"

"Articulate as always," Dante said. "Anyway, first, please, all of you accept my thanks for making time in your day on such notice. I see you all look appropriately puzzled as to why you're here, as well you should. If you gentlemen can be patient for just a bit more, I'm still waiting – Ah!"

Leo Schilling appeared at the opening in the screens, taking in the posh surroundings with the same cowed look of a first-time visitor to Notre Dame.

Dante introduced Schilling around the table, then, "Gentlemen, this is Mr. Bick's attorney."

The Shanahans frowned in unison.

"Did you hear something we didn't about us being replaced?" Sean asked.

Dante settled himself in his chair, nodded Schilling to sit alongside. "Mr. Bick … *Senior.*"

The Shanahans looked at Dominick, Dominick looked at the

Shanahans, then all three looked at Schilling, then they looked to Dante.

"So now we have to fight the father and the daughter?" Sean asked.

"We've *all* – myself included – made a grievous misstep in this affair, gentlemen," Dante said. "Because this contest has been over a will, we keep treating this affair as if it's over a, well, a will."

"It *is* over a will," Sean barked, and Terry set a calming hand on his arm which, unsurprisingly considering Sean's temperament, did nothing to calm him. "God, I hate when you do that," Sean said, flicking Terry's hand away.

"Well, it is about a will … and it isn't," Dante said. "We keep forgetting that the decedent is not deceased. Mr. Bick Senior is alive, if not well then on the mend, and, as I would certify if asked, of sound mind. And he has decided to take an active role in this issue."

Terry nodded understandingly. "On his own behalf."

"Exactly."

Their waistcoated server appeared inside the screens. "Welcome back, Doctor."

"Ah, Michael! Good to see you, again. Gentlemen, if you don't mind, I'll get us something to start? Michael, it's a bit warm out there today, I think something light, don't you?"

"The caprese?"

"Excellent. Make it a platter. Gentlemen, it's a simple dish, but the tomatoes and peppers come in from the farms each day, and the mozzarella, it's so fresh I've often accused them of milking the buffalo in the kitchen, haven't I, Michael?"

"Yes, you have, Doctor."

"And have Thomas select an appropriate aperitif from the cellar as an accompaniment. I trust his judgment. We'll order a bit later."

As Michael withdrew, Sean's ruddy face grew a little ruddier: "Mind if I ask who the hell's paying for this shindig?"

"I'm a bit curious myself," said Dominick. "I'm just afraid to ask."

229

"I thought this would provide a more conducive atmosphere for discussion," Dante said. "There's something about conference rooms …" He shook his head, tsk-tsked a bit. "I find the psychology of conference rooms polarizing. The brief cases snap open, the papers are slapped on the table, the two sides square off … It's no longer a discussion, it's a war."

"I would've been happy with Applebee's," Dominick said.

"I'm sure you would have," Dante said.

Sean was tapping the table impatiently with his butter knife. "You still didn't answer –"

"I think it only fair you should split it," Dante said.

"*We* should split it?" Sean dropped the butter knife.

"You and Mr. Castellano."

"And why would we do that?" Terry asked.

"Yeah," Dominick said, "why would we do that?"

Dante took a sip from his crystal water glass and fiddled with his silverware as if the immaculate arrangement was off in some small way.

"Because, gentlemen, this little gathering is in service to your respective clients, and in that regard, I believe you'll find we'll have an agreement on the matter before dessert."

Which brought another exchange of looks around the table.

"We did go back to our clients after the deposition as you suggested," Terry said, looking quite unhappy about it.

"And?"

"They want to push forward."

"Hire their own forensic expert no doubt."

Terry nodded.

"It's a waste of money, you know."

Terry nodded again.

"Not to mention they'll look like jackals which will hardly reflect well on you gentlemen."

Terry looked painfully resigned.

"I'm feeling left out," Dominick said. "Can I be an animal, too?"

"Just a half of one," Dante said. "How about a horse's ass? Because when the details of everything which transpired between Emeline and her brother come to light, Emeline won't look any better."

"You said something about a settlement," Sean said.

"No, I said an *agreement*. Mr. Schilling tells me that Mr. Bick Senior, being the concerned paterfamilias that he is, has been reconsidering the situation. Mr. Schilling?"

Schilling, Dante guessed, with his quiet little practice of wills and mortgages and such, probably didn't get many of these dramatic moments, and certainly not in such lush surroundings. He could see the old lawyer trying to hide an I'm-loving-this smile behind a face of TV-legal-drama-learned gravity as he handed out blue-bound documents to the Shanahans and Dominick.

"I have," Schilling explained, "at my client's request, drawn up a revised will –"

"*Another* will?" Sean said.

"*Another* will?" Dominick said.

Terry smiled and nodded an "of course" kind of smile-and-nod.

"– properly witnessed. Also attached are several waivers. If your respective clients agree to accept Mr. Bick's conditions, they waive any right to contest this new will now or at any time in the future. Mr. Bick is, as we speak, currently negotiating the sale of his business. Whether or not Mr. Bick Junior retains his position there will be entirely up to the new owners. If the new owners terminate his son's employment – or his son chooses to leave the store – Mr. Bick Senior will provide him with a severance equal to six months pay. Whether Bick Junior stays at the store or not, Mr. Bick will also – on receipt of the signed waiver – pay off the outstanding mortgage on Bick Junior's house, and put aside a sum of fifty thousand dollars in trust for his grandson to be used exclusively for educational purposes."

"And if our clients don't sign the waiver?" Sean asked.

"Then Harlan Junior and Dorothea get nothing. The terms are similar for Emeline. There being no outstanding mortgage on Mr. Bick's house, upon receipt of her signed waiver he will deed the house over to Emeline free and clear, and also provide her with a sum which should cover twelve months of utilities, maintenance, property taxes, and living expenses. If she wants to continue on in the house thereafter, it'll be up to her to figure out how. Mr. Bick will also provide a trust of fifty thousand dollars for Emeline to be used for any educational or training purposes she may choose."

At that point, Michael reappeared with a platter of caprese salad, the wine steward with something white and freshening to go along with it. Dante gently shooed them out, assuring them the party could serve themselves. He poured himself a sip of the wine, a Chardonnay it smelled like, took a taste. "He never fails me, that man," then poured himself a full glass and offered to pour for anyone else.

"Screw that," Sean said, perusing Schilling's handouts. "I could use a double scotch."

"I'm doing some quick math," Dominick said, "and that leaves a lot of the old man's estate unaccounted for."

Terry nodded in agreement. "What happens to the rest?"

Schilling no longer felt any need to hide his smile. "He lives on it."

"What do you mean he –"

"Mr. Bick intends to buy a house in a senior citizen's community in south Jersey."

Dominick was shaking his head, dazed. "Buy a …?"

"Cape May County," Dante said. "Lovely area, actually. Have you tried the mozzarella?" Dante put a few bits of the seasoned cheese and tomatoes and peppers on his plate, took a small bite of the glistening white cheese. "A delight. I'm telling you –"

"Fuck the mozzarella!" Dominick blurted, then realized he was being a bit loud and choked his volume down. "That creaky bastard's in an old folks home and now you're telling me he's going off somewhere –"

"Cape May County," Schilling said.

"Who the fuck invited you?" Dominick demanded.

Schilling settled back in his chair much as Dante had, popped a lump of mozzarella in his mouth. "You were right about the cheese," he said to Dante, then turned back to Dominick. "Mr. Bick invited me."

"And you're telling me your, your, your *client* that Emeline's been babying for the last couple of years is going to live by himself –"

"No doubt Mr. Bick will engage a home health care provider of *his* choosing," said Dante, "but for the most part, I can assure you he's quite capable of looking after himself. Dr. Singh, who oversees the facility where Mr. Bick currently resides, is quite prepared to testify to that fact should anyone choose to raise the issue."

Sean was rapidly flipping back and forth through the new will, but Terry had been more carefully studying it page by page. "This business about any remaining assets on Mr. Bick's passing …"

"Ah, yes!" Schilling seemed to have been waiting for this, and his smile grew a little wider. "Any remaining assets at such time as Mr. Bick should pass will be liquidated –"

Dominick let out a long, unhappy breath.

"Liquidated!" Sean said. Terry leaned over to show Sean that particular clause, but Sean pushed him away. "It's not going to make me any happier reading it myself, Terry! What happens to the cash?"

"As the will states –"

"Just lay it out."

"– the proceeds from the liquidation will be put into an educational trust for the children of the names you see on that attached list."

"Who the hell are all these people?" Dominick said, scanning the list.

"Current employees of Mr. Bick's stores, and retirees."

Sean was rubbing his forehead so hard Dante thought he'd peel the skin off. "So Dad's leaving it to his employees?"

"You're not listening, Sean," Dante said. "Not his employees."

"Their children," Terry said.

"Ah!" Dante exclaimed, "I see Michael has returned. You were right, Michael, the caprese was an ideal choice, and, as usual, excellent. Yes, we should order. What is Carl – Carl is the chef, gentlemen, a true *artiste, tres splendide* – tell me, Michael, what gastronomic wonder is Carl accomplishing with the chicken today?"

* * *

On the plaza in front of the office tower, Leo Schilling took Dante's hand in both of his. "Beautifully played, Doctor."

But there was more to it than simple professional admiration. He saw it in Schilling's face: *thank you for my friend.*

Dante nodded; it was understood, and Schilling toddled off.

Dante turned to see the Shanahans walking off in the other direction. They each had their copy of the Bick will out, and Terry kept trying to point things out to Sean on his copy only to have Sean bat his hands away. "I've got eyes, Terry! I can read! I went to law school too, ya know!"

And there was Dominick, standing alone in the middle of the plaza, looking down at his scuffed Oxfords, his overstuffed, gaping briefcase tugging at his arm, his lips pursed, and he seemed to be nodding and shaking his head over some interior dialogue only he could hear.

Dante started for the curb to hail a cab.

"Think they'll go for it?" Dominick called to him.

Dante shrugged.

"I'm afraid to ask, Danny, but what – or should I say *who* was it got the old man to decide to take a hand?"

"Let me ask *you* a question: why did you bring this case to me? The delayed fee aside, you had to know that just because it was coming from you meant there'd be a better than fair chance I wouldn't even consider taking it."

"Oh, I was pretty sure you'd take it."

"Really?"

"It was about a damaged family. And when it comes to damaged families, Mr. Pignatello, I consider you the expert."

Dante wasn't quite sure how to take that.

And then Dominick smiled. There was something rueful about it, something even a bit bitter … but, in the end, it was still a smile. "I'm going to have a hell of a time explaining to my firm how I got sandbagged by my own expert witness. And you know once word about this gets out, you might have scared some business away from your door. Still …"

"Still?"

"Tastes bad just saying it, Danny … but, goddamn you, you did a good thing in there. Even if I got a bit screwed in the process."

Dante stepped to the curb and flagged a taxi. "Care to share a cab?" he called to Dominick.

Dominick shook his head. "I'll walk. I'm in no rush to have the partners hand me my head."

Dante started to climb into the car, then stopped. "Oh, Dominick! If Emeline and Bick Junior agree, that's the end of the case and, I'm afraid, your firm's contingency. My fee, however, and my expenses, per our agreement –"

"I remember: thirty days." Then still with that oddly blended smile, he raised his right hand, elevated his middle finger, and gave it a jab. Yet something about the gesture seemed more salute than insult.

* * *

Dolly Moffitt was waiting in her office door for Dante. She couldn't seem to pull her eyes away from his toupe-less topside. Then, as he stood with her at the door, he could see the Dolly Moffitt calculating machine whirring behind her eyes. After a bit, she nodded. "Yeah, that could work."

She closed her office door behind Dante, gestured him to sit on

235

her sofa next to Eldon Stewart who was wearing the same Crayola blue suit he'd been wearing when he'd first introduced himself to Dante.

Dante waved off the offered seat. "Hello, Mr. Stewart, good to see you again. Don't mind me, Dolly, but I just had lunch at Vincent's – Do you know Vincent's, Mr. Stewart? No? I didn't think you would. Anyway, a sumptuous feast, Dolly, divine as usual, and if I sit I'm certain I'll nod off and wouldn't that be embarrassing for us all? And then we wouldn't get to settle our business, and we do have business to settle, right, Mr. Stewart?"

Whatever it was Stewart had been expecting, Dante could see this wasn't it. Maybe a contrite Dante, subdued, whipped. Scared. But the ebullience was throwing him, even worrying him a little, and that only made Dante more ebullient.

"The other thing, Dolly dear – and this is why I really can't sit – is I'm excited."

Moffitt took her seat behind her cluttered desk. "Excited."

"Yes yes! You see, naturally I've been running Mr. Stewart's proposal over and over in my mind, just over and over and over, Mr. Stewart. It really set me to thinking. By the way, I hope your client appreciates how aggressively you've been pushing his proposal. But, as intriguing a concept as it is … Well, Dolly, sweet Dolly, I think I have something *better*."

Which was something, Dante knew, that always pleased Dolly Moffitt's ears. She tilted her chair back slightly, crossed her legs, cocked her head slightly to the side, and interlaced the fingers of her hands across her middle. This was Moffitt's g'ahead-and-pitch-me pose.

Dante paced the cramped office in a rather obvious pretense of being rabidly enthused. "I have to admit, I took my cue from Mr. Stewart here; a follow-up to *Shadow Hunter*. Only this would be something more personal, more revelatory. It would reach beyond the shadows to pull the key player in *Shadow Hunter* into the light." Dante gave it some flare by miming a dramatic reaching out and pulling in.

"And that would be …?" Moffitt asked, already knowing.

"The Shadow Hunter himself: *me!* This would be something of a, well, I suppose you'd call it a memoir. It would tell the story – the true story, mind you – of a frighteningly ambitious man, a man so cripplingly self-conscious about his humble background that he spent the better part of his life – the better part of his entire *life,* Dolly! – constructing a monumental fabrication as to who and what he was. And then our protagonist hears about these grisly killings at Bailey Beach. Is he shocked by the horror of it? Moved by the tragedy of it? No! Motivated strictly by mercenary motives, he forces his way into the case because he sees the opportunity to make himself into a celebrity. And he's such a master bullshit artist – I mean a Rembrandt of bullshit this man is – that he even manages to convince the Bailey Beach police he's important to the case … which he is decidedly *not!*

"And he does become a celebrity, a talk show fixture, a bestselling author, so on and so forth. But then comes the third act, and this, Dolly, this is where the book catches *fire!*

"At the peak of his fame – the very tip-top peak – he is threatened with exposure – here's the nifty twist, Dolly – by the very man he helped – correction, by the very man he *didn't* help to catch. And this threat, Dolly, this threat forces him to face what a sham he is and has been for years, and just how empty this glittering bauble he's made of his life really is. So – and I know how much you like a happy ending – as a form of, oh, what would you call it? Contrition? Atonement? Spiritual exorcism? He executes what may be the only act of integrity in his life and undertakes the exposure himself."

"In a memoir," Moffitt said.

"See how I brought it around full circle? That might make a good title: *Beyond the Shadows!*"

Moffitt smiled. "I was thinking maybe, *Out of the Shadows.*"

"Even better! What do you think, Mr. Stewart?" Dante asked the sour-faced man slumping into the sofa. "Don't you think that's better than your proposal? Do you think it would sell, Dolly?"

"Possibly."

"I could have an outline for you by next week if that'd be a help."

"It would, Dante, thank you."

Dante dropped on the sofa next to Eldon Stewart and patted him on his knee. "Sorry, Mr. Stewart, but obviously this work wouldn't require the participation of your client. So …"

Stewart's mouth opened and closed a few times, then, "You're bluffing."

"Am I?"

"You think just because you waltz in here without wearing your rug, you're gonna make me think you became some goddamn saint overnight? Bullshit. I don't think you'd flush yourself down the toilet like that."

"Dolly, dear, you said you needed a draft by when? November? Mr. Stewart, check in with Dolly in November and see if this was a bluff. And if you're thinking of pressing your client to perhaps beat me to the punch, well, granted, he does have quite a bit of spare time on his hands down there in Rahway. But, not to belabor the obvious, and to put it in words you'll understand, your client is fucking nuts. I wouldn't count on getting anything usable out of him by November … if at all."

Dante gave Stewart another friendly pat on the knee, stood, and made for the door. "Dolly, lunch soon? We'll hammer out the details?"

"Call me tomorrow," she said, "and we'll set it up."

"Good, good! Oh, and Mr. Stewart? I would be very much appreciative if you'd convey a message to your client for me."

"What's that?"

"Tell him I said go to hell. I'd be very much surprised if they didn't already have a room reserved for him."

* * *

238

Dante tried to keep a discrete distance from the closed door of the Shanahan & Shanahan conference room, but the reception area wasn't very large, and the voices inside carried, one more than the others.

Most of the vocalizations coming through the double wooden doors were low, indecipherable rumbles, but Dorothea Bick's voice would occasionally cut through with a painful clarity. Dante couldn't pick out complete sentences, but did hear, "Are you kidding me? … crazy old coot … I've never heard so much bullshit … Who the hell do you work for? … whole bunch disbarred …"

It went on like that for twenty minutes or so, then silence, the sound of shuffling chairs, and the doors were flung open. Terry Shanahan was first out, looking drained, as exhausted as if he'd been running laps. He passed by Dante without a word or a glance, passing through the office suite doors to the otherwise vacated floor outside. Sean was right behind him, his pale face now a choleric red, pausing just long enough to give Dante a this-is-all-your-fucking-fault glare before he stormed off after his brother.

And then came Dominick Castellano. He walked slowly, casually, a silly grin on his face. He stopped at Dante and set a hand on his shoulder. "What's that thing the gladiators used to say before they started chopping each other up?"

"*Te salutamaus morituri;* we who are about to die salute you."

Dominick's grin grew a little wider, and he gave Dante's shoulder a parting pat. "You said it, brother. They're all yours."

Dante tugged at the bottom edge of the vest of his three-piece, shot his cuffs, then glided into the conference room closing the doors behind him.

Emeline Bick sat across from him, even more slumped than usual, red-eyed, a small kerchief twisting in her birdlike little hands, a pathetic, helpless look on her face. She looked up at Dante's entrance, lips trembling, "Save me!" in her watery eyes. Dante gave her a comforting smile, wondered how much of it was true and how much of it was Emeline the manipulator, and made for the head of the table.

Harlan Junior and Dorothea had been sitting with their backs to Dante when he'd come in. As Dante passed them by, Harlan never looked up. He was slouched in his seat, but there was nothing defeated in his posture. He seemed strangely ... relaxed. Relieved. Dante understood: the war Harlan had never wanted was now over.

Dorothea, however, was leaned tensely forward on the table, her anger so iron-forge hot, Dante could feel it burning through her caked-on makeup in pulsing waves at him. For a second, he looked at her coiled posture and thought she might lunge across the table for his throat.

Dante sat back in his chair, neatly crossed his legs. "So."

"This is all your doing," Dorothea spat, "this bullshit deal."

"I'm not a lawyer, Mrs. Bick. Harlan's father worked it out with his own attorney."

Dorothea's blood-red-painted lips curled into an ugly, accusing smile. "You're going to sit there and tell me you didn't have any part in this?"

"I offered counsel to Mr. Bick _ "

"Huh!" and she tossed herself back in her chair, looking confirmed in her suspicions.

"– but the decision was his, as are the terms. Understand something, Mrs. Bick: I was engaged by Emeline's attorney for a contracted-for fee. Whatever any of you choose to do or not do going forward won't change what I'm to be paid. In other words, I have no vested interest in the legal outcome here. Take your father-in-law's offer, don't take it; I'll get paid the same."

"Good fucking job, sweetheart," she snarled at Emeline. "You hired him and he screws *all* of us. That's great, terrific. Nicely done, Em."

"Is that how you see it, Emeline?" Dante asked.

Emeline sniffled. "I ... I don't really understand ..."

"You feel betrayed?"

Behind the sniffles and the hankie dabbings, her little eyes were hard. She wouldn't say it, but it was there.

240

"By me … and maybe by your father. Well, I'm sure you're probably feeling whatever your kin across the table are feeling. Right, Harlan?"

Harlan only shrugged, something which brought him a sharp elbow poke from his wife.

"I doubt any of you would believe this, maybe at some future point you'll understand, but your father only had the best interests of all of you in mind."

Another "Huh!" from Dorothea.

"I'll respond to that by asking all of you how any of this has been in Mr. Bick Senior's interest? Was any of this fight – *any* of it –" and Dante moved his eyes from one of them to another, fixing them, demanding an honest self-appraisal "– carried out because you thought this was somehow good for that gentleman tucked away in a facility in New Jersey? None of this was to benefit that man. You acted as if he were already dead."

And at that, they all – even Dorothea – shrank in their seats a little. But then Dorothea firmed, emphasizing her question with hard jabs at the table: "Just what the hell're you here for?"

"After I leave, each of you will confer with your respective attorneys, and, if I'm any judge, you'll each get the same advice. With Mr. Bick Senior's mental capacity no longer at issue – and I assure you, it is no longer at issue – you'll either have to accept his arrangement and get something, or refuse it and get nothing."

"Or fight it," Dorothea said coldly.

"Your prerogative, Mrs. Bick. You can contest my report, the report of Dr. Singh at your father-in-law's facility, you can bring in, at some expense, other mental health professionals to examine him. You can engage another law firm if you're dissatisfied with your current representation. I'm telling you that all you'll accomplish is to run up some bills as well as present yourself in the worst possible light. But this is America; you're free to embarrass yourself however you see fit."

241

Her retaliation was to hit the question again, harder, sneering: "What the hell are you here for? You just come in to crow about how you fucked us all over?"

Dante smiled tolerantly. "All of you have expended a great deal of time, energy, and not inconsiderable monies to do each other damage in this affair. In my view, you each have three options going forward: you can continue to try to hurt each other; or, you can walk away from each other."

"You said there was a third way to go?" asked Harlan.

Dante nodded, smiled softly back at him. "Build bridges. Like it or not, however you choose to deal with each other or not, you're connected. Nothing will ever change that. Emeline will always be your sister and aunt to your son. You will always be her brother. Your son has a grandfather who loves him and misses him. And he also loves and misses his son." And now he fixed his eyes on Dorothea: "If, for whatever reason, you choose to walk away from each other, or, worse, continue to war with each other, you'll do as much damage to yourselves as to each other. Trust me; I know."

Dorothea's eyes narrowed suspiciously. "And you care so much because …?"

Even if I could explain it, I'm not sure you – especially you – could understand.

Dante stood and headed for the door. "Let's leave it that I'm available to help any of you, all of you … if you want the help. Your attorneys have my contact information. I hope I'll hear from you."

A gratified snort and a snicker from Dorothea. "So that's it! You came trawling for business! Jesus, you don't have any shame, do you, mister?"

Dante stopped at the door. "Excuse me?"

"Yeah, you're happy as hell to help us … for a *fee*!"

"Well, Dotty," and Dante hit the "Dotty" hard, making her flinch, "I really do want to help." He smiled as he reached for the doorknob. "But I'm not a saint."

* * *

242

About a half-hour past Bailey Beach on the Garden State Parkway is an exit that, if you turn east off the ramp, takes you to Seaside Heights on the Jersey shore. Turn west and soon you're passing through Holiday Village, a fifty-five-and-over retirement community. The joke in Jersey – which may be a joke but is still true – is Holiday Village is the place in south Jersey where north Jersey goes to die.

Holiday Village is a sprawling network of wide, quiet streets lined by neat, boxy little homes, all of them one floor (no stairs for all those arthritic knees and hip replacements), and girdled by a thick band of sundry medical offices, medical supply stores, probate attorney offices, eateries with early bird senior specials, and funeral homes.

It was close to six by the time Dante turned the Camry onto his Aunt Connie's street, but the summer sun was still high, bright, and hot. Except for one overweight man on a personal scooter with an equally overweight basset hound sacked out across his feet, the street was empty. It was the time of day when most residents were either watching *Wheel of Fortune* or off at an early bird dinner special.

His aunt was high up on a ladder leaning against the side of the house, her denim shirt splotched with sweat, her flushed face under a flopping sunhat, her hands in Minnie Mouse-sized work gloves digging rotting leaves out of the rain gutter.

"Aunt Connie!" he called, walking across the sandy lawn. "What're you doing up there?"

She made a big show of throwing her arm across her eyes. "Whoa! Wear a hat! That thing's tough on the eyes!"

"What-are-you-doing-up-there?"

"These gutters aren't gonna clean themselves, Danny."

"You'll fall and break a hip, and then where'll you be?"

She was stiffly coming down the ladder. "In the arms of this handsome Mr. Clean-type guy in the nice suit standing on my lawn. I can't wait for him to whisk me off to the ER in those big strong arms!"

She hugged him. It was a bad fit; she was a head and a bit more shorter than he. But he liked the way she felt swamped in his arms.

"I'm gonna get sweat all over your nice suit," she said, finally pushing off. She waved at the big man on the scooter as it whirred by. "That's Mr. Woltz. That's what he calls walking the dog. He used to really walk the dog, then they both got too fat, but he missed making his rounds. So ..." She dabbed at her sweat-shiny cheeks with her sleeve.

"Look at you! You'll get heat prostration."

"Make up your mind: am I gonna bust my hip or get heat prostration?"

"You'll get heat prostration and fall over and break your hip."

"I need something cold to drink. I got Coke; how about a glass of Coke?"

Dante didn't drink soda, but he said yes.

She sat them out on the awning-covered back patio in a couple of lounge chairs with tall plastic glasses filled with ice and soda. The patio was fenced off to pen in a silver-and-white shih tzu who'd immediately flung itself on Connie's lap as soon as she'd sat down. Connie fanned herself with her hat, closed her eyes, let herself cool off. "It's too damn hot to have this animal on my lap, but she missed me while I was working out front. I don't have the heart to kick her off. You live alone, don't you, Danny? You should get a dog. I always had a dog."

"I remember."

"Remember Cindy? No, I don't think you were coming around when I had Cindy. Big German shepherd, black all over, like a wolf. Scared the hell out of people just 'cause of how she looked. But you know that damn dog used to hide behind me when the lady up the block came by with her wiener dog. She could've *eaten* that dog, but it scared the crap out of her.

"Hey, you want something to eat? I got a half a tray of leftover lasagna in the freezer. I got cold cuts you want a quick sangwich."

"No, thank you."

"Didn't you have a different car at the cemetery? You got a whole fleet or what? You doing that well?"

"I don't have a car. The other one was a rental. This one belongs to a friend."

"I'm surprised."

"About?"

"Not that you don't have a car. I hear that; I hear a lotta people in the city don't have a car. I'm surprised you're close enough friends with somebody they'll lend you their car."

"Just because that's true doesn't mean I'm not insulted."

"I wasn't trying to zing you, Danny. You just don't seem like someone with many friends." It was said with concern.

He rattled the ice in his glass.

"Ya know, Danny, this is the most I've seen you in – . I don't even know. What's going on?"

"I'm taking your advice, Aunt Connie: physician, heal thyself. I had a vision in my head of the kind of person I wanted to be."

"Is that a bad person?"

"Some of him is. But the worst part about him was the way he thought he had to erase everything he was before. Like it never happened."

"How do you do that?"

"That's what I'm learning; you don't."

"So now you learned that. Whaddayou do next?"

He looked at the shih tzu stretched out on his aunt's lap, perfectly content as Connie absently rubbed one of the dog's velvety ears between her fingers.

Want to trade lives, mutt?

"I'm not sure I know. I just know I can't keep going on the way I have been."

"You made yourself into one kind of person. Maybe you can make yourself into another."

"Maybe someone less …?"

"Arrogant? Condescending? Snobby?"

"You're not making this easy, Aunt Connie."

"It shouldn't be."

"Touché."

"See? Right there; *that* was snobby. Ok, I'm busting you a little bit. So, is this your way of saying you're gonna be here for Christmas?"

"Christmas is a long way off."

"Fine, then let's start with something a little smaller. One of your grand-nieces is having a birthday this weekend."

"I got the message."

"My daughter Joann's girl."

"I've never met —"

"Then this is a good time to get introduced."

She smiled at him, but it was actually something of a dare.

"I'd like to ask someone," Dante said.

"A date? A little moral support?

"Something like that."

"More the merrier. It'll be fun."

"Ok. Now explain to me: what the hell is a Chuck E. Cheese?"

"Let's just say that for this new you, it'll be a trial by fire." She laughed, and the way the dog rolled over on its back pawing at the air, Dante got the feeling he (and now it was obvious it was a he) thought it was funny, too.

"I don't know about you, but I'm hungry," Connie said. "You don't want the lasagna, treat me to dinner. Just let me change my shirt. We'll go to the Blue Fountain. They got an all-you-can-eat early bird, we can just make it."

He forced some kind of smile, said something that sounded enthusiastic.

This change thing isn't gonna be easy, is it?
Fuck no.

Epilogue

She lived in a stretch of modest but comfortable row houses in Hoboken, one of those old Jersey riverfront towns which had battled back over the last twenty years from being a home to closed factories to becoming a chic Manhattan ancillary. Dante stopped the car after he turned onto her street, looked at the time on the dashboard clock. It was almost ten, late enough to be rude, but he also knew he was trying to rationalize his way into turning the car around and heading upriver to the Lincoln Tunnel entrance. He looked over at Rachel, asleep in the passenger seat, snuggled against the chill of the air conditioning under his blazer, and knew he was about to use her as another excuse not to do this.

If you don't do it now, you probably never will.

There wasn't an open stretch of curb, so he eased the Camry down the narrow street, double-parked in front of her place, left the car running as he climbed out and closed the door behind him as quietly as he could. He checked to make sure Rachel was still asleep before he headed up the walk, stood on the little stoop, and pushed the button for the doorbell.

When there was no response after a few moments, he convinced himself he'd done his due diligence and was about to turn back for the car when the curtains across the window to his right flapped and he saw Edie in the window, framed against the blue light of a TV. She stood there unmoving, and Dante wasn't sure if she had problems making him out in the dark, or she was debating closing the curtains and going back to her television. She ran her fingers through her short hair, then she disappeared, the light over the front door came on and he heard the several locks unlock. She opened the inner door but left the screen door closed.

"Good evening, Edie. I'm sorry to disturb you this late."

"You're a little off your usual stomping grounds. Did we open some world-famous gourmet restaurant I didn't hear about?"

He pretended to smile at that.

She nodded at his toupe-less top. "You forget something? Or you just get caught in a strong wind?"

"I thought I'd try it for a while, see how it fits."

"It looks ok. But then, I always thought it did."

"You were always generous."

"To a fault."

"Yes. May I come in?"

"No."

"Oh. Dominick told me you were seeing somebody —"

"He's not here. I just don't think you should come in." She crossed her arms, leaned against the door, her face, hard in the blue light from inside, seemed to be studying him. "So. What is this?"

"Well, I was sort of in the neighborhood."

"Seriously?"

"I was down at Connie's."

"Your Aunt Connie?"

"One of the grandkids was having a birthday at something called Chuck E. Cheese."

She chuckled. "I thought you looked a little ragged. I would've given my eye teeth to see you in a Chuck E. Cheese."

"Then Connie had some of the family over to her house after. It was her way of ... reintroducing me to the family."

She unlocked her arms and slipped lightly outside onto the stoop. Dante felt obliged to back down the few steps to the walk.

"How'd that go?" she asked.

"There were a few oh-Mr.-Big-Shot-finally-came-to-see-us comments."

"Well-deserved."

"Yes. But ..."

She cocked her head, waiting.

"It was ... nice. A lot of stories about the family. About my mother and father. I ..."

"Yes?"

"I can't remember the last time I laughed that much."

She smiled, then, in a way that gratified him; she seemed happy for him, and in that he felt one old wound heal. And then she grew serious. "Don't lose it a second time, Dan." She squinted down the walk, into the dark at the idling car at the curb. "Is that someone in your car?"

He cleared his throat. "A friend."

"Was she at Chuck E. Cheese with you?"

"Yes."

"No wonder she's tired. She must be a hell of a good friend."

"We'll see."

She grew firm, again. "Be nice to her." And, again, he sensed it was meant well.

The front light was drawing flying insects now, and Edie batted at them as they flitted between her head and the light. "Well, you shouldn't leave her out there –"

He cleared his throat, again. "Is ... my son home? Would you please tell Dante I'd like to speak with him?"

She took a long, meditative breath; ah, so we finally get to the point. She sat down on the top step. "He prefers Danny."

"I don't blame him."

"And he's not home. He's spending the night with a friend. Let him enjoy it."

"Yes. Well ..." He brought out his wallet, extracted one of his business cards, took his Meisterstuck from his breast pocket and began writing on the back of the card. "Would you give him this? These are my personal numbers on the back; I didn't know if you had them." He handed her the card. "Could you ask him to call me, please?"

She didn't take the card. Backlit as she was, Dante couldn't quite make out her face, felt more than saw she was hardly impressed. "Only Dante DiMarchese would leave his business card for his son."

"Please, Edie. I'm trying."

Something in her attitude changed, softened; he hoped that was her feeling the truth of it. She took the card. "I'll ask him – *ask* him to call. I won't force it, Dan."

"Fair enough. Well ..."

"Well." She stood, stepped back toward the door. "Good night, Dan."

He nodded his good night, stood there while she stepped back inside, the door closed, the locks locked, the front light went out.

Rachel felt him slide back into the car. "Where are we?" she asked, not quite opening her eyes.

"Still not home. I had to make a stop. Go back to sleep."

And she did.

He took the car around the block and then back onto the road that would take him to the tunnel, across the river, and home.